LP
W
FIC
BRA

3874900

Brand, M   W9-AQK-867

Old Carver Ranch

8/13

HICKORY FLAT PUBLIC LIBRARY
2740 EAST CHEROKEE DRIVE
CANTON, GEORGIA 30115

SEQUOYAH REGIONAL LIBRARY

3 8749 0073 26117

OLD CARVER RANCH

Center Point
Large Print

This Large Print Book carries the
Seal of Approval of N.A.V.H.

OLD CARVER RANCH

Max Brand®

Center Point Large Print
Thorndike, Maine

PROPERTY OF
SEQUOYAH REGIONAL
LIBRARY SYSTEM

This Circle Ⓥ Western is published by
Center Point Large Print in 2013 in co-operation with
Golden West Literary Agency.

Copyright © 2013 by Golden West Literary Agency.

First Edition, August 2013.

All rights reserved.

The name Max Brand® is a registered trademark
with the United States Patent and Trademark
Office and cannot be used for any purpose
without express written permission.

Printed in the United States of America
on permanent paper.
Set in 16-point Times New Roman type.

ISBN: 978-1-61173-792-9

Library of Congress Cataloging-in-Publication Data

Brand, Max, 1892–1944.
Old Carver Ranch : a Western story / Max Brand. — First edition.
pages cm
ISBN 978-1-61173-792-9 (Library binding : alk. paper)
1. Large type books. I. Title.
PS3511.A87O43 2013
813'.54—dc23
                                                    2013015390

Acknowledgments

"Old Carver Ranch" by John Frederick first appeared as a seven-part serial in Street & Smith's *Western Story Magazine* (8/26/22-10/7/22). Copyright © 1922 by Street & Smith Publications, Inc. Copyright © renewed 1950 by Dorothy Faust. Copyright © 2013 by Golden West Literary Agency for restored material. Acknowledgment is made to Condé Nast Publications, Inc., for their co-operation.

Chapter One

Be they never so courageous in ordinary circumstances, there are few horses that can be trained in such a way that they keep a steady nerve in the high places, but Major was one of those brilliant exceptions that prove a rule. He came to the very edge of the precipice to snuff the keen air of the cañon, and then hooked a forehoof over the rock and stretched himself like a cat, while the sunlight slipped and glided over the black velvet of his hide and modeled the shoulder muscles in long flutings.

"Now, look here, Major," said the rider, a man who was as shaggy as his horse was sleek, "them treetops ain't going to suit my taste at all. You young fool, keep clear of this bunch of empty air, will you?"

The words were fierce, but the tone in which they were uttered was entirely nonchalant and the rider swung forward to see what lay below. He saw the cliff drop sheer for a hundred feet then put out a steep apron that gradually broadened and decreased in pitch until it rolled out into the beginnings of hills, sliced and carved where the storms had worked gullies.

But what interested the big rider most as he leaned forward was a dark line of shrubs, apparently about knee-high and dipping in and out well down on the slope of these hills, keeping a front as even as though men had planted the hedge. It was timberline that the rider saw, and that was so welcome to him. Here the trees had struggled to the highest point of which they were capable, and here they paused, a tangle of dwarfed veterans perhaps a foot and a half high and five centuries in age. Spruces, pygmy pines, artistic willows, and a few other species made up that advance guard. The line swung on at an even height on either side of the rider. Not a shrub stepped out in advance of the phalanx, for in a single season storms would have harrowed it to death.

The rider regarded this timberline with infinite satisfaction, and then turned and glanced over his shoulder. It was easy to explain his pleasure by following that backward glance. A dozen ragged peaks climbed toward the sky, each as shorn as mountains can be above timberline, whipped by storms, clothed only in winter snow. Beyond and among those visible peaks, Tom Keene was recalling cañons and breakneck slopes in the summit region over which he had passed. No wonder, then, that his eye dropped gratefully to the forested sides of the mountains farther down, where the sturdy lodgepole pines began at ten thousand feet and continued in dense groves to two thousand feet lower, where their rather pale green merged gradually in bigger and nobler evergreens.

Tom Keene was not satisfied with a general glance, however. He uncased a pair of field glasses and probed the distant woods with them until, half a mile down in sheer descent and five miles in an air line, the glasses focused on a little shack barely distinguishable in the distance and among the trees. But no sooner had he marked this wretched little habitation than the horseman drove the glasses back in their case and whirled black Major away from the cliff. A moment later they were laboring down the precipitous descent. And on the way Tom Keene was thinking pleasantly: *The old man'll never know me. Never in the world.*

Far different, indeed, was the seventeen-year-old stripling who had left that same shack ten years before. The smooth face was now clothed in a black beard that began close beneath the eyes and terminated in a square trim just below the chin. Six feet and two inches of bony frame had broadened and deepened and hardened until Tom Keene stripped to a hundred and ninety pounds of iron-hard muscle.

But the physical changes had been the least of all. It was his brain that had developed. Greater, far greater, than the distance his eye glanced down to the shack from the mountain top, was the distance his brain looked back to find his younger self starting into the world for adventure greater than he could find in practicing the arts of

9

woodcraft or tending his father's line of traps in the winter or descending into the lower valleys of the cattle range to work in spring and fall roundups.

So great was the change that he could hardly believe that he was the same man. It was another identity that had become his. Somewhere in the ten years that other self had died, and the new Tom Keene had been born into the world, resourceful, cool-nerved, skeptical. He had worked with his hands ten years before, but now those hands were no longer degraded by the cut and burn of a rope because they must be kept supple for the cards—supple and practiced for the cards so that a separate intelligence seemed to dwell in each fingertip. And the world was a most easy place to make one's way in if one had sufficient wits for it. It was so easy that it was criminal to keep entirely to the flowery path. Tom Keene, for instance, found money but no amusement in playing cards with greenhorns. And therefore he never did it. He chose, rather, to match his wits against men who were as much professionals as he, shrewd, fox-eyed men who could put their emotions behind a mask and keep them safely out of sight during the entire course of a card game.

Falling in with such as these, he found that his course was to play the part of the rough-mannered simpleton until he had inveigled the expert into a game, and until the expert, as always happened, had purposely lost a few stupid hands—bait money. But, when he began to trim Tom Keene, he found the yokel transformed into a dexterous trickster. The play might run very high in an encounter such as this—eagle against eagle—and, though Tom usually won, he occasionally lost, also—lost frequently enough to keep his money reserve low. He knew that he would always continue to lose, and that he could never be a truly great gambler, because he could never become an entirely heartless machine. The beard masked him somewhat, but nothing could mask the fires in those black eyes of his, once his enthusiasm was roused. If he kept to the game, it was not so much because he had the usual gambler's dream of the "million-dollar tableful of boobs", as it was that he loved the cards for their own sake.

Tom liked a straight game, letting chance favor who it would, but most of all he loved to sit in with three or four of his own kind, each man making the deck all but talk, each perfectly aware that the others cheated, each determined to back his own skill against the best tricks of his competitors, and this battle carried on quietly, with all done smoothly, politely. Such an evening to Tom Keene was like a happy hour to the painter; he felt himself rise to the greatest heights, the inspired heights.

For ten years, then, he had followed the fortunes

of life as they came to him by the medium of the gaming table. For ten years he had constantly promised himself to return to the old place, take his father from labors that the aged man must now be growing too feeble to continue, and place him in comfort in some town.

That good thought was the source of the cheery whistle of Tom as Major struck a long, fairly level slope—the last slope leading to the cabin of old Keene—and flew along it, rejoicing in the opportunity to stretch his legs after so many hours of climbing up and down. But, resolved to surprise old John Keene with his appearance, Tom drew rein a considerable distance from the cabin, dismounted, and, leaving the stallion behind him, stole forward on foot.

John Keene was not in the clearing beside the cabin, however, and, when Tom slipped around to the little horse shed behind the cabin, his father was not there. More than that—the only hay in the little mow was a forkful or two of time-yellowed, musty stuff on the floor. There had not been a horse in the shed for many weeks.

A chill of alarm now spread suddenly through the big man, and, running out, he observed that no wisp of smoke issued from the smokestack that sagged above the top of the shanty. The shutter that secured the window in time of storm hung now from one rotting strap. Behind it, the glass of the window was broken and patched with spider webs. With a shout of dismay, Tom ran to the door, sent it crashing down with a kick, and thundered: "Dad! Where are you?"

And then he saw the old man lying on the bunk. He raised one hand in greeting. That was all his strength sufficed for. A death light, so it seemed to Tom, shone on the haggard features.

Chapter Two

He fell on his knees beside John Keene, overcome by a great pity and a great remorse, and he caught the hands in his. Age had drawn the skin tight on those fingers, but, above all, how cold they were on this joyful spring day, so full of sunshine beyond the door. The whole body of the trapper was so wasted by a hard life and a long one that there now seemed barely a spark burning within and sustaining the misty light that gleamed feebly out of the eyes.

One hand fumbled faintly for freedom, and, as Tom released it, it was raised in a sign that seemed to bid him be quiet. At the same time his father closed his eyes and compressed his lips. Tom knew that the dying man was rallying by tremendous effort to recall so much of life as would permit him to speak a few words to his son before he reached the end of the long trail.

In that interim, not daring to watch the silent struggle, no less bitter because of its silence, Tom looked over the familiar room. It seemed to have shrunk since he last saw it. The little stove that had stood on three legs now stood on none at all, but was supported on a platform of small logs roughly squared by the axe. The gun rack contained the weapons, those which he remembered out of his very infancy, unaltered, and still showing every evidence of care. The axes, bright of edge, were tied in a bundle, backs together. The scrap of rag rug had been tramped upon until that last vestige of the checkered pattern now was gone. He turned to the corner cupboard, in the lower part of which dishes for cooking and eating were kept, and the upper part of which had ever been sacred to a few belongings of his father. Even now he thrilled as he glanced at those upper doors with the dark and polished spot from much fumbling at the keyhole.

Below, he saw the bunk that had been his, and he started on observing the blankets neatly folded and piled on it with the sun-yellowed copy of *Ivanhoe* on top—exactly as it had been when he left ten years before. So astonished was he by that sight that he automatically touched his thick beard as though he wished to make sure that ten years had indeed elapsed. In the meantime, a faint murmur from the form beside him made him turn.

"Tom," said the whisper. "Come closer."

He leaned near to his father. "Keep your grip, Dad," he said. "I'm back here to stay as long as I can help. Your hard times are over. Lord knows I've been a skunk for staying away, but now I'll make up. Fight hard, Dad. Fight hard and give me a chance to help."

The old man pressed the face of his son between his trembling hands as though by their touch, rather than the use of his rapidly dimming eyes, he could recognize his boy. "Heaven be praised," he said. "For two days I've wondered why the Lord's kept me here lingering along like this. But now I see. Tom lad, it's a pile easier to die when . . ."

"Who talks of dying?" Tom thundered, leaning still closer, striving, so it seemed, to dart life from his fiery eyes into the body of John Keene, or to supply it with the vibration of his bass voice. "You ain't going to die. You're going to live. Remember when you said that you'd never seen five hundred dollars together at one time? Well, listen to this . . . listen to this." He tore from his waist a money belt, and he pounded it on the floor with a great jingling so that the whole shanty quivered.

"D'you hear? D'you hear? There's twice five hundred. And there's more where it came from. Why, what're you talking about dying? Here's something that'll make your heart warm again, Dad." And over the bony hands of the sick man he poured a tide of golden coins that cast a faint glow, it seemed, like the light of a sunset.

But John Keene felt the gliding metal and heard the strong voice of his son unmoved. "How come you by all that money?" he murmured. "If I could live to get down into the lowlands and . . . yes, it sure might be some help to me, Tom, if I ain't a dying man now. But where'd you get that money?"

A dozen lies leaped to the teeth of Tom Keene. Should he say mining, trapping, cows—there were so many possibilities that he paused, and then he saw that the eye of his father had cleared and was looking into his face like a ray of light plunging into turbid water. And in spite of himself he bowed his head.

"Looks like I ain't been through enough yet. This had to come before I finished," the father murmured. "Leastwise, you couldn't lie to me, Tom, and that's a tolerable big comfort. I reckon you never took nothing from them that couldn't help themselves?"

"Never," Tom said, and he added: "Just keep this talk about dying out of your mind. You're going to live. I'm going to make you, and I'm going to take care of you . . ."

"Son," broke in the dying man, "don't you know that I can't take nothing that don't come out of clean hands?"

"Tell me straight!" cried Tom. "What have you gained by working your heart out all your life? Who's thought any the more of you for all that?"

"I've thought a pile more of myself," the old trapper said. "And it does me good right now. I'm stepping along in the edge of the night, Tom, and any minute I may step off the cliff and never land back in daylight again. And times like this it sure lays a comfort on a gent's heart to know that he's been honest. Besides, by working hard every day and serving God, I've laid up a treasure . . . two treasures, Tom."

"Treasures?" the son asked incredulously.

"One is a good name," said the old man. "You can't find the like or that treasure in gold, my lad. You lay to that. And the other treasure you'll find yonder, inside of that cupboard. Not now, Tom. Don't go for it now. Wait till I'm gone, and then you'll find it. It's the thing that made me so rich I could give away to other folks all my life. It made me so rich that I wish to heaven, Tom, that you and me could change places . . . for your sake. Son, when you . . ." He choked, and Tom caught the meager body in his great arms. "It's only a step," the trapper went on, panting now, "but it's a dark, dark step to be taking, Tom. If only I had some light to show me . . . if you'd get a . . ."

He relaxed, and Tom placed the dead body back on the bunk, closed the mild blue eyes, and folded the hands together. Then, stepping across the room, he flung himself down where he had slept so many years and lay quivering, for the grief was to him like a scourging. He writhed under it. Of what use were his big hands now? All the might in his body had not been enough to breathe into his father enough strength to last him another minute of life.

Those ten years that had passed so carelessly, so joyously, now lay like ten burdens on his heart, for while he played in the sun, the old man had been dying. Winter after winter the length of the trap line had shrunk as the power of the trapper diminished. Year by year his earnings dwindled toward a point. He had been forced to give up the horse that had been his link with the life of the town in the lower valley. And, still uncomplaining, trusting to heaven and that great tomorrow of which he had so often spoken in the past, he had come at length to the hour of his death.

And the proceeds of a single night of Tom's work would have kept the old man in comfort for two years. Here an ugly suspicion came to Tom. It brought him sharply to his feet and made him stride to the old kitchen table, in the deep drawers of which the cornmeal and the white flour were kept. He jerked them open with such violence that a faint dust of the meal rose to his nostrils with a sweet odor. But that was all. The tin bottoms of the drawers were of a polished bareness. With sweat rolling down his face, Tom looked back on the emaciated features of the dead man. Was it starvation? He would never know. That ghost could never be laid. But at least bitter want had hurried the end of John Keene.

He went to the cupboard in a daze. The key was not hanging on the string, but that was nothing. He fixed his fingertips under the edge of the door and ripped it open. Treasure? Inside, he swept his hand on bare shelves until he struck a book that he brought out to the light. It tumbled open in his hand, the film-thin pages slipping away on either side, pages of close print. It was a Bible that had opened to the Psalms, and his eye caught on this place: *I will sing of loving kindness and justice. . . .* The book slipped from the hand of Tom and crushed, face down, against the floor.

"Loving kindness . . . justice!" he cried in fierce mockery. "Does that look like it?"

The walls of the little shack gave back his loud voice with redoubled volume, and, in the silence that followed, his heart shrank suddenly. He picked up the book, turned it, and found that by chance the place had not been lost. Again his eye struck on the line: *I will sing of loving kindness and justice. . . .*

And an odd thought came to Tom Keene that those words might have been brought twice to his attention with a purpose, that it was indeed well for him since the place had not been missed.

He sank slowly upon his bunk and glanced down the page.

Chapter Three

There were three priceless things that, from of old, were the apples of the eye of John Keene. One of them was this little Bible, time-worn, yellow of edge, and frayed. This he had by indirect words commended to his son as a gift.

But the other two treasures had not been mentioned. Tom took them from the wall where they had hung, side-by-side, symbols of the honest heart of the dead man. One was a medal for heroic service in the Army of the Confederate States, and the other was a faded picture of Lincoln. When the grave was dug, Tom placed the two relics on the breast of the trapper and so lowered him into the pit.

It was the first gray of dawn, that coldest and most cheerless time, when the last sod was heaped above the grave. But it was the rose of morning when Tom finished chipping in the inscription on the flat stone that he had dragged to the spot. He stood back with the cold chisel in one hand and the single jack in the other hand, and scanned the ragged letters that he had made.

Here lies John Keene.
He lived square,
and he died with clean hands.

Then he swung into the saddle, and made off down the familiar trail that was unchanged in the slightest degree by the ten years. He was very hungry, very tired, and he would willingly have pushed the black stallion hard to hurry on to the next village, had it not been that the horse was quite as weary with fasting as he. And he would not abuse Major. Three years ago he had had the foresight to invest in the crippled, high-blooded yearling, and his reward was the king of horses now under the saddle.

So, letting the honest Major take his own time— which was a steady gait on the rough, mountain trail—Tom tightened his belt to the last notch and then amused himself with watching the progress of the dawning morning over the peaks, how the shadows melted away in the hollows like pools drying up with magic speed, and how the air grew momentarily warmer as the sun climbed higher and the trail dropped lower.

But this was a poor way of killing time for a man with the spirit of Tom. He leaned, drew from the saddlebag the Bible, and opened it again at random. He had found in it, the evening before, words both stern and beautiful, but now what his eyes discovered started him frowning. Half a dozen times his hands twitched to hurl the book into the neighboring ravine, but each time he managed to look back into the text until the list of the Ten Commandments was finished. After which his comment was a single word repeated once or twice with peculiar variations in the tone. Then he dropped the Bible back into the saddlebag.

But a moment later he was impelled to lean and make sure that none of the pages had been doubled back by this rough treatment, and, when he sat back in the saddle once more, he found that he did not require the printed page in order to recall those commands to his mind, one by one. Of the ten, there were few that he had not violated at one time or another. He reviewed those violations carefully. They were all excusable, he declared to himself. For instance, though he had thrice killed his man, he had been cleared of any blame by a jury of his peers. Nay, he had even been thrice thanked by good and law-abiding citizens because he had rid the community of evil-doers.

But, in spite of that flattering reflection, the printed words jolted across his memory and took on a voice and sang against his ear in rhythm with the steadily padding feet of Major: *Thou . . . shalt . . . not . . . kill.*

Tom Keene swore again. But his throat was dry, and there had come into his mind a second self, most unfamiliar and infernally disagreeable, which sat in judgment upon all that his other self did and said and thought. That new self, on the inside, had an irritating way of agreeing with the printed words. Indeed, it was almost like an echo.

Shawker might be alive to this day, intoned that small, inward murmur, *if you'd given him a chance. You might have been able to tear the gun out of his hand and then . . .*

His throat had grown drier. He gritted his teeth, flung back his big shoulders, dragged down a deep breath, jerked his hat lower over his eyes, scowled like a villain into the shadows of the wood—but, do what he could, he was unable to summon up the old, carefree, hearty soul that had been his. His past began to hang on his mind.

Is this the treasure that my father has left me . . . this devil of remorse? thought poor Tom. Then, unable to resist an odd impulse, he jerked his Colt .45 out of the holster and hurled it into the cañon as far as the strength of his long arm would carry. The moment it had swished from his fingertips, his heart leaped into his throat in dismay. Down it sped in a swift, bright arc and clanged into a wreck on a stone far, far below.

It was a shock that brought Tom up short. "Have I gone batty?" he asked himself. "What's wrong inside of me?"

It was the book, he decided a moment later, that had made him ruin the best old gun that ever punched a way into a gent's hand.

But book and gun were presently forgotten as his mind harked back to his father. In his sullen, restless youth he had often been irritated by the calm of the trapper. He had wondered how a man could cling so contentedly to a single spot for half of a long lifetime. He had rebelled against the smiling, quiet ways of John Keene. Those were not his natural ways. Soul and body, he had taken the mold of the dark-eyed, beautiful girl who had married the trapper and died of a broken heart in the loneliness of the mountains.

But that could not be charged against his father, he decided. Nothing could be charged against that blameless life, and to the very end the old trapper had been able to pour out a strangely effective influence upon all who came near him—all save his own wife and his own son. They alone had been too near, it seemed, to see him as he was. But on all others, to a greater or a lesser degree, fell the influence of that—what should he call it?— loving kindness was certainly the expression.

It came to the big man with a start, and a little chill of awe ran through him. He was glad to see, above the trees of a nearby hollow, the windings of a pale blue twist of smoke. He swung Major to the side and made for the house or campfire, whichever it should prove to be, at a round gallop.

Chapter Four

It was a cabin upon which he broke from the trees, a cabin surrounded by a spacious clearing of several acres. Many of the stumps had been dug out. All around the cabin itself there was a fine

24

stretch of loamy ground, the nucleus and core of what would one day be a rich little farm, no doubt. Toward the edges of the clearing there were increasing numbers of stumps, around which the plow had been driven so close to the trunk as to show that all side roots had been removed. The work of clearing was still going on, for yonder was a new-felled tree as yet untrimmed, and on the trunk of another pine the axe man was working with a will, swinging the heavy axe with a long, loose stroke that did the heart of Tom Keene good. He loved to see sturdy muscle at play; it made his own muscles flex and relax in sympathy with the labor.

In answer to his hail, the fellow turned a tanned, happy face toward him—a man of thirty, perhaps, arrow-straight, hardened, but as yet unbent by the labor of hewing out his home. He sank his axe in the tree and came at once with an eager step that told that he was glad to see a stranger.

"How's chances for breakfast?" asked Tom. "I'm plumb starved."

"Your chances are riding on the top of the world," said the woodcutter. "My brother ain't hardly through finishing up the breakfast dishes. You come along in with me, and I'll see what we can do for you. What's the news with you, partner?"

Tom Keene glanced inward upon his mind. The greatest events of his life had happened this past twenty-four hours, and yet nothing would be news he could tell to another man. He wondered at this greatly. How many other men talked only of things that little concerned them, and buried in silence their real feelings and all that was really vital to them?

"News?" he said. "I been out from any town for quite a spell. I guess I ain't got any news."

He saw the lithe-limbed homesteader picking out the important points about Tom's make-up with a keen eye, dwelling on three things chiefly—the unusual, thick black beard that gave so many years of dignity and importance to Tom, the bulk of shoulders and length of arm, and above all the empty holster in which his cherished Colt had hung. Such a man as Tom was not apt to be seen without a revolver, and if he were without one, there must be a significant reason.

All of these were the comments that, Tom knew, went on inside the brain of the other, but Tom could have laughed aloud. How trifling a thing was a beard or a gun or length of arm, to be used as an index of the mind and soul?

He put the black Major in the shed while his host admired the magnificent body from which Tom stripped the saddle. Then they went to the house. The breakfast dishes, indeed, had not been cleaned. They were still jammed in a heap at one end of the roughly made table. The larger portion of the length was occupied by ponderous books, over which leaned a young fellow as like Tom's first acquaintance as one pea is like another. He had the same lean, sinewy contour of body, the same eagle-thinness of feature, the same bird-like quickness of eye. The main difference was that the face that he turned toward Tom was somewhat pale, the brows separated by a heavy, perpendicular wrinkle, and his glance, for the very first instant, was a little suffused with thought. His thoughtful frown blackened at once to a scowl as he started up with as much guilt as indignation, Tom thought.

"That's the way the dishes are getting done, is it?" sneeringly inquired the woodcutter. "I might've knowed if I'd listened close. I didn't hear no racket."

"There's plenty of time," said the other, who appeared many years the junior of the pair. "We ain't so close to dinner time as all that, are we? Howdy, stranger!"

He looked to Tom with a smile of welcome that, beyond doubt, was as much assumed to turn the wrath of his brother as to greet Keene. The latter was seated in due form at the table, and the elder brother turned to the stove where, by lifting the lid, he found that the fire was out.

At once, he whirled on his younger brother with a flush of rage. "The fire's out!" he exclaimed. "Blowed if you ain't sat right there in arm's reach of it, almost, and let the fire go out!" He ground his teeth as this incredible fact worked its way home into his mind.

"I had something to do besides feed a fire," said the younger of the two. "I had something to do that was more important than that, Hal. You know it, too, if you'd stop and give yourself a chance to think." He indicated the ponderous tomes on the table with a gesture that was not altogether without a tinge of self-conscious satisfaction.

"To the devil with the books and to the devil with the law," Hal said. "You got no business making a bargain with me if you ain't going to keep it, Jack. You come here agreeing that, if I do the chopping and all the work except a few of the little chores, you'll have everything shipshape inside the house, and that you'll still have time for your studying. I ain't aiming to cut off on your studying. I'm proud to have you aiming to be a lawyer. But I say I'm blowed if I'm going to get the short end of the bargain all the time."

They faced each other with clenched fists.

Jack ground his teeth in turn. "Are you going to expose all of our family history?" he asked with biting sarcasm. "You might begin further back and tell the conditions under which Father left you the money to start up on this place with me. Why don't you tell that, too, as long as you're in a humor to communicate the details of our family arrangements to every stranger who happens by?"

"You can't bulldoze me with none of your big

28

words," Hal said, hotter than before. "We was to have beans for dinner, and you know it, and them beans ain't been put on. Didn't I pick them beans over last night . . . which was your work? Didn't I put 'em to soak last night . . . which was your work . . . just so's you could have a straight shot at your law reading, which you're always howling for?"

"I can't help putting the study of law a trifle above the importance of wood chopping," Jack observed with a glance at Tom Keene that invited the latter's approbation.

"You can't, eh?" roared Hal. "Well, it's about time you did start putting wood chopping above your rotten books! I ain't seen you do anything but read most of your life, and yet you ain't got anywhere. . . ."

"I can do anything you can do with an axe or a horse or a rope," Jack said fiercely, "or with my fists!"

"Eh?" grunted Hal. "D'you mean that?"

"I don't have to repeat a thing in order to mean it," Jack said with a sneer, and he fell back a little and dropped his hand on his hip in what Tom could not help feeling was a rather oratorical attitude.

"Jack," cried his brother, "if it wasn't for a stranger being here, I'd teach you a thing or two that maybe ain't in books! You been just aching for . . ."

"For a what?" asked Jack.

"A licking," Hal said.

"You ain't man enough."

"I'm twice man enough."

"Lemme see you do something besides talk."

"Then . . ."

They leaped together with muffled shouts of rage and crashed against each other with a shock of their big bodies that made the cabin quake. So confused were they by their anger that they were unable to strike directed blows, and, before one fell, Tom Keene tore them apart with such violence that they staggered away to opposite walls of the cabin.

"Gents," Tom said, "I sure hate to step in between when folks is having a little argument, private-like. But right now I got to say that it sure ain't nacheral . . ."

"Curse your hide!" Hal thundered, swelling with redoubled anger as soon as he saw that he could turn it toward some more legitimate object than his brother. "What call have you got coming in here and breaking things up?"

"And tearing my shirt!" cried Jack. "Your advice wasn't asked, was it? No one appointed you judge, so far as I know."

"Friends," Tom Keene said, recalling with all his might the dying and beatified face of his father, and striving hard to banish the temptation to war from his mind, "I'm a peaceable man, and

I don't want no trouble. All I'm trying to do is ask you if you ain't acting like a pair of young fools . . . ?"

"Fools?" cried Jack. "Call me a fool, and I'll smash your dirty beard into your face, stranger!"

It was an involuntary act. No forethought lay in it. No malice was behind the hand. No plan made him double the fist. And yet the big left fist of Tom Keene was doubled, and, before he knew what he was about, his long left arm had twisted back and then struck out with the speed of a rattler trying to strike two gophers before they can both escape. That bony mass of fist was avoided by the blocking arm of Jack so that it did not shoot through to his face, but it was deflected to his chest and landed on that target with sufficient force literally to lift Jack from his feet and fling him with a crash against the wall of the little house.

Then, knowing instinctively what was coming from the other side, Tom pivoted on toe and heel and started to punch with his right fist which landed on Hal's abdomen as that bronzed athlete came hurtling through the air to the rescue of his brother.

The blow deposited him in a gasping heap on the floor, but at the same moment Jack, rebounding from the wall, landed solidly on the side of Tom's jaw and staggered him. By the time he had recovered his footing, both Hal and Jack

31

were tearing in at him like two fighting terriers.

Well for Tom Keene then that his precarious mode of making a living had forced him to study with utmost care all methods of self-defense—so-called. He met Hal with a long stabbing left to the face that converted his nose to a red blotch and stopped him as though he had run into a wall in the dark. And then he twitched across a right hook, short and nasty, that landed cleanly on the point of Jack's chin and dropped him on the floor on his face, a limp and quivering mass. The next second, heaved into the air in the grip of those long, iron-hard arms, Hal was sent crashing down upon the body of his brother, and both lay inert, slowly regaining their scattered, stunned senses.

As for Tom, he retreated, dismayed by what he had done, and sat upon the edge of the table, staring down at them. It had been a wonderful treat, this moment of exercise. And he was assured that the promptings of it had come from the wicked spirit that had in the first place driven him out from his father's honest cabin and made him exchange the peaceful life of a trapper for the wild and turbulent life of a gambler.

Out of the bottom of his heart came the words with which he greeted the stunned brothers as they staggered to their feet. "Gents, I'm plumb sorry. If I could make it up to you, I would. But I got this to say . . . it seemed pretty hard to me that two brothers should stand up like that and light into each other. It sure did seem hard. I ain't any sky pilot to do preaching, understand? But I wasn't one of them that had a brother born in his house. I've had to get along without one. Maybe you think that's easy? Well, it ain't. A gent that has a brother born in his house is plumb lucky. Why? Because he's got a sure enough friend made to order and guaranteed. He . . ."

"You've talked enough . . . enough!" Jack snarled. "Get out or . . ."

"Take your hand off that gun," Tom Keene said, rising from the table. "Take your hand off that gun, friend, or I'll sure enough pulverize you. I"— he attempted to justify the old fierce impulse that rose in him according to the new lights that were dawning in his nature—"ain't going to stand by and see you do murder. Not me, Jack. And, if you don't let go of that gun, I'll take it away from you and jam it down your throat!"

The last words came in a roar, with a flash of teeth through the beard, and Jack, appalled by that voice of thunder, hastily dropped his fingers from the gun and stood like one about to be stricken by a blast of lightning. The stain from his face dripped down to his shirt while he listened as Tom continued.

"Boys, it seems to me like I see what you're starting in to do here. You're going to concentrate chiefly on making this farm a go, Hal. You're going to practice law over in Gridley, Jack. If the two of you will pull together, why, they ain't hardly a thing that you couldn't do. You could have everything smooth as silk inside of a couple or three years. But, gents, I'll tell you where you got to watch yourselves. Him that don't trust other folks, ain't going to be trusted by them. That's sure plain!"

The thought burst upon Tom like an inward light. He saw that the two brothers had forgotten their bruises and their wounds in the battle against him. He saw that they were listening, fascinated. That they were as much hypnotized by the display of emotion on that rough and bearded face as by his words, did not occur to him. But a glory fell on Tom Keene and glittered in his wild eyes and made him tremble until his beard quivered.

"Partners!" he cried. "When I think of what you two have got by being brothers, I sure envy you. There ain't no bar between you. You don't have to sit across the table making talk that don't mean nothing and chattering about stuff that's just news of other people. No, sir, for you can sit down there and open up and talk right from the bottom of your hearts. You don't have to be ashamed of showing yourselves the way you are. You can learn out of each other. Why, if you'd trusted each other and had faith in each other, you'd've been able to break me in two and throw the pieces out the door. D'you believe me?"

They were afraid to deny him. They could only gasp.

"God made you strong enough to make each other stronger," Tom said as the belief in his own words took hold on him like a torrent. His voice rose and crowded the cabin. "All you got to do is to give your hand freely to your friend and believe him. Them that you believe in will believe in you. Partners, if we had faith in one another, this old world could be as happy as a dream."

Chapter Five

It was noon before they would let him leave, and, when he insisted that he could stay no longer, Hal went out and saddled black Major. Tom turned on the younger brother.

"Partner," he said, "I been talking like I was a pile older than I am. And I been talking like I was a good man. I ain't."

Jack watched him carefully, thoughtfully. After that first moment of battle, he seemed vastly attracted to the stranger.

"I ain't denying that," Jack said, "till I hear what else you got to say."

"What would you say was my way of making a living?" asked Tom.

"Why, preaching, I'd say," said Jack. "I suppose you're on your way to take up your work in a church right now?"

Tom jerked off his money belt. It fell on the table with the weight of a heavy fist. "How d'you think a preacher got that much money?"

"In a town," Jack answered. "Folks in a town would pay that much money to hear the sort of things that you can say."

"Do you think they would?" Tom asked, wondering. "But why should they pay me anything?"

"So you could use it to help the poor, of course."

"Suppose I used it to help myself?"

Jack laughed softly. "Anybody could see that you're honest," he said. "Anybody could see that you're a pretty good sort of a man."

Tom Keene sighed. "I'll tell you something," he said. "My father died because I left him in want when he was an old man. And this money, yonder, is the money I got by being a sharper at cards. That's the sort of a good man I am." As he spoke his confession, shame and sorrow burned into him. "I've been a thief, Jack . . . except that thieves have got to use some sort of courage. They got to take a chance on being caught. But I've been a gambler. Nothing is any lower than that."

"A long time ago," Jack said, his eyes wide, "a lot of good men have been pretty rough characters, but they repent and make the best sort, they say. They know what being really bad is. A man that's born a saint . . . why, he don't know what temptation is."

"I tell you this, son," Tom Keene said, "a gent

can't get over a thing by just repenting. It won't work at all. The things you've done that are wrong stay with you. They're part of you. Everything that a gent has ever done is a part of him, just like his eyes and his ears. He can't forget. It grows with him. I'll never be over being sick for what I've done in my life. I've done a pile of bad things. But worst of all, I'm a murderer."

"I don't believe it!" Jack cried, nevertheless shaken.

"I am," groaned Tom. "I've murdered my own father. I broke his heart waiting for me, and then I killed him with starvation. Why, a murder with a gun ain't nothing compared to that sort of thing. And d'you know why I'm telling you all this, Jack?"

"I don't know," Jack replied humbly.

"Because it'll make you remember me and what I've said," said Tom. "You got interested in what I've talked about, but you been just interested in the words. Now that you know the truth about me, you'll remember everything and believe. It ain't the words I've spoke that'll do any good in this old world, Jack. It's something behind the words that counts. I tell you, son, we all got a fire inside of us. Sometimes that fire gets into our words. Sometimes it gets into what we do. But I can feel it burning inside of me . . . the want to help other folks and keep 'em from doing what I've done and to teach 'em to have faith and trust in one another.

I ain't got no words to pour that fire into. But God will help me to show it to folks, and God will help me to stand it when they laugh at me. But you, Jack, you'll remember?"

"Why will Hal remember without knowing this?" asked Jack. "Why shouldn't he know the truth about you, too?"

"Because he ain't got your head on his shoulders," Tom said. "If he knew that I'd ever been real bad, he'd lose all trust in me. He'd think that I was play-acting all this. You see? But you look deeper. Because I'm smudged up, you'll be more apt to think I may have something worthwhile in me. D'you know why? Because you're smudged up yourself, Jack."

The younger man started back from him, indignant and surprised.

"I mean it," said Tom. "You're using your brother mighty shameful, Jack. You think that gents that don't know nothing about books can't amount to much in the world. But I tell you, Jack, that your brother is a mighty good man. He ain't open-minded like you, but everything that's inside his mind is good stuff. You got to do your part. You think you ought to get a pile of praise because you're reading books and getting ready to practice law. You think that, because you're boosting yourself along, everybody had ought to give you a lift. Well, Jack, that's a devil of a good way for a gent to ride for a fall, I can tell you. You got to be more humble . . . you got to think about making your brother comfortable while he works like blazes to give you a home. And if you only half try, he'll be so grateful, Jack, that the tears'll plumb start in his eyes. Meantime, here he comes. Before he comes . . . I know you'll be needing money. Here's a hundred. Spend it just for your books. So long."

He strode out of the cabin, leaving Jack breathing hard, confused by a dozen conflicting emotions of gratitude, anger, suspicion, happiness.

Outside, Tom took the black horse from the hand of Hal. And into the latter's unwilling fingers he stuffed his money belt.

"Look here," protested Hal, "you've done more good for us than you can make out, already. D'you think that I'm going to take . . ."

"It belongs to you or to nobody," Tom said. "I'll tell you why. A dying man told me to give it to the first good man that I met along the road. And I guess that you're him, Hal. So long!"

He was in the saddle and away before Hal could open his lips to protest again.

Among the mountains rode Tom Keene. The day faded. The evening came on with a soft wind blowing upon him through a gap in the range of peaks before him, and the wind was fragrant with the perfumes of the evergreens. The stars were beginning to walk out into the eastern sky. And a mighty happiness was beginning to strike through Tom's soul.

"And," Tom cried, "to think that all my life I been working as hard as I could to take things, and never guessed for a minute that the greatest fun of all was in giving things away!"

The road climbed. And his thoughts climbed with it. To Tom it seemed that the dark lowlands behind him represented the dark years of his life, the cruelly selfish years. But, beyond the tops of the mountains, just before him, the stars were crowding down against the shadows. There was beauty before him. Why had he never paid any attention to such things before? Because he had kept his eyes too constantly fixed on his own welfare. And now, the minute he lifted his eyes from himself, a weight lifted from him, a weight of worry about his welfare. Let each day take care of itself. He would only, hereafter, labor to sow the seeds of happiness and faith in one another among his fellow men.

So thinking, he reached the top of the divide. Below him was a valley. He saw the sprinkled lights of a town straight ahead. And in that distance, every household was reduced to a single, meager spider thread of golden light. A dozen people, perhaps, were represented by each shaft of light. And in a great outflowing of compassion it seemed to Tom Keene that the blackness of the rest of the village was typical of the lives of men.

Happiness was confined, in every house, to only a golden instant here and there in the blackness of the days.

But if he could waken them to the truth—if he could kill suspicion, envy, greed, hatred of one another—then the besieging darkness would roll away.

He lifted his voice into tremendous singing, and Major, as though in response to a prick of the spurs, spurted into a swift gallop down the slope.

Chapter Six

It was two or three months later. Tom himself did not know, for he had long since lost all track of time. He counted existence only in terms of the good he could do in the future, and the evil he had done in the past. Just as he had poured his whole strength into the game of taking by skill and cunning, so he now poured it into the opposite game of giving all he had.

He studied the Bible, not as extensively as he might, for study did not come easily to him. Moreover, he fell into the habit of dreaming over the poetry of the Great Book, with instinct for its power and suggestiveness. Out of it he quarried the proofs with which he fortified his theory. But, on the whole, he was able to do very well without reference to the Bible or quotation from it. He was making his own religious way and gathering his own adherents by the preaching of his simple belief that the clue to golden happiness for all men is faith and trust in one another.

He carried his voice everywhere. In mines, in cow camps, in lumber gangs he appeared and held forth, and men listened. They listened to him in the first place, because he was so big and his beard was so tangled and thick. They listened to him in the second place because his voice was so ringing and loud. They listened to him in the third place because, otherwise, if they taunted him or interrupted him, he knocked them down with two fists that were like two boulders, and they listened to him in quiet wonder because his words bore the stamp of his sincerity, which made them current coin for any mind, no matter how simple, to grasp.

"If you believe in your brother, your brother will believe in you. If you give with a free hand, you cannot help getting back what you give."

Such a doctrine was simplicity itself, and a simple doctrine is the best for a man who wants to make converts. Once in a mining camp, as he was talking after supper to the long table lined with miners at their coffee, he was interrupted by a man who knew him as an ex-gambler, and this fellow stood up and accused him in round terms. And when he was through and the miners leaned forward to hear the denial and weigh the proofs, they were astonished to hear, instead, an admission of the truth. Such a man was to be believed.

Rather than scoff at Tom Keene for his past, they believed him on the theory that he who knows what sin is from practice, should be more able to talk of it to others.

He was riding in a country new to him, a country of neither dead flat nor mountains, but rather of pleasantly rolling hills, with stretches of arable soil between, and some forest and much good grazing land. In the distance, a town was announced by the pricking of the church steeple above a hill. Closer at hand was a house by the road, with a little girl of twelve, perhaps, her bare legs and bare arms brown, singing like a bird near a well.

Tom Keene drew rein. All that is beautiful, he had found, gives a man strength. And he smiled as he watched the child and listened. She sat with her legs dangling on the inside of the well, and with a stick and string she fished for imaginary prizes in the airy depths below her. It was no doubt a disused well. On the far side of the house was a windmill swinging its shaft and creaking busily as a changeable wind swung the fan slowly back and forth.

She leaned, slipped. Tom saw two brown arms flash in the air as she turned and caught at the edge of the well stones. Then she dropped from sight, and her scream was chopped away in the middle by a splash.

Major, inspired by the unaccustomed touch of

the spurs, cleared the fence in a tremendous bound. Tom was out of the saddle in the instant, and stooped above the well. Far below, past the dried mosses on the stones of the old well, was the dark circle of water with a swirl of green to mark the spot where the child had gone down.

At that moment the girl showed again, her clutching arm thrusting above the water. Had she been clear-headed, she could have caught a crevice of the stones at the level of her head and there supported herself for some time, but she was blind with panic, and Tom had only a single glimpse of the wild face before she went under again.

The next instant he was going down the well with reckless speed, wedging his boots into the rough projections of the stones and cursing the spurs and the high heels that hampered him. He reached the bottom in time to thrust his right hand far down and tangle his fingers in her hair. He drew up. It seemed that a dead weight floated toward the surface. Then her face was exposed, wonderfully changed. Indeed, death could not have altered her more. The brown was vanished from her face. He saw colorless lips, closed eyes, and a small, pinched, pretty face.

Still higher he raised her. Weakly her arms dangled behind her. When he called, the crowding echoes made his voice an immense murmur that was confused to his own ears. But he managed to get his arm under her shoulders, and with some effort he worked her up until she could be placed across his shoulder.

As he labored, he jammed one of her arms against the stones, and this brought a sudden outcry of pain from her. He saw that the arm was hanging crooked. The bone had been snapped in the fall. That wail did not last. All in a moment she shook back the hair that straggled around her face. She clasped his neck with her other arm, and when he panted out—"Hold tight, little one, and don't be afraid."—she actually managed to summon up a wan smile to assure him of her courage.

He began to climb. His boots had touched the water at the bottom, and now they slipped half a dozen times on his way up. He was in constant danger of falling from his place. Moreover, it was hot as an oven where the sun had heated the stones, and they now reflected the heat. The descent had seemed short. But the climb up was prodigiously long. Even his huge muscles began to ache before he was halfway up.

And, partly to give himself more courage, he said to the girl over and over: "You're not afraid, honey?"

She would answer in a voice made small with the pain that she was suffering: "I'm not afraid."

A voice came running from the distance, crying out. And as he neared the top, a woman leaned, calling—"Mary! Mary!"—and then a scream as she saw Tom and his burden.

But what a plucky young one it was. She raised her head. It had fallen a moment before on Tom's shoulder, and a faint moan of pain had come from her. But now she looked up and cried: "I'm all right. I'm 'most as good as new."

A moment later Tom placed his burden in the arms of the woman, and all three were laughing and talking at once, weak with joy and thrilling with the saved life—until Mary dropped back her head in a dead faint.

They put her down on the ground, and her mother opened her dress at the throat. But Tom started up and pointed over his shoulder.

"Where's the nearest doctor?" he asked. "We've got to have one here. Her arm's broke bad, lady. It ought to be set right away, I guess."

"He's only two miles away, around that hill, yonder. But I doubt that he will come. We owe him too much money already, and I can fix . . ." She broke off.

Tom was already in the saddle, and Major rose like a bird and cleared the fence. His leap carried him into the center of the road, and then he swerved and spurted away at a sprinting gait for the doctor's.

Tom found the man of medicine reading comfortably on his verandah. He was a little, stern-faced person, equipped with powerful glasses and a precise manner. His appearance was finished off with a narrow gray beard, carefully trimmed.

He uttered a wail and dropped his book at the sight of Major soaring over the fence, smashing to bits some of the choicest rows in the vegetable garden that the doctor cared for in his leisure moments.

In the next instant big Tom Keene vaulted out of the saddle and landed with a crash on the porch. "A broken arm," he said. "Where's your things?"

And he rushed the doctor into the house, stammering protests at every step of the way.

"I'll get my horse and buggy," began the doctor. "But who's this for?"

"Up the road, here. I dunno their names. A pretty woman and a sight prettier girl. They say you've been there before. And . . ."

"The Carvers!" the doctor cried. "I can't go. Mercy is one thing, and human kindness is all very well . . . but it can be run into the ground. By the eternal, I'm not going, sir. They owe me for scarlet fever and measles and whooping cough. I've doctored their horses and their cattle. I've gone to them in fair weather and foul. But last year I drew a line and swore that never again would worthless John Carver command my services when . . ."

At this point it became difficult for him to continue his observations, for he was scooped up inside the arm of big Tom Keene and carried, all his five feet two of dignity wriggling and writhing, out to Major, where he presently found himself deposited in front of the saddle.

"You infernal rascal," began the doctor. "I'll have you tarred and feathered for this. I'll have you hanged from the highest cottonwood tree in the county. I'll have you . . . whoop!"

His voice ascended to a yell of terror as Major, hardly encumbered by the additional burden of the doctor's spare body, hurtled into the air and cleared the fence, leaving the wrecked vegetable garden in much the same manner as he had entered it.

The doctor had scarcely finished commending Tom's eternal soul to the care of the Creator when he found himself borne up the road at a terrific speed, and, looking up in terror at the blowing black beard of his captor, he was forcibly reminded of some of those genie who make the enchanting and terrible tales for children. He had not more than accommodated himself to the facts of the case and begun another exposition of the dire calamities that would happen to Tom for his outrage, when the horse was halted with jarring, scraping hoofs in the middle of a cloud of dust, and the doctor was jerked to the ground and his case of instruments and his black official bag thrust into his hands. Above him towered a grim-faced giant.

"Look here," Tom Keene said. "There's a little

girl in this house that's got a busted arm. Fix her, and I'll see that you're paid for the job. But, if you do a shabby piece of work, I'll come and knock your house into a pile of shingles and set the place on fire and throw you on top. I mean that. Now get in there and start working."

The doctor gazed apprehensively upon this thunderer, then turned and fled for the door of the house.

By the time Tom had entered the room where the child lay, he found that the doctor was an infinitely changed man. He had shed his irritation and his offended dignity like a worn-out coat. He was moving about the room with a precision and speed incredible to Tom. In a marvelously short space of time, he saw a narcotic administered to the plucky little sufferer, and then the making of the splints and the applying of the bandages went on apace.

Tom was made as comfortable as possible in a shirt and vest belonging to Mr. Carver. As for the wife, she could not speak to the rescuer without tears. Tom accordingly avoided her.

At length, from the sick room issued the doctor and stood again on the porch, rubbing his hands together and sunning himself in the last warmth of the day while he walked up and down and hummed a little tune under his breath. Mrs. Carver followed him with grateful and rather apprehensive eyes, as though she dreaded the mention of the bills, which was sure to be forthcoming. But the doctor was too self-contented at that particular moment to refer to disagreeable subjects.

"A very pretty fracture," he announced, "but it's going to heal . . . with proper care . . . as clean as a whistle, Missus Carver. Mind you, I say with proper care. Your husband can't come storming around the house. Mary'll have to have quiet for a time. Understand?"

"Yes, Doctor," Mrs. John Carver murmured.

Kings do not elicit the humble submission that is paid to physicians. "And now," said the doctor with a strange mixture of amusement and anger as he faced Tom Keene, "I'm going to leave you and walk home."

Tom followed him a little distance down the road. "I guess," he said, "that I acted like I was bull-dogging a yearling more'n going for the doctor. But, you see, Missus Carver told me, to start with, that they owed you a bunch of money, and that they had no right to send for you."

"They hadn't," the doctor snappily replied, "but, heigh-ho, I've come, and the job's done. Not a bad job, either." He was so delighted with the work he had just accomplished that he could not refrain from walking with the springing step of a youth and whistling a bar of an old air. "As for your own actions," went on the doctor, "I am of a school in medicine that does not keep such a strict eye upon the manner in which a thing is done as upon the fact that it is accomplished. A broken bone is a broken bone, and, though one may put on his splints in one way and another in a different way, the important thing is that the bone be made to knit. Well, sir, you were sent for a doctor. You got him, and you brought him home." He laughed again, while his good humor amazed Tom. "The way you got me doesn't really matter."

"I'll pay for the . . ."

But Tom was interrupted by a great-voiced explosion from the doctor. "You'll pay for nothing!" He paraphrased somewhat clumsily: "What are you to Hecuba or Hecuba to you? No, sir, I'm not the man who'll be found wanting in charity. Matter of fact, I do three dollars of work for every one I'm paid for. And, if I do such work for others, why not for sweet little Mary Carver. Heaven bless her."

The heart of the big man warmed to his companion. "You're a good man," Tom said, "a mighty good man."

"Nonsense," the little fellow said, and thrust out his chest with a great air. "I'm a doctor . . . that's all." He added: "What did I hear Missus Carver telling me about your climb up the well . . . up the well? Good Lord, sir, what do you mean by telling me that I'm a good man? Nonsense. Tut, tut, tut! You'd pay me for the work, eh? Never in a thousand lifetimes, sir. And who are you?"

"I'm a tramp, more or less," Tom said frankly. "I go about enjoying life, you might say, in my own way. But I'm sure interested in that little Carver girl."

"So's everybody in the county," said the doctor, "for a braver and a clearer-eyed and a more trusting and gay little body was never born, upon my honor."

"But from what you said," Tom went on, "and from the looks of that big house and the buildings around it, her folks ain't in as good shape as they might be so far as money goes."

"Money?" exclaimed the doctor. "Why, once they were millionaires, I hear. John Carver's father was a king in these parts of the world. There was only one strong law, and that was his word. That was John Carver, the First. But John Carver, the Second, is a different story. He started wild as a boy, gambled most of his father's money away, and then he got married and began to hate his wife because he couldn't support her. You may have met that type of man here and there? The lowest of the low, in a way. They are cruel to those who are dependent on them, simply because they cannot provide for the dependents. Well, that's the way with John Carver. You ask me if he is a scoundrel. I say no. You ask me if he is dishonest, I say not to my knowledge. But I'll say this . . . that he leads a strange life, with his pocket full of money one month and not a penny the next. But, no matter how much money he gets, never a cent of it goes to the paying of his just debts, confound him!"

Tom took his leave of the physician and set his face toward the Carver house. There, he knew, was a job cut out for him.

Chapter Seven

With the unsavory picture of the Carver household in his mind's eye, Tom Keene turned back toward the house. As he walked along, he eyed the big, rambling building with a growing interest. Some houses are just so many stones or boards put together, but others have a distinct personality that may be recalled or noted when the form is not in the observer's eye at all. The house of the Carvers was such a one.

It was built in that period when the mid-Victorian romancers were most in love with the Gothic and the pseudo-Gothic, and everything that tended toward the mysterious and the exciting. Architects in this same period were prone to erect tall houses with as many gables as possible, and with lonely rooms set off in turrets at the corners. In this manner, the house of Carver had been raised. Half the panes of glass in the upper windows were gone, and the elaborate carving that edged the cornice, where the fancy of the workman had led him into the creation of odd monsters, had broken away in sections and fallen to the ground.

In fact, never had Tom Keene seen a house that so adequately expressed a fallen estate. It was large enough to have housed forty. Instead, it did not house four. All the out houses, as well—barns, sheds of all kinds, which had once been erected on the most princely scale to house horses, to stow away immense quantities of winter food for the cattle, and to cover the machinery needed in the operation of a great estate on which both farming and cattle raising were conducted—all of these buildings showed even greater disrepair than the dwelling. Their backs were broken by time and neglect. Their sides sagged in. Long boards had fallen here and there. Indeed, the farm buildings were in such condition that they were past help. At a glance, even the most ignorant person could tell that it would cost more money and time to repair than it would to rebuild.

A peculiar melancholy invaded the mind of Tom as he considered these details. Floating between him and the fact as he saw it, was an image, like a mirage, of the place as it had once been, when everyone who drove over either hill into view of the Carver house must have slackened the trot of his team to a walk to enjoy the prospect spread before him, and to envy the power and the vast wealth of those who lived behind the shelter of the trees in the great house.

What is so melancholy as the sight of fallen greatness? And what, Tom could not help asking himself, had been the root of the weakness? In what direction had the first Carver built upon sand? But at least this much was true: no matter how utterly the family had fallen, in the person of Mary Carver the line had put forth a lovely blossom, before its death.

Such thoughts haunted the steps of Tom as he turned again from the road and walked up the path to the porch. He noticed on either side, what he had not paid heed to before—that this open ground was stubbed over with the stumps of trees. No doubt these were originally planted here to furnish shade, and the improvident present owner had chopped them down to furnish wood for the stove!

In the front hall Mrs. Carver met him, a little flushed, a little large of eye. "I guess you'll be hungry about this time of day?" she asked him. And there was a timidity about her question that made him look at her again.

"Always carry a pretty good appetite around with me," Tom answered.

"I . . . ," began Mrs. Carver, and paused. She clasped her hands nervously before her, and her flush died out to a wretched pallor. "There ain't much to offer you," she finally managed to say. "I was expecting to have . . . John . . . out from town with a lot of things, but he ain't come yet, and right now there's hardly . . ."

"Don't you go apologizing," Tom said heartily. "You don't have to start worrying and cooking to make me happy. Boiled potatoes and boiled pork is a feast for me. Don't have to be breast of chicken . . . no ma'am!"

Still she paused. The gloomy thought obtruded itself in Tom's mind that the woman might be actually begrudging him food.

She was making a great effort, and at length, with her head bowed and her eyes turned to the floor, she was able to say: "I can offer you flap-jacks and . . . and tea."

And all at once Tom saw things that had been present to his eyes before, but to which he had remained blind. He saw her thinness of face, which made her cheek bones so prominent; he saw the stoop of her hollow shoulders. Above all, he remembered the strange lightness of the body of the girl. But no sooner had the ugly thought presented itself to him than he shut it away. It could not be in this day and age. Men might commit strange and awful crimes, but he had never yet found one fallen so low that he actually allowed his family to suffer for the lack of food.

But the woman was cringing and shrinking before his horrified gaze. It had been worse than the laying on of whips for her to tell him this shameful truth about her husband.

Sweat poured out on the forehead and from the very armpits of Tom Keene. He fell into a hot agony of shame for the whole race of men that had produced the wretch named John Carver.

"I was only joking," he managed to say. "I couldn't . . . I couldn't stay and . . . and have supper with you-all, anyways. You see, I got to go on. I'm due right now in town. I got to . . ."

But she bowed her head and rested her face in her hands. She wept.

It was agony to Tom to watch her. It sent queer pangs of sorrow through him. He was ashamed. He felt as though he had been abashed before a multitude. He stepped to her and laid his quivering hand on her shoulder. Heaven above! How sharply the shoulder bone struck through to the heavy palm of his hand.

"Don't do that," Tom said huskily. "Please don't do that, lady. Look here. I'm coming back . . . quick."

"No, no!" she cried. "You don't mean you're coming back to . . . to bring us something? Oh, if I took charity, my husband would be furious with me. He has a terrible temper, and he would lose it if he dreamed that I . . . you see, he can't help it because we're this way. He really doesn't know . . ."

Tom Keene ground his teeth. "If I should do anything for you, lady," he said gently, "nobody in the wide world would ever know about it unless you wanted to tell 'em yourself."

"You . . ."

"You just raise up your head and stand on your two feet and forget that you're afraid, Missus Carver," he insisted, and he drew her hands away from her face.

"But I never can look you in the eye," she said miserably. "I never can. After what you've done for me . . . for Mary . . . for poor John himself . . . and then to think." Tears ran down her thin cheeks again, and she wavered a little.

By thunder, thought Tom Keene to himself, *she's plumb weak. She's pretty near starved.* He said aloud: "I'm going to be back not so very much after it's dark. Will you keep a-smiling till I come? And will you start a-smiling now, lady?"

She managed a miserable smile, obediently, and, with his heart smiting him, Tom turned away and went hurriedly out of the house.

He looked on the world in the glory of the sunset time with a joyless eye. It was a bad world. There was a vast predominance of evil in it, or else this poor woman and her child could never have fallen into this condition.

Throwing himself into the saddle of Major, he sent that glorious animal plunging down the road. And there was revolt in the heart of Tom—there was war in his heart. But, whether he wanted most to help the woman and her child or wring the neck of John Carver, he could not tell.

Chapter Eight

Tom Keene stood in the middle of the village street. The silken black of Major was his background; the big horse towering with head thrown high. On the one hand was the lit entrance to the gambling hall; on the other hand was the bustle of Porterville's leading saloon, and in the distance, along that crooked street that had first been laid out in all its winding by leisurely cattle who wore the trail to the water hole, the smoke from a score of smokestacks and chimneys wound up into the sunset sky. The windows began to be blocked out in yellow squares as lamps were lit. Porterville was entering upon a peaceful night.

Men were either in their homes or in the hotel a little farther down the street, thinking of supper. Only a scattered few took this odd time of the day to patronize the saloon or Will Jackson's gambling house, where the cards talk "plain talk that any honest gent can understand." There was nothing moving in the street other than a thin, blue-white cloud of dust that the wind had lifted up and was rolling along between the houses, puffing it leisurely into varying forms.

How could the village be pleasantly roused to answer the will of Tom and come out here from dining table and saloon bar and gambling machine to listen to his words? The means he adopted were means that he had used before and always with the greatest success. He patted the neck of Major and pointed to the nearest door, the door of Jackson's.

Major snorted, then walked obediently to the designated house, tapped on the door with his forehoof, and, when it was opened, advanced a half step into the interior. There he maintained his ground, in spite of curses, until he had emitted a long and ringing neigh, after which he withdrew, rearing back with the agility and balance of a cat. Naturally half of the men in the room came to learn the cause of this strange performance, and they crowded out of the door to see Major step across the street to the big, bearded man who waited there, and who straightway pointed out the saloon.

Whatever game was on, it was well worthwhile stopping to watch such a trained performer at his tricks. They saw Major go to the saloon, thrust the swinging doors open with his nose, and stride half his length into the saloon. Again he neighed, and again, in his retreat, he was followed to the doors by a mass of curious men. Still he was sent on by Tom until he had climbed the front steps of half a dozen houses and neighed inside their doors, and by this time his purpose was accomplished.

Rumors, that will pierce walls of stone, traveled easily among the flimsy shacks of the town and brought man, woman, and child into the dust of the street. Here they saw Major take up his position and saw big Tom Keene swing up into one stirrup, sitting crosswise in the saddle so that he could speak more easily to the gathering crowd. The shaft of light from the open door of Jackson's fell full upon him. And because they had gathered to see tricks, they stayed even when he began to talk about good will and trust in one another, and charity.

Here, however, they wavered. All the eloquence of Tom could not really avail when there was hanging in the balance against him the fragrance of suppers cooking on a score of stoves. The rear edges of the little crowd began to give back and thin out, and a man who had spent somewhat too much time and money in the saloon cried: "If you got that sort of a lingo, why don't you wait for Sundays? Expect to waste our time in the middle of the week?"

The word was instantly taken up by a burly chap who roared: "If you want money, why don't you work for it?" And he began shouldering his way through the front ranks toward Tom, delivering a steady volley of curses as he came. He, also, had spent overmuch time in the saloon, and his liquor urged him to find action. And so he came toward Tom, a red-headed fellow, hair on end.

By this time, disgusted at the profanity of the man of the red hair, the women had sifted quickly out of the little mob and Tom saw his entire audience about to fall to pieces. His course of action was swiftly determined. He swung his leg into the saddle, twitched Major around, and, as the people scattered with shouts of alarm from his path, he bolted straight at Red Head, scooped him up from the ground, bore him cursing and raving to the water trough by the saloon, and quenched his oaths with a gurgle in the unsavory waters. Holding him by the boots, Tom soused the drunkard up and down while the crowd yelled with joy. Their sense of humor was not pitched many notes above this in the scale, and their yell rose to a wail of hysterical joy as Tom completed the lesson by tumbling Red Head into the dust.

He rose, clotted with mud, but, when he reached for his revolver, it was torn from his hands by a dozen willing townsmen.

"If you can't handle him without a gun, you sure ain't going to get a look in with a gun, Red," they assured him. "Give him a chance to talk, boys."

Every soul who had turned away was swept closer than ever around the speaker.

"I sure got to apologize for raising such a dust," Tom Keene panted out. "But, you see, boys, Red plumb forgot that they was ladies present, and he had to be gagged."

It brought another laugh from the onlookers. They were willing to laugh at well-nigh anything, now. And in another moment Tom was deep in the heart of his talk.

"Boys," he said, "I'm a gent that reads the Bible,

but I ain't up here to talk about God Almighty. I figure that He can get along tolerably well without. What I got to say is to you ladies and to you gents about a way of living happier. I'm up here talking for charity. I'm up here to show you folks that you got to help others. Lemme see one man in the crowd that ain't had help. Lemme see one man that don't owe something to the world."

The announcement of his subject cast a chill upon the interest and the enthusiasm of the crowd. There was to be no more ducking of individuals into troughs. They began to turn their minds back toward the matter of the waiting suppers. And Tom, quick to see the wavering attention, and that those on the outskirts of the crowd were again beginning to move away and thin out, at once picked upon a victim. He selected the most prosperous-looking man he could find. He was one of those persons who, being very large in front, are forced to rock back onto their heels. This gives them a seemingly bold and honest carriage. His dress was that of any cowpuncher. But he had on a necktie instead of a bandanna, and the necktie gave him an opportunity to display a huge diamond that glittered and gleamed even in the faint light of the evening and caught the eye of Tom Keene. He pointed directly at this imposing citizen of Porterville.

"You, there, partner," he said. "How much do you owe the world?"

"Not a cent," said the plump cattleman readily, slapping his fat palms together with a great noise. "But, on the other hand, there's quite a handy pile owing to me. If you're going around doing justice, friend, you might stay here for a while and help me collect some of the bills that are owing!"

This ready retort brought a laugh from the crowd. They favored the big man with a glance of approval, and then they turned with a new challenge to Tom, daring him to find a just answer to this complaint. He regarded the complacency of the fat man with the most profound disgust, cast about in his mind for a counterblow, and then demanded sharply: "Name one of them bills, partner."

"Well, sir," said the fat man, "I don't mind naming one that won't hurt nobody's feelings to be named. Jack Harper owes me two hundred dollars. Get that coin from Jack, will you?"

There was a peculiar smile on the faces of every man in the crowd, and yet the women were shaking their heads solemnly.

"Is Harper here?" asked Tom.

"In spirit, maybe," said the other. "You got to raise the dead to get that money for me, son."

This levity on such a grim subject caused a shade to pass over the faces of the crowd. Plainly they did not take any too kindly these references by the fat individual to the debts that were owing to him from a dead man.

Tom instantly bore in on his opponent. "Didn't you have no security for your money?" he asked.

"Nary a cent," said the rancher.

"You gave him two hundred without nothing to show for it?"

"I sure did."

"Well, sir, what made you give it to him?"

"Because I was sorry for him. I wanted him to get along."

"D'you give two hundred to every man you're sorry for and want to see get on? Don't you ask any questions? D'you let every worthless beggar . . . ?"

"Worthless beggar!" shouted the fat man. "Who calls Jack Harper a worthless beggar? Why, he saved my brother Paul's life two years ago! That's how much of a worthless beggar he was!"

"Ah," said Tom. "He saved your brother's life?"

"He did. Everybody here knows it."

"Partner," Tom said, "is your brother's life worth two hundred dollars?"

There was an indignant snort from the fat man, but he fell silent while all attention focused with renewed vigor upon Tom, since he had cornered his enemy and given this happy turn to the argument in his favor.

"And if you go back over the other debts that are owing to you," Tom continued, "you'll most generally find that you gave away money because you got security, or else you gave away money because you owed a debt of another kind to somebody. But I tell you what, friend, that two hundred dollars won't ever be begrudged by you to Jack Harper. No sir. I know the kind of gent you are. I'm simply putting this to you in another light, and, when you see what I'm driving at, you'll be the first one to dig down in your wallet and give to the poor in the town. What I say, boys, is that every man-jack of us owes a lot. We've all had friends that have helped us. We've all been in tight pinches. And we'd ought to remember those times when other folks come along asking for charity. The reason you're happy is because others want you to be happy."

"Wait a minute!" called a sharp voice. "Nobody never done any kindnesses to me . . . not that I recall particular. I've fought my own way. You ain't talking to me, stranger!"

It was a cripple, a slumping, wry-faced, bitter man.

"Don't you owe nothing," Tom asked fiercely, "to the mother that brought you into the world and that loved you and raised you and kept you strong enough to live? Don't you owe nothing to her? Didn't she give you no helping hand?"

The cripple lowered his head as though striving to avoid a great light that had been shone in his face. He winced away out of sight.

Tom turned back to the others. He found that their attitude had changed. At first he had amused them, then he had impressed them with his physical strength, and then he had overawed them by his rough and ready methods of argument, and they were more or less afraid that, if they spoke, he would fall upon them and expose weaknesses of which they did not think.

"Look here, friends," said Tom. "Out here, west of the Rockies, we don't keep our coin locked up because we feel plumb hostile to other folks. It's just that we don't know where we can help. Them that are poor don't go around telling us what we could do for 'em. That's my job, boys. I'm going through to tell you what a lot happier you'd all be if you gave a hand to them that ain't as strong as you are. If you make another man happy, you're going to make yourself happy. And there ain't a man on earth, I guess, that ain't worth help. You can't make a mistake. If the rain comes out of the sky, it ain't wasted. The sand drinks it up, the sand feeds the mesquite, and the mesquite is what makes life on the desert possible. Same way with kindness, boys. Even if it don't show no results . . . it helps in the long run. I want you to open your hearts. That's the main thing. Usually I don't ask no more. But tonight I got to ask for money to help them that won't and can't help themselves, simply because they are just too proud to beg. Boys, it ain't often that I ask for money to help folks. I most generally want nothing but a hearing. And if I'm asking tonight, it's because there's a reason."

He swung down from the saddle, drew from his pocket an old crownless hat, and, fixing this in the teeth of Major, he started the horse through the crowd. It was an original manner of passing the hat and the crowd responded to it well. Nickels and dimes and quarters and even dollars jingled musically, and the hat was sagging limply with the weight when Major brought it back to Tom Keene. He counted it swiftly—$7 gained for the Carvers. It was not a great deal, but it would buy the woman raw provisions for a week.

In the meantime, a dozen men had clapped him on the shoulder and asked him into the saloon for a drink. Plainly they considered his talk simply an ingenious manner of begging for his own purse. It was this spirit and a wholly cynical tone that Will Jackson, leaning in the door of his gaming house, called: "You got it on me, partner! I risk cash to get cash, but all you put up is words."

Tom turned and walked directly to the gambler, with Major following close at his shoulder, as always. "Friend," Tom said, smiling, "is that praise, or d'you aim to get this seven dollars that Porterville has just turned over to me?"

Will Jackson sneered again. He was not, in fact, a cheerful sort. Besides, he did not have to be pleasant in order to make money. He ran a square game until he saw big prizes in the offing. Then, to be sure, he showed his dexterity of fingers in forcing the goddess of chance to take his side.

But, in case anyone cared to challenge his methods, the same nimbleness of finger and wrist, used in a slightly different fashion, conjured a gun out and directed a stream of lead at the antagonist. He leaned in the doorway now, with his arms folded, calmly looking up and down the bulky form of Tom Keene.

"Maybe," he said, "when you ain't picking up the easy money with your jaw work, you fill out here and there with a turn at the cards. Is that your style, Bill?"

"My style," Tom said gravely, "is something that I guess you wouldn't care to listen to. But if you want to play for the seven dollars I have here, I'll take the chance."

"Suppose I win?" Will Jackson said. "That'll be charity used right at home, eh?"

"You can't win," Tom said. "They ain't a chance in the world of that. Don't go arguing yourself into thinking that you can."

"I can't?" said Jackson. "You got something on the cards?"

"Yes," said Tom, "the Lord is on my side. He won't let me lose."

Will Jackson stared and then snorted with disgust and surprise. Such talk as this he had never heard before. "Come in," he said.

An old man laid his hand on the shoulder of Tom as the latter advanced toward the door. "D'you know," he said, "that the sheriff might be sort of interested in you, son, if he knowed that you was getting money for charity and then spending it at a gambling table?"

"Spending it?" Tom laughed. "Why, man, I haven't the slightest idea of spending it. Come in and watch me win. And every cent I win goes to the poor." He turned to the gambler. "What's your name?"

"Will Jackson," said the latter.

"It's a black day for you, Jackson," Tom stated. "Name your game."

Chapter Nine

Of all the occupants of chairs in the gaming house of Will Jackson, those who played at only one table did not break up their game at the summons of the black stallion. At this table sat three men, one obviously a cowhand, one rather too pale to have led a life in the open, and another who was some years younger than the other two in appearance.

All three were haggard, but the eyes of the cowpuncher and the professional gambler were alight with victory, and the eyes of Jerry Swain were dark with despair. Ever since the night before he had sat at this table in this identical chair and fought for fortune.

In the beginning she had favored him with smiles. By midnight he had won a full $1,500 without exhausting the purses of the other two, and then, feeling that his great time had come, Jerry Swain had started to recoup all his losses of the past. Those losses had been many, with short intervals between. Only the pocketbook of a man as rich as Jerry Swain, Sr., his father, could have floated him through crisis after crisis in which he found himself involved as result of his passion for the cards and desperate adventures with them. But a year before, his father had warned him that he would never again pay an I.O.U. signed by his son at a card table. As a result, Jerry had been forced to stop playing at the very time when he was certain that the luck was about to turn. It had run too long against him, and now there was sure to be a break.

But he must have capital available with which to nurse his winning streak through lean places when he next sat in. So, for a whole year, he had raked and scraped and begged, until he gathered a handsome purse together. Last night he determined that the time had come. In his pocket was a solid bank of greenbacks—nearly $1,000 with which to plunge—more, indeed, than he had ever possessed before. And, as has been said, he saw that capital more than doubled by midnight. By dawn, every cent of his winnings was gone.

Still he struggled on. By midafternoon his money was cut to $100. By late afternoon he had signed an I.O.U. for $200. Why be a piker as long as he was in at all? And by evening he had signed away $300 more.

He owed $500 in paper, and then he began one of those reckless, blind plunges that even the best gamblers will sometimes start upon when they feel that things must begin to turn their way. But matters would not change. The money slipped away. The $500 melted gradually and at length, as Tom Keene entered the house, with a crowd of the curious about him, the last cent of Jerry Swain's money floated into the pockets of the professional.

He pushed back his chair and leaned his sagging shoulder against the wall, staring in sullen hatred at the other two. He was not a good loser, this millionaire's son. Few of them are. He had encountered too little resistance in his youth to be able to endure it now. And he glared with malice in his eyes at the gamblers who had won. They were profuse in their regrets that he should have to leave the game when his luck was certainly on the verge of turning.

"Never seen such a bad run of luck in my life," they said to each other.

That was poor salve for the grim mood of Jerry Swain. He knew that his run had been bad. He also knew that his tactics in the past few hours had been extremely stupid. Worst of all, he was beginning to feel that, no matter what he did with the cards, he would have been helpless in the hands of these two. Oddly enough their winnings were almost equally divided. Or was it altogether odd? Had they not agreed to pluck the goose in equal shares?

The thought brought such a fury storming up into his brain that he could not endure to sit at the table and face them. He stamped across the room, thereby giving the pair a chance to wink at each other.

"Fifteen hundred!" said the pseudo-cowpuncher.

"Seven hundred and fifty seeds apiece," said his pale-faced companion. "And lucky that we got away with it, at that. You sure drew it pretty wide last night, Shorty."

"When I let him get a thousand ahead? Why, I know the boob. He was dreaming of millions when he seen the coin begin to come in. He was born to be a loser, because he ain't got the nerve to win like a man or to lose like a man."

"What about the five hundred in paper? Will it mean anything, d'you think?"

"Will it mean anything? Are you nutty? Ain't his old man the gent that owns most of this here county?"

"And ain't his old man the gent that said he wouldn't pay another I.O.U. that his son signed at a card table?"

"The devil he did!"

"The devil he didn't!"

"What'll we do, then?"

"I dunno. But I figure that if we put on the screws we can make the hound dig up. There must be a pile of coin around that house, and young Swain ought to be able to get his hands on five hundred iron men."

"He's got to!" snarled the other. "We'll show him up in front of the whole town if he don't."

The same thought was spinning busily through the head of Jerry Swain as he joined the circle of spectators around the table where Will Jackson in person was sitting down to relieve the prophet of good will of his $7 of charity money.

"Mind you, boys," Will said, "if I win this stuff, I'll give twice seven bones to some gent that's off his feed in the town. But it just peeves me a little to see anybody get so chesty. It sure peeves me." He drawled the words. In moments of emotion his mouth twisted far to one side, and his voice issued solely through his nose, which gave it a rich violin quality. Now he fixed his baleful, pale-blue eyes upon Tom Keene and dealt, his slender fingers flashing like magic over the pack.

But, thought Jerry Swain, what could these fellows know of the terror of defeat? Neither of these had a father waiting to question him. Neither of these had to make an accounting or wait for the signature of another before his check could be honored. And in the big ranch house, Jerry Swain, Sr., would be waiting even now, for his son was not home for dinner on the second consecutive night.

The $500 had seemed little enough when he signed those treacherous slips of paper, but now the sum grew in importance momently. It became greater and greater—$500! A cowpuncher would have to work for a year to make that much. And he must have that sum before he went home.

He could not put off the two who had lost to him. He could not. They were known men, fierce, ready to fight full as freely as they were ready to gamble. Such as these would not accept promises.

Had he a friend of whom he could ask money? No, his only friends were the whining hangers-on who preyed upon him. Not one of them would come to his assistance when he was in need. Only when he was flush they knew him well. He vowed that instant that he detested every one of them. For that matter, he had no love for a single human being. And most, of all he hated these calm men sitting at the table and playing so carelessly, as though they had the resources of millions behind them.

He watched with verminous glee while the cards flashed and fell. Out of that game one of the two must come out the loser. He would wait until he could see on whom the blow fell.

In consideration of the fact that Tom's capital was only $7, the bets were small, very small to begin with. With every hand the deal changed.

Tom Keene was losing steadily. His seven shrank to six, to five, to four. Was it a trick of the light, or was the sweat really beginning to shine on the forehead of the bearded man?

Jerry Swain decided that it was sweat of excitement, and his malignant heart gloated at the sight. Here was pain. No matter in whom, it helped to pay back for what he had suffered.

At the table, Tom Keene, reaching to cut, had felt beneath the middle finger of his hand—that dexterous and highly sensitized fingertip that the long absence from work with the cards had seemed to make more true and delicate in touch than ever before—and under the tip of that finger it seemed to him that he felt a crimp in the side of the pack, such a crimp as a man makes when he has run up the pack and wishes the cut to fall at this place. He hesitated, then he struck squarely into that crimp and cut. That hand then was lost before it began. They were betting only dimes and quarters. But the cards that were floated to him across the table were now so good he had to bet higher, to save his face. That hand cost him fifty percent of his remaining capital. He had $2 left.

Then came his deal, and he sent his thoughts in quest of an answer to a great question. If he sat through this game, playing honestly, he would be trimmed of what was left, and Mrs. Carver would go hungry. But would heaven approve of cheating at cards, even to cheat a cheat? The old gaming instinct was hot in him. The gambler—and the cause of Mrs. Carver—triumphed.

The Lord forgive me, Tom Keene thought, and promptly and deftly stacked the deck.

Chapter Ten

In ten minutes he had won $20. In ten minutes more he had won $100 while the crowd, forgetful of waiting dinners and calling wives, watched, spellbound. Long before, Will Jackson had realized what was happening. He had caught a Tartar. Ordinarily he felt that he could have cleaned up this thick-fingered rascal in no time, but tonight things were against him. His hands were stiff. And he lacked adroitness of mind, also. As a matter of fact, he was furious when the crowd, which had come expecting to see him deftly and painlessly relieve the stranger of his money, stayed and beheld the great gambler of the village suddenly trimmed.

Then, for just a moment, he lost his head. He plunged blindly, dealt a straight hand, bet the limit of Keene's stakes on a full house, and saw four of a kind take away his money. He was $500 in the hole when Tom Keene pushed back his chair.

"Poker," he said, "is all very well in its own way, but it's a terrible slow game, Jackson. Suppose we try the dice. If you still insist on losing your money to charity, why, Jackson, let's go double or nothing at the dice, because my time's not my own. I'm a busy man, Jackson. I can't bother around here with small potatoes."

Jackson turned white under the badinage. If he could have found a pretext, he would cheerfully have pumped a stream of lead into his tormentor. Forcing himself to smile, he found the dice and led the way to a table covered with green felt, with a high wall at the rear for the bounce of the little cubes.

The devil was in it—the very devil. In a single roll he had a chance to clean the stranger of everything. The dice were given to his dexterous hands by the toss of a coin. Fair and true he rolled them, saw them click lightly—he could call them, even against that wall, nine times out of ten—and then saw them fall back, not seven, but ten. And the bearded stranger scooped up the stakes.

He was $1,000 dollars richer than he had been when he entered Porterville at sunset.

"Once more!" Jackson pleaded.

"It was double or nothing," Tom Keene said. "That's the finish, I guess. Which, any way you look at it, is a lesson for you, Jackson. Luck is one thing, but God Almighty is another. So long!"

Take it and be hanged, Jackson thought, but he followed to the door, saying softly: "Now that you got a thousand, I'll be watching your charity, stranger. Go just as far as you like. There's the Muldoons down the street. Bill Muldoon has been out of work a month, sick with a fever. I guess they could use a hundred or so. Don't let that hold you back if you're set on giving coin away."

"Is there any friend of Muldoon's here?" asked this astonishing itinerant preacher.

A long-faced man appeared, frowning dubiously. "I know old Bill, I guess," he said. "What about it?"

"Here's a hundred for him," Tom Keene said. He shoved it into the hands of the other, and, in the clamor of surprise that followed, he side-stepped through the jam and gained the street. There he swung into the saddle on Major, and the beautiful stallion, breaking into a jog trot guided by voice and the pressure of the knees alone, passed slowly down toward the far end of the village.

He left an admiring and stupefied crowd behind him that, as he melted into the dusk, turned upon Will Jackson and greeted him with a tremendous guffaw. It did not make so much difference that the home champion was beaten so long as the beating had been administered with such immense good nature.

"The White Mask himself couldn't have made money any easier," they declared, referring to a successful and mysterious robber who had operated through the mountains for some years.

Of all the people in the town, only one failed to show a desire to stand around and talk about what had happened. That man was Jerry Swain.

Slipping out to the hitching rack at the side of the house, he loosed and threw the reins over the head of his bay mare, and, while all eyes stared down the street toward the form of the stranger disappearing into the darkness, Jerry Swain picked his way around the back of the houses and cut toward the road in the direction Tom Keene had started.

He spurred the mare to a frenzy of running and at length jerked her to a halt in a hollow where a young grove of pines shouldered close together in a thicket of greenery. He wedged the horse back among these and brought out his revolver, for he had noted, when Tom Keene left the gambling hall, that he wore no gun. His reasoning was simple. He needed $500. Yonder came a man who professed that he wanted no money for himself but simply collected it for others. In that case, Jerry would relieve him of the wallet. He could also use very well the spare change outside the $500. If only the fool hadn't given away that hundred to Muldoon. It irritated Jerry as though the $1,000 had been his from the first instant.

His heart began to jump. And presently it leaped into his throat, but a white fire was rising through the trees on top of the nearest hill to the eastward. That white fire grew into a broad moon, and Jerry cursed. The light would make it easy to recognize him. He slashed holes in his handkerchief, and then decided that it would be too complicated, take far too long, to arrange a complete mask with eyeholes. Indeed, at that very moment the hoofs of a horse beat heavily over a small bridge a short distance down the road, and Jerry hastily tied the handkerchief over the lower part of his face. That would conceal him sufficiently by moonlight. His mare, however, must not be seen. She was too well known, both for her beauty and her speed. So he dismounted and kneeled behind the first line of the trees.

Over the hilltop came Tom Keene, looking immense as a giant on the top of the black horse, with the great moon behind. He jogged slowly into the hollow. Jerry could hear him humming. And what a terrible man this joyous monster was, and how huge his shoulders loomed as he came down the hollow. Suppose . . . ? But there was no time for supposing, no time for the terror that lurked inside Jerry to come to the surface. Here was his victim at hand. He leaped out and presented the revolver, shouting: "Hands up, curse you, or I'll blow your head off!"

The hands of the big man went obediently up, and the great black horse stopped.

"Inside your vest pocket you've got a wallet. Throw it here!"

The wallet thudded lightly in the dust at his feet. After all, how easy it was. What fools men were because more of them did not do this.

He kicked the wallet open, and with a glance

down he saw the edges of a neat stack of bills. And he laughed contentedly. Laughter, however, was not the thing that he must use. He informed Tom Keene, with a burst of curses, that he had better get out of the hollow and ride straight on. "Because, if you try to break back to town, I'll drill you clean," declared the amateur road agent. He drew the wallet closer with his toe. "And keep them hands up!"

The big man had started to lower them, but now he obediently made them rigid again, and with a low word to the black horse he passed on. Scarcely had he gone by when Jerry stooped toward the wallet and scooped it up with his left hand, still directing the revolver carelessly after the victim. As he did so, a shadow struck across the moon-whitened road, and he glanced up in alarm to see a monstrosity flying toward him. Tom Keene had whirled in the saddle and now leaped with both arms stiffly outstretched.

The revolver barked from the hand of Jerry, but it was a random shot fired without direction—a mere convulsive twitch of the forefinger over the trigger. The next instant a mountain, literally, fell upon him and crushed him to the earth. The revolver was torn from his grip. He was jerked up to his feet again by a force as resistless as that which had beaten him down, and the cold nose of his own revolver was thrust into his stomach.

"You rat!" Tom Keene cried, and wrenched the

handkerchief from Jerry's face, well-nigh breaking his neck with the violence. At the same time he pressed the muzzle of the gun into the hollow of the robber's throat.

"No, no, no, no!" gasped Jerry. All his breath departed from him as though he had been plunged into cold water to the chin. He slipped to his knees in the dirt and held out his hands to Tom. "No, no!" wailed Jerry Swain. "I . . . I . . . I can't die. For heaven's sake don't k-k-kill me! My father will . . ."

"Get up," the big man said, gesturing recklessly with the gun.

Jerry obeyed although he had scarcely the strength to stagger to his feet. "My father is . . . ," he began.

"I know who your father is," Tom said. "I seen you back in Jackson's. They told me about you. They told me that you were a hound. And now I see that they're right. They told me that you were a fool. Stop shaking . . . I ain't going to shoot you. Seeing you act like this makes me sick . . . like you was carrion between me and the wind. It sure takes the stuff out of me to see you shake like that."

Jerry Swain marvelously recovered by that assurance. He found it possible to stand straight. "If you don't tell, I can . . ."

"I'm not going to tell," said Tom. "You don't have to buy me with promises. It's simply because they tell me that your father is an honest man that I'm not going to tell. But what I want you to listen to, Swain, is this. They laugh at you when your back is turned. D'you think that you have any friends back there in Jackson's? I should say not. You're simply the easy mark. They pluck you and turn you out. Then you go back to your father and get more money out of him. You're simply the means they use of getting stuff out of your father. Understand? And when your back is turned, they laugh at you louder than ever."

"It's not true," gasped out Jerry, writhing with shame as he had never writhed before. "They know that I've helped too many of them out when they were low."

"For everything good you've done, they thank your father, if they thank anyone. You can lay to that, kid."

Jerry Swain groaned. Then his thin, handsome face contracted with rage. "Curse them," he said. "I'll get even with 'em all."

"Start in getting even with yourself, Swain," Tom advised. "Take a look at the way things are drifting. You're headed for a fall. I know there ain't much chance of changing you, but I'm playing for long odds. Swain, you got one chance in twenty of making a man of yourself. I'm turning you loose in the hopes that you'll be man enough to find it. So long!"

Chapter Eleven

The head of Jerry Swain remained bowed in humility just so long as it took Tom to ride over the next hill. Then he raised it again and shook his fist in the direction of the generous enemy. Having been caught and shamed in the commission of a crime, he felt only a deep malignancy toward his discoverer. Besides, like most weak men, he hated Tom for his strength of mind and body. Last and not least, the money that he had held in his hand for an instant was now torn away from him again, and he saw himself confronted once more with the unenviable necessity of facing his father. At that thought his whole soul quaked hardly less than he had shaken when the cold muzzle of his own gun had been shoved into the hollow of his throat. He dreaded his stern father hardly less than death.

All the way home he revolved possibilities in his brain, but he could arrive at no good argument or excuse. There was nothing for it but to go to the rancher and ask for $500 in cash at once. Otherwise, he would have to answer for it to the men to whom he owed the money. And, much as he dreaded his father, he dreaded that pair still more.

He could tell now, by the slightest effort in retrospect, that they were practiced sharpers working together, hand in glove. The backward glance very often clears the most confusing puzzles. He could also see, by the same glance, that they were a hardy pair, and that they would be very apt to present their claims for money with guns. A coward himself, he felt instinctively that all other men were both brave and desperately careless of such a matter as the lives of others.

In the quandary in which he found himself, his mind also reverted sometimes to the warning words of Tom Keene. They, also, were true. He had been used as a fool and a gull by the gamblers at Jackson's. And he cursed both them and himself for it, without extending any thought of gratitude toward Tom for the insight.

It was true. All his life they had simply despoiled him, at the same time piling him with ridiculous praises and calling him the best of game sports and good losers. And all the time they talked, his money flowed. No wonder they were glad to see him appear at the bar in the saloon or at the gambling table in Jackson's. No wonder they fought for a place in his company. He was better than the goose of the fable. He laid golden eggs for the nearest. And he could remember, now, a thousand looks and winks and murmurs exchanged among his companions. How great a gull he had been.

In the bitterness of his heart he wished, like Nero, that the men of the world had only one neck. Never again would he trust anyone or anything.

Not even his own relative should be admitted into his confidence. Tom Keene had aimed to introduce humility into the heart of the young rancher. Instead, he had planted inexhaustible hatred.

As he turned from the road into the avenue of lofty poplars that led to the big house, and that was his father's particular pride, he saw, sure enough, two shadowy horsemen riding out from the trees. They ranged alongside him.

"We missed you," they said, "and we thought that maybe you was in a rush to get home and grab the money to pay us. You see, we know how plumb set you are on paying off all your debts quick."

He returned no answer, but, going first to the stable and throwing the reins to the Negro there— for it was a point of his father's pride that his family should not have to care for their own horses—he came back to the front of the house.

"We'll be waiting right here," the two gamblers told him. "But make it *pronto*, will you? We ain't used to being out this late in the dark."

And their low, mocking-laughter followed him as he went slowly toward the front steps. Slowly, slowly he dragged himself up to the door, praying for an inspiration, but, when he stood in the hall, he knew that there was nothing for it except to tell his father the ugly truth.

And he went straight to the library and did it.

Jerry Swain, Sr., was there, as always at this

time of night, buried in his big chair by the fire, and with weary but indomitable face, forcing his eyes along the page of the book. Around him stretched the specially bound tomes of his library. There was a sprinkling of fine volumes of hand-made paper bound in parchment. And yonder a long set flashed in spotless white pigskin. Other and soberer bindings in morocco and in heavy brown calf swept in almost numberless units around the capacious walls of the room. Every book was a chosen volume. A special librarian had selected them. Every book was a known book. There were no fascinating obscurities. There were no light and intriguing memoirs, no ranges of gay fiction spiced with love and danger.

The librarian had leaned toward history. There were, of course, translations of the classic historians from Herodotus and Cassio. And all the modern, most lengthy, and most dry writers found their place. Philosophy found her place in bulk, also.

And here, seated before his fireplace, with great dictionary on the one hand and a stiff-backed chair to keep him to his task, old Jerry Swain, in his sixty-fifth year, marched relentlessly ahead in his course of reading, which was to take him through every one of the volumes in the big, high-ceilinged room. Heaven alone could tell how he hated it. He had not the gift of letters, but, just as he had sat the saddle twenty hours out of twenty-four in his youth and made his herd grow, so now he sat for a definite length of time every day in this dismal library and scourged his mind on to fresh labors.

In a corner of the room sat his evil genius, the high priest of the demon, Culture. He was a little, white-headed man with the round, rosy face of a boy. His voice, also, was as light and high a tenor as it had been in his tenth year. His eyes had never dimmed in the poring over books, which had made up his life. No glasses had as yet been proved necessary to him. But with unfaltering hand he turned page on page. And he would twitter on with a joyous nonchalance about profundities. Arabic and Hebrew were his playthings, and in his careless moments—his after-dinner hours of relaxation, so to speak—he indulged himself by mining in the treasures of Sanskrit. But in his real moments—then there was nothing but abstruse mathematics worthy of occupying his brain.

Sometimes poor Jerry Swain looked upon his mentor as a giant encased in the body of a pigmy. Sometimes, he revolted against the hideous labor of following print until his eyes blurred, until his head swam. But always with a fine sense of duty he brought himself back to his task. He would not die until he became a cultured man.

"What is a man without history?" a traveling United States senator had said in a speech that Swain once heard. "And what is a man who does not know the masterpieces of literature? Nothing! A hollow shell!"

To Jerry Swain this fierce assertion was of the utmost importance. He was at that period beginning a new life in which the chief purpose of his energies was the accumulation of an atmosphere that would separate him forever from his past. That past was of a nature that made Jerry sometimes shrug his shoulders and glance quickly around, almost as though he feared that someone might peer in upon the memories that he was calling up to mind. To be sure, he had built his fortune upon a broad basis of hard work, but he had helped himself along from time to time by methods of a rather grim nature. No one suspected. But, staring up into the face of the senator, Swain listened with a believing spirit.

And poor Jerry Swain took that announcement to his heart. He was only a hollow shell if the senator were to be believed. And he must be believed. Jerry had voted for him. He was never to know to the moment of his death that the sentences that changed the course of his life were never written by the senator, though they were spoken by him. They were not even written by the senator's secretary. They were composed by the senator's assistant secretary, who was a girl freshly out from college with an ignorant world before her to be uplifted.

But the result was that Jerry Swain, Sr., sat now

deep in the third volume of Gibbon, his mind reeling as monotonously sonorous sentences rolled on and on like waves in the sea—ground swells in the middle of the vast Pacific.

Yesterday, for recreation, the white-headed, young-faced demon in the corner of the room had given him *Tristram Shandy*. And the rancher had waded industriously through some fifty pages of that whimsical masterpiece before, having found some dozen themes announced and abandoned in that time, and struggling desperately and in vain to find a theme of the story that was announced to him as a novel, the poor man closed the book and leaned in his chair as far as the stiff back would allow him and whispered softly: "Swain, are you going mad? Are you losing your brain?" So he had left *Tristram Shandy* and reverted to the more soporific style of Gibbon.

Sometimes, the little man in the corner talked to him about his reading. Of course he never talked about anything so simple as Gibbon. But he would talk about the sources of Gibbon. Personally he had not much use for English.

"If Shakespeare had only walked in the shoes of a Roman, how great his plays would have been," he was accustomed to saying. "Don't you agree with me, Swain?"

That little tag-end question about an agreement, he rarely left off, even if he had just been quoting raw Arabic. And Swain never failed to mumble an assent.

It was at one of these moments, in time to save him from an answer, that his son entered.

Chapter Twelve

To say that Jerry Swain was only glad to see his boy because he made a timely interruption, would be no doubt too much. Yet certainly it may be said that never had he laid a book aside with greater satisfaction than he did now as he turned toward Jerry, Jr.

He looked Jerry over with an eye of approbation. He always saw the face of his dead wife in the handsome features of his boy, and for that reason he loved him and forgave him a thousand sins. He never was able to see that there was as much feminine weakness as there was feminine beauty in the features of young Jerry.

But this night, coming into the library flushed with the wind and evidences of riding, the son was as dear to the father as well-nigh any human being can be to another. He did not even weaken and change his attitude to suspicion when the boy began with the time-honored formula: "I'd like to talk to you a minute alone."

"D'you mind letting us have the room for a while?" asked the rancher. "We won't be long, Tomkins."

"Tush!" chirped the octogenarian, rising as straight as a sapling and clasping in his fleshless arms the burden of a Sixteenth-Century first edition. "Be as long as you please, Mister Swain. I'm trotting up to my room for the night." And he went with a sprightly step through the door.

Some of the rage that was burning in the youth overflowed in the direction of this absentee. "The little grafter," he snarled. "I should think you'd get tired of paying for his board and room. What the devil good is he?"

"He directs my reading," the rancher said with dignity. "He's rounding up culture for me, Son, and doing everything but putting on the brand for me so that I can call a few facts my own. But look here, Jerry, it seems to me that you have nothing but knocks to give everyone around you. I wish you'd get over that habit. It's not good. A man without friends is like a cripple without crutches."

"I, for one," Jerry said viciously, "will get on without 'em, just the same."

"You will?"

"Yes, I need no help."

"You don't? And where would you be without what I'm going to leave you one of these days?"

"That's true," Jerry said, immediately backing down, as usual, the instant his father showed the slightest sign of heat. "And, as a matter of fact, Dad, I've come to you tonight needing help bad."

"Ah?" said the father. It was all he could do to

keep from saying—"Good."—so whole-heartedly was he a man of action, and so greatly did he yearn to put his shoulder to the wheel if his son needed him. But he continued: "Well, boy, tell me what's gone wrong with you."

"It's money," Jerry said. "I've got to have five hundred. Because . . ."

"Never mind," said the rancher. "Don't bother with explanations. Good Lord, Jerry, aren't you my boy? And is five hundred anything to me? No, I thank heaven, I can write my check for a hundred times five hundred and never miss it. Never miss it!"

How he rejoiced in this chance to boast a little. How it warmed the very cockles of his heart to talk to his son of his power, without having the freezing eye of Tomkins watching from the corner ready with a question.

"Things are looking up all over," went on the father, taking checkbook and pen from his pockets. "Money is going into the bank account steady and sure. We got our drift fences out, lad, and we catch every stray dollar and herd it the right way." He laughed at his own fantastic metaphor. Then he pulled his glasses down lower on his nose and prepared to write. Heaven opened for his son. He was past the gate of danger. If the old man asked for an explanation later on—well, he would have time to think up one.

"But," Jerry, Sr., said suddenly, "what do you

want this for? How come you to . . . ?" He pulled the glasses off his nose. Glasses were all very well for looking at print, but he still preferred to trust the lenses that nature had given him rather than peer into a human face through glass. He saw that his son was grown pale as cloth. It sickened him. Fearless himself, the sight of fear in his son maddened him. All at once he roared: "You've written another I.O.U.! You young blatherskite, have you done that? If you ain't . . . !"

Bad grammar flooded his tongue in moments of emotion. He was stopped not by the protestations of his son but by the latter's horrified silence and what he could see with the naked eye.

"Jerry, why did you do it? Will you tell me?"

"Dad, it was a queer turn in luck . . . and . . . things have got to break for me someday."

"You lie!" thundered the rancher. "You can't force luck to come your way. Luck goes where it isn't asked. Why, you blockhead, you . . ." He stifled again with his rage. "Not a cent!" he bellowed. "Not a cent! I'd see 'em dead first."

"Good Lord," groaned the son. "My honor, Dad!"

"A snap for your honor! Honor doesn't sit in at a card table, you idiot. If you lost money there, go pay it out of your own pocket. You'll get nothing out of mine."

"But . . . Dad . . ."

"Get out!"

Before that raised face, Jerry, Jr., shrank back to the door. But for the first time in his life he dared to delay in the presence of the terrible old man.

"Dad, I think it means murder if I haven't the five hundred. They . . . they'll kill me."

"Kill you?" the rancher thundered. "Are your hands tied? Haven't you got a gun? Kill you? Good Lord, are you afraid? Didn't I teach you to shoot myself? Get out of the room, and if you ever ask me again for gambling money, I'll skin you . . . myself!"

And the very roar and heave of his voice carried Jerry, Jr., through the door and into the hall. There he leaned against the wall, sick at heart. What could he do? He decided that his best luck might be found in an attempt at light-heartedness. Straight out of the house he proceeded and down the steps and confronted the two on horseback, where he had left them.

"Boys," he said glibly, "I'll tell you how it is. The old man is a little hard pressed for cash just now. Some big deals he's pushing through have really tied up about every cent he has, and he . . ." He was interrupted by derisive laughter.

"D'you think we're as thick in the head as that, kid? Nope. We'll let you in on a few facts. We laid in close to the windows, and we heard what the old man had to say when you gave him the rise for the coin. And what it looks like to me is that we'll never get the stuff. And if that's the way of it, Swain, we'll have it out of your skin."

They were suddenly advancing on him, two grim, savage-faced men.

"On my honor!" poor Jerry cried. "On my honor, I'll get it for you if you give me time and . . ."

"How'll time help you?"

"My allowance . . ."

"Ain't five hundred a month . . . we know that flat enough."

"I'll get it some way. I'll get more than five hundred. I'll pay you interest."

"We ain't money-lenders," they said coldly. "We want the five."

"It'll grow to seven-fifty in a month, boys. I swear it will!"

Suddenly they desisted. The promise seemed to have lulled their angry suspicions. "Look here," they cautioned him. "Inside of a month and a day, we'll come back. If the coin ain't waiting for us at Jackson's in two envelopes, all sealed up and addressed, half to each of us, first thing we'll do will be to spread the word around that you've double-crossed us, and that your I.O.U. ain't worth a hoot. Then we'll come out and get you, Jerry, and when we finish with you, the cat can have what's left if she can find it. So long!"

Their hoof beats drummed away. Jerry Swain grasped for the nearest tree, and leaned against it until his head cleared of the swimming thoughts and the dark fear. But in the end he knew one blissful fact before all else. He was free for a month—thirty days of sunshine.

Before the end of that time something would turn up. It was a perfect eternity. He turned back to the house with an almost jaunty footstep and ran up the steps to the big room that was reserved for him in the corner of the house. From the window he looked out along the line of the poplars. And then, to one side and the other, he glanced down at the jutting wings of the big, red-roofed barns. What a huge estate was his, and what a power would be in his hands when it came to his turn.

What would he do? First he would find the two gamblers and smash them. Secondly? Secondly he would find the big man with the black beard, big Tom Keene, and make him burn for what he had said and for what he knew. Such a man's knowledge was not safe.

Chapter Thirteen

The load that black Major carried out of Porterville that night was not the bulk of Tom Keene alone. Bags and bundles and parcels of a dozen descriptions bulged around the saddle and jounced softly against the sides and back of the great stallion as he went on down the road after the interruption of Jerry Swain. And when they reached the shadow of the great house, it required some time for Tom to take off the bundles and so arrange them that he could make one immense armful of them. Then he went to the kitchen door and tapped loudly.

In answer, he heard a chair squeak as it was pushed back. Then footfalls went slowly down the hall, and the light of a carried lamp wavered through the door and approached him. Mrs. Carver opened the door to him and jumped back with a cry of surprise and alarm at the sight of the giant with the shapeless, shadowy heap in his arms. The flame leaped in the chimney of the lamp as she sprang back, and by that light she saw the face of Tom.

She stood by in silence, then, while he put down his load. Her quick eye recognized the contents of every parcel by its shape—the bread, the flour, the sugar, the butter, the side of bacon, the ham—for she had grown to know the shape in which Mr. Tucker did up his articles from the general merchandise and grocery store of Porterville. And when all was done and Tom rose, dusting the flour from his hands, he looked up and saw that tears were streaming down her face.

"Lord, Lord," Tom soothed gently, and his voice at its softest went booming and humming through the room. "What's wrong now? Have I hurt your feelings, Missus Carver, by bringing out these things?"

She turned away from him to put the lamp on the table, but she remained with her back to him for a moment, and by the quiver of her shoulders he knew how she struggled to regain control of herself. At length she could face him, but only by looking down at his feet. She was crimson to the hair with shame.

"I know," she said, "that I've got no right to refuse it while Mary is lying in there sick. I've got no right to tell you that I can't take it. But . . . what will John do when he finds out? He's a proud man . . . he's a terrible proud man, and he'll near die with shame when he learns about how . . ." Her voice trailed away and choked to silence.

"Look here," Tom Keene insisted, "there's no need that he should ever know." And he thought grimly to himself that he would like to wring the neck of this proud man who wandered about the country as he pleased and left a starving family behind him. But he went on to make the acceptance easy for poor Mrs. John Carver. He took her arm; he smiled down into her face.

"Lemme tell you something, lady," he said. "Them that are too proud to take help are most generally the ones that are too quick to give help. They want to give and give and give. But the minute that they can't give, and when they have to be plumb uncomfortable for the lack of things they need, they still won't let anybody give 'em a helping hand. Now, you and your husband, I'll bet, have done a sight of good for folks."

She caught eagerly at that straw of comfort. "Yes, yes," she said. "In the old days, I've heard John tell how his father used to stake the boys when they were down and out, and then he would never take a penny back for it. He could have half of the good gold mines in the mountains if he had let the boys go out with grubstakes, but the stake that he gave them were always just gifts that they could pay back when they pleased. Yes, Porterville owes a lot to the Carver family."

To the Carver family. The heart of Tom Keene shrank as he saw the poor woman taking refuge behind the good deeds of her husband's ancestors.

"I suppose," she went on, "that I could even take such things as this as our right." Then she added with a changed voice: "But you ain't from Porterville. We got no claim upon you."

He placed his great kind hand upon her shoulder. "You start fixing up a snack for the little girl. I'm going to go in and talk to her. Don't you worry about having no claim upon me. Lord, Lord, I ain't giving anything myself. I just collect . . . and then I give the collection where I think it might help the most. Claim upon me? Why, Missus Carver, every woman in the world has a claim upon me."

"Why is that?"

"It was a woman that brought me into the

world," he answered. "For her sake I got to do what I can for the rest. And that includes you and the little girl in yonder room. Now you get busy with the stove and stop worrying."

He was gone before she could protest again, and, once he was gone, she started to work with a feverish speed. A fire soon smoked and then roared in the stove; in a few minutes bacon was hissing in the pan, and a fragrant mist spread over the kitchen.

It spread farther still and pried with a stealthy finger into the front bedroom where the injured girl lay. But, half famished as she was, even the smell of food did not entirely distract her from the big man who had saved her from the well, and who was now sitting beside her bed. Mrs. Carver, carrying a tray loaded down with food, paused outside the door and listened intently to them.

The big voice of Tom Keene was sounding steadily, and he was telling her about the black stallion that he rode. He had made up his mind, he was saying, that he would raise a colt for himself and make it know him so well that it could almost read his mind.

"So I went out to a big horse ranch," said Tom. "They had 'most a million horses, it looked like, that spring. And all of the mares, pretty nigh, had colts running at their sides. Well, I went right through the herds with Smithson. He kept pointing out colts that looked fine to him, high-spirited colts, because he wasn't raising no ordinary weedy range stock. But it didn't take me more'n a minute to see that 'most every one of them wasn't what I wanted."

"How could you do that?" asked the girl breathlessly.

She had been moaning faintly but steadily with the pain when Mrs. Carver left her. Now the torture of her arm was forgotten.

"I could do that," Tom explained, "by looking at the heads. The head of a horse, if you know what to see in it, means just as much as the face of a man. I was looking for a face, you might say, and pretty soon I found one that I wanted. I told Smithson that he needn't take me no further, but, when he seen the colt I was pointing to, he set up a holler . . . 'Why,' he says, 'I'd be ashamed to let you get off my place with a colt like that. Why, son, he's all legs. He ain't going to be good for nothing.'

" 'Well,' I says, 'I figure that he'll be good enough for me.'

"And I was right, Mary, because that turned out to be Major. Listen!" He whistled. The sound of a short, eager neigh floated quickly back through the open window. "That's Major talking to me now," said Tom.

There was a cry of delight from the girl. And then her mother came in with the tray.

Pain was forgotten after that. It was a gay party

for half an hour, and then Mary, overcome with weariness and the pain of her hurt, fell asleep almost in the midst of laughter. Tom leaned over her, arranged her pillow, drew up the covers, and he and the mother tiptoed out of the sickroom. In the dining room they sat down again.

"You've been in sickrooms before," Mrs. Carver said with feeling. "I can see that you've taken care of a sister, maybe?"

She had started to say daughter, and then a second and closer look at Tom revealed that he was far younger than she had thought him to be. The black beard gave him an appearance half a dozen years, at the least, older than he really was.

"I have no family," Tom said. "My father is dead. I never knew my mother's face . . . and that's all!"

"You're all alone then?"

"Tolerable lonely," Tom answered. "But I keep stirring around. That's a pretty happy way to live, Missus Carver."

Mrs. Carver made no answer to that remark. She remained thoughtful for some time, merely nodding and smiling when he talked, and answering his direct questions rather shortly. And when he asked what her husband was doing that kept him away from home so much of the time, she merely sighed and shook her head. He did not press that point.

A few minutes later he saw what had been on

her mind to keep her so quiet, for she said suddenly: "Have you never thought of settling down?"

"Settling down?" Tom laughed. "I wouldn't know how to do it. Some birds pretty near live on the wing, you know. And I reckon I'm that way. I like change, you see."

She shook her head. "A rolling stone don't gather no moss," she declared solemnly. "You'll be coming to no good end if you keep roving, a young fellow like you."

"Maybe it's dangerous," agreed Tom, and he swallowed a smile.

What if she should ever come to know exactly in what capacity he had roved in the old days?

"D'you know what you'd ought to do?" she asked suddenly.

"Well?" Tom said.

"Stay right here on the ranch with us."

"What? Me?"

"Exactly! Why not?"

"Why, I dunno," Tom said, "except that I figure I'd ought to be moving on in the morning."

"Where to?"

"I'm not quite certain. Just the way the wind blows at dawn will tell me, I suppose."

"Them that don't bide in one place," Mrs. Carver said oracularly, "will come to repent it sooner or later. That's the trouble with my poor husband. Anybody around here can tell you what the Carvers was once. But they ain't the same now. John's father stayed still and worked. And everything that he set his hand to turned into money. But John is always a-roving. And look at the way we are now." She cast out her work-reddened hands to the empty box of a room, with its cracked ceiling. "Look what the Carvers have come to. Just look at it, will you? And all because he has to keep stirring around instead of staying put. I never knew what I was marrying . . . never dreamed it. But you . . . you're different. You got a kind eye and a quiet eye. A body can talk to you and show you where you're wrong if you keep gadding. That's why I want you to stay here."

"Well," Tom said gravely, "I sure take it kind of you to ask me this way."

"Ah, lad," she said with a tremor in her voice, "I can see the good in you standing up and looking me in the eye. But why I offer you the place is this . . . it's a good ranch. There ain't any reason why it shouldn't pay. But it's meant for farming and not for running cattle. There's a good hundred and sixty acres down in the ravine bottom that's as rich land as you ever seen. All it needs is a plow and a handful of grain to show what it can do. But John won't bother none with farming, and the place ain't big enough to range many cows on. But you . . . if you was to stay on steady here and take a hand, you could make a pretty piece of money for yourself and us, too. I wouldn't make you no hired hand. But I'd give you a share in all that you made. Don't that sound like good business talk to you?"

"What would John Carver say?"

"He'll take my advice. It's time that he did."

Tom raised his head and stared at the blank, black rectangle of the window glass.

"I'm going out for a walk," he said, "and, when I come back, I'll come with an answer for you."

Chapter Fourteen

He had felt himself called upon to go through the world ministering to the needy with his doctrine of faith in mankind, and how could he shrink his destiny to the problem of this single family?

Heading toward the mountains, he started to walk until the problem should be settled. On the one hand, there was the call of the road. On the other hand, there was the need of little Mary Carver.

She should be cared for and reared tenderly. Would the drunken wastrel, John Carver, do his duty by her? No, for all of him the girl and her mother, also, might be dead even now for lack of food. His gorge rose. And the unChristian-like desire to murder boiled in him when his mind dwelt upon Carver.

So he fought the question back and forth as his long legs covered the distance toward the mountains. Blind with his own thoughts, he was walking in the higher mountains against the light of the dawn almost before he knew it, and then he realized, with a start, that he could not get back to the ranch before sunup. In fact, he could hardly get back before noon. But they would find Major still with them, and, so long as the horse was there, they would know that he had not deserted them entirely.

Luckily he had slipped the gun he had taken from Jerry Swain into his belt before he started. And therefore he breakfasted heartily on stupid mountain grouse, the easiest of all game to shoot because they can be stalked almost to arm's length. After breakfast on grilled grouse, he selected a place where his head would lie in shadow and his body in sunshine, and was instantly asleep.

When he wakened, it was past noon, a drowsy, ambitionless time of day, and, when he came to a shining pool patterned with shadows, he could not resist the temptation, and he slipped out of his clothes and dived in. He found bottom a full fifteen feet below, and he was so delighted by that deep, clear water that he idled there until the hottest part of the afternoon was spent.

But when he donned his clothes again, he was nearer the solution of the problem, and he had decided that, come what might, his place was in the home of the Carver family until Mary Carver was sure of a better future than at present opened before her. Besides, though he might amuse or even uplift ten thousand in the same space, might there not be a more solid satisfaction if, at the end of a year or more of gratuitous labor, he could so far restore the ranch to a paying basis that Mary might be assured of an education of one kind or another, and her mother secure from hunger, at least? That was the goal that he established for himself. When he went down again from the mountains, it would be to enter upon a course of severe labor not to end for many a weary month.

But, for now, surely it was permissible if he dallied a little longer among the mountains in the old freedom that was so clear to him, hunting his food when he was hungry and exploring here and there as his fancy led him. So he gave up the thought of returning for the rest of the day, and, having registered a good resolution for the future, he closed the door on what was to come, and enjoyed himself. Most of the afternoon that remained to him, he spent in trailing a young grizzly, slipping along the trail of the bear and lying prone in the rocks to watch the deftest of mountain hunters, saving the loafer wolf alone, rip the heart out of a tree and devour a bee's nest, honey, wax, stings, and all. Again he lay in the rocks above and kicked his heels together in childish pleasure, seeing the method in which the bruin tore up a big ant hill, moistened his right forepaw, and laid it down so that the brave ants, issuing, swarmed upon it and were successively licked off in multitudes.

The one elderly thing about Tom Keene was his great black beard, and under that beard was the careless soul of a youth of twenty-seven. Every moment of that vacation from the Carvers and their needs was a golden treasure to him. He slept that night as he had not slept since he left the old life, and he wakened luxuriously late in the morning and started down the back trail. Once, with his face turned toward home, however, he swung off with his long stride and kept steadily on. He dropped out of the mountains into the lower foothills at midmorning. He was striding among these when Jerry Swain, Jr., sighted him and struck in on his trail.

The night before Jerry had determined to leave the country and take a long vacation far to the north. He had actually acted on the panic spur of the moment and galloped away. But on the road sober reflection had a chance to work in him. Distance would not save him from the pursuit of such men as those to whom he owed his debt. Distance would not save him, but, while he was away, they might choose to carry their claims to his father. What would happen when Jerry Swain, Sr., was hounded to pay the gambling debts of his son, the youth could not exactly say, but he knew it would be one of two things. Either the two claimants would be kicked out of the house abruptly, or else they would be paid and Jerry, Jr., would be disowned as an unworthy son. Neither eventuality was profitable. The kicks that the two crooks might endure from his terrible father they would be very apt to repay the son with chunks of lead. So Jerry, rising that morning, had reluctantly and mournfully started toward home by the most roundabout way through the hills. He wished to be alone as much as possible so that he might strive to think out a solution of his problem. Out there away from other men, perhaps inspiration might pop into his head.

And so it was, coming over a hilltop, that he dropped into sight of the big form of Tom Keene striding away below him. At once Jerry reined back and rode carefully. It was most unusual to see a man going on foot through the mountains, particularly a man who owned such a horse as Tom Keene was known to possess. Besides, it tickled Jerry to trail the black-bearded stranger. With all the power of heart and soul, Jerry hated the big man. He had been detected in the commission of a cowardly crime by Tom, and, because the latter had permitted him to depart unpunished, he hated him only the more. No small spirit can endure to be pardoned by another man. It seems to be a threat hung perpetually above his head. And a sneaking hope came to Jerry that he might be able to run down the mystery of Tom

Keene on this bright morning. At least, there was no better way in which he could drive from his mind the thoughts that haunted it.

Unaware of the careful rider, Tom kept steadily on until he heard, far before him, the baying of a pack of hounds. He listened to the chorus with amazement. It was not like the mingled cry of other packs he had heard running on the trail of mountain lions and plagues of the cattle ranches. It was a deeper-pitched, more mellow call. It came to him very faintly. A moment later the change in the wind extinguished the sound save for a delicate echo that lived an instant along the hillside.

And as this faded in turn, he saw a horseman spur over the next hill and plunge into the hollow, looking behind him with unmistakable dread as he bent over the horn of his saddle and urged his horse on.

When he turned his head again, Tom saw, with a shock that the face was completely covered by a white mask. It could be no other than that safe blower and highway robber who he had heard mentioned the night of his arrival in Porterville. Yonder the hounds cried far away on his trail. And here he rode on a fast-failing horse. That he should be masked was natural enough, with the pursuit so close behind him. But that he should have retained the white mask that identified him was a mystery.

However, there were ways of explaining it. Tom

had known criminals before, who kept some betraying article of dress simply because they felt that their luck was wrapped up in the wearing of it. And this man, no doubt, had heard himself referred to so often as The White Mask that he had begun to feel that the secret of his power and of his success was in the wearing of the telltale mask.

That wonder held the mind of Tom Keene for only an instant. Then he raced across the hillside shouting loudly for the fugitive to stop. The answer was a stream of curses, and then the sun winked on the bared revolver.

On the hillcrest behind them, young Jerry Swain jerked his horse frantically to the shelter of some projecting rocks, and then, fearful of a stray bullet, he craned his neck and looked out to watch the progress of the battle.

It was short lived. The gun in the hand of the robber barked twice before Tom Keene's weapon made answer, but that answer was effective enough. The White Mask turned halfway around in his saddle, hurled the gun far from him as his arms flew up, and then pitched for the ground. He struck it heavily, a limp weight, and rolled over three times, coming to a pause in a crumpled heap.

Tom reached him instantly, tore from his face the mask, and exposed to his own eyes and the eyes of Jerry Swain, in the distance, features that he recognized by the photograph that hung in the Carver house. It was John Carver himself!

Chapter Fifteen

Next, in horror, with the very spirits of Mary and Elizabeth Carver at his shoulder, Tom Keene looked to the wound and found that it was ugly indeed, but by no means mortal. The slug had torn its way through the deep shoulder and had missed the lungs. The weight of the heavy slug had been sufficient to knock the rider off balance, and the fall to the ground had jarred the senses out of him. Already he began to recover, and his first action was to reach for his face, where he found the mask gone. Next his hand went inside his coat toward the place where a revolver had been, which Tom had already found and removed.

Then, calmly enough, he said: "I'm done, I guess. But where did you grow . . . out of the ground?" He glowered at Tom sullenly until a change of the wind brought to his ear the approaching clamor of the hounds. Then his bravado vanished and he turned white. His glance over his shoulder was a horrible caricature of the pretty, quick side looks of Mary Carver. "You'll keep off the dogs?" he pleaded to Tom. "You'll not let the dogs get at me, stranger?"

Then speech returned to Tom Keene. "Carver," he said, "you're a goner."

"You know me, eh?" Carver gasped out. "I . . . I

don't recollect your face exactly. But . . . partner, if you'll give me a hand back into that saddle right now, I'll split the coin with you. I'm loaded with it, pal. Look here . . . and here." He stuffed a hand into his coat pocket. He drew it out filled to the fingertips with fluttering greenbacks. "Quick!" he gasped out.

But Jerry Swain, his face savage with his own need as he beheld that money, was astonished to see the big man shake his head in response to the unmistakable gesture.

"How'd you get the money?" Tom asked.

"There's no killing on it," panted out John Carver. "I swear there ain't. They've told their lies about me, but I've never killed a man in my life. Lew Gibson they lay to the account of The White Mask. I never killed him, friend. Heaven blast me, lying right here, if I did. I've blowed safes, and I've stuck 'em up now and then . . . but I've never done more'n shoot into the air to give 'em a scare. Will you believe me? And will you give me a hand?"

"Carver, you . . ."

"But it's real money!" Carver shouted, seeing denial in the face of the big man of the beard. "It ain't the queer. You think it's the queer? Take a look. Listen to me . . . they's five thousand on me . . . five thousand! I'll split it with you fifty-fifty."

The deep baying of the hounds floated closer. A

spasm of uncontrollable terror shook the wounded man, and, dragging himself up, he embraced the knees of Tom Keene with his one manageable arm.

"Partner," he sobbed, "for heaven's sake . . . for heaven's sake!"

"You couldn't last an hour in the saddle . . . not half an hour," Tom Keene said.

But the other had seen the pity mixed with the horror and contempt in Tom's face.

"You know me . . . and you know that I got a family. The finest woman a man ever had for a wife. She'll die grieving if they get me. And my little girl, partner . . . my little girl Mary will have to grow up shamed and . . ."

"Shut up!" groaned Tom. "Ain't I been thinking about them things?" He looked up to the clouds blowing through the sky for a solution of the wretched problem. And the suppliant used that chance to reach for the revolver lying on the ground, his face grown as subtle and savage as a beast's. Tom looked down in time to grind the weapon into the dirt with his heel. And the robber snarled up at him.

"It's true," Tom Keene decided. "If she grows up with the world knowing about the kind of a father that she has her life'll be ruined." And a wild thought was passing through his brain—he had taken one life from the world, the life of his own father. Suppose he should restore another in his place? "Carver," he said, "you've been a lying, lazy hound to your wife and your kid."

"I know. But I've never had a chance to go straight," whined Carver. "I've never had a chance. I never could get far enough ahead. But now I could stay straight, partner. I swear I could if . . ."

"Don't swear," Tom said savagely. "You ain't fit to swear and be believed. But what I'm going to do . . . look here, Carver. If you was to go back on what I'm going to make you promise, I'd come and cut your throat."

"Go on," Carver sobbed, still looking over his shoulder toward the point from which the baying of the hounds could be heard.

"If I get you out of this, you'll stay by your home. You'll do your best to take care of your wife. You'll give your girl a good education, eh?"

"I . . ."

"Don't swear, I say. I guess you'll do it. If you don't, I figure I'll come back and finish you up, Carver. But now tell me this. How close have they been to you? Could they see you clear?"

"Not nearer than to make out the color of my horse."

"Never seen your face even through a glass . . . never had a chance to size you up?"

"I wore a mask all through. How could they see?"

"They could see that you didn't have a beard,

117

that's what I'm asking for. But if they ain't been close enough for that . . . I'll try." He leaped into the saddle on the roan as he spoke. "Remember," he called, "I'll be watching what you do, Carver, even if I have to watch you out of a grave!"

And, so saying, he sent the blue roan across the hollow at full speed. He dipped out of view around the corner of the nearest hill, and John Carver busied himself with cutting away his coat and bandaging his wound to stop the flow as well as he could. He was not half finished when a pack of hounds darted over the crest of the hill behind him and shot straight down to the point where he was seated at his work. Short and heavy of leg, with long and sweeping ears, a gait steady and clumsy, a half dozen of the dogs appeared—true bloodhounds.

And terror stopped the hands of the robber. "But it's the scent of the horse that they've got," he told himself. "They ain't going to bother none with me."

Sure enough, they swerved to the left and dipped into the hollow while a rout of a full score of riders came in hot pursuit. The leader shouted directions. Two thirds of the men went on with the hounds. The others swirled around John Carver.

His story was simple. He, John Carver, had been walking across the hills when he heard the distant baying of hounds, and, almost at once, he had seen the rider of the blue roan, a big, black-bearded man, come over the crest of the hill, looking behind him and spurring his horse on in all the fashion of a hunted man. This, in conjunction with what he had heard of the robbery of the Mayville bank on the preceding day, had convinced him that it might be the famous White Mask himself. Therefore, he had run across the field and drawn his revolver, but the rider refused to halt in answer to his command and, instead, had gone for his gun. He, John Carver, managed to fire twice, but both shots unluckily went wide, while the robber, firing only once, had struck him to the ground, and now he lay there, fainting, a martyr to the law. The stains on him, and the hounds sweeping away at full cry on another trail—these were sufficient items to convince even the stern-faced, stiff-whiskered sheriff in charge.

"Get back on the trail," he commanded, "and start riding. You, partner . . . what's your name?"

"John Carver."

"You'll sure be remembered when we run the hound down. You'll come in for your share of the reward. It ain't every man that has the nerve to run out single-handed and try shots with The White Mask."

"Thanks," John Carver said humbly.

"Pete," ordered the sheriff, "and Bob, give Carver a hand. One of you stay with him, and one of you start on and get help out here for him . . . a buckboard or something to take him in. Carver, you sure you ain't bad hurt?"

"I'll live through it, right enough," said John Carver. His upper lip writhed back from his teeth. "Only got one request to make, Sheriff."

"You got a right to talk, Carver. What is it?"

"When you get within gunshot of the hound, don't show him no mercy. Shoot to kill, boys."

The sheriff waved his hand. "You leave that to me, son. We're either going to get him this trick or else salt him away with lead. Come on!"

They stormed away down the trail with a shout, and Carver, watching them go, noted that every man was mounted on a horse far fresher than the blue roan. He gave a great sigh of relief to think that he no longer sat in that saddle. As for the big man of the black beard—it mattered not what were the causes that had made him shift places.

The world is plumb full of nuts, anyway, John Carver thought to himself, and dismissed Keene from his thoughts.

Chapter Sixteen

His two guardians had submitted surlily enough to the order of the sheriff, and still, as they debated which should ride into Porterville or to the nearest house for help, their eyes turned after the noise of the departing bloodhounds. Yonder was excitement greater by far than the excitement of any fox hunt or boar chase. Yonder, also, was exceedingly great profit. Yet they were too manly to whine audibly at the disappointment. They came quickly to agreement as to which was to ride in. One departed. He had hardly dropped out of sight across the hilltop when another horseman came in view, riding up at a brisk canter and coming almost from the direction in which the hounds had disappeared.

It was Jerry Swain, Jr.

"What's happened? How do they lie now?" cried the man from the posse eagerly. "Did you get a look at 'em?"

"At what?" asked Jerry.

"At the posse . . . and The White Mask. . . ."

"What d'you mean?"

"If you don't want to foller 'em, stay here with this gent that got plugged for trying to stop The White Mask. You stay here with him . . . that's easy enough. I'll light out after the rest of the boys."

"Sure," Jerry said. "Go on if you like. I know Carver. Hello! Sorry this happened. Are you badly hurt?"

"Nothing fatal about it," John Carver answered. "Sort of cracked, but not plumb smashed."

The man of the posse waited to hear no more, but, secure in the belief that the newcomer was an honest man, he whirled his horse and darted away after the dying noise of the hounds. Jerry Swain

121

was instantly on the ground and helping to arrange the bandage. The thanks of Carver were profuse, and the groans and the curses that he showered on the head of The White Mask were equally thick.

"What sort of a looking man is he?" asked Jerry. "Did you get close enough to see that? Or was he wearing his mask?"

"Not when I seen him," Carver said. "Big fellow, Swain. He must weigh close to two hundred, and he looks strong as an ox. Sort of man you'll expect anything from."

Jerry Swain, remembering that encounter in the dusk and the crushing arms of the preacher, blinked.

"And he's got a big black beard," Carver said. "Matter of fact, it'll be hard for him to get away the next time, now that his face has been seen this once."

"It will, right enough," said Jerry. In his heart he marveled a little at the villainy of Carver in so calmly shifting all the blame and furnishing this exact description of his rescuer. Yet, when he examined his own conscience, he was sneakingly aware that he would have been apt to do exactly what the elder man was doing.

"Here," he said kindly, "I'll brush some of the dirt off of this coat." He started to drag it from under Carver, but the latter deftly put his heel on it and then—but merely as though bracing himself—dropped his usable hand on the revolver that had fallen to the ground near him.

"Never mind," he said cheerfully enough. "Let it rest where it is."

"What's the matter?" asked Jerry. "Got something in it you don't want people to see?" He was favored with a glance of murderous intentness after this speech.

"Nothing worth seeing," Carver said. "But I can manage to take care of my own clothes yet a while. What d'you think could be in it?"

It was a delight to Jerry, this interview. He felt the cruel pleasure of the fisherman playing with the fish and knowing that in a little while he will be able to land it, no matter how the fish may battle in the meantime.

"Well," he said, "I had an idea there might even be something quite useful in that coat."

Carver started. "Useful to who?" he asked sharply.

"To anybody."

The color of the robber changed. "Swain," he said huskily, "what are you driving at?"

"Money," Jerry said suddenly.

The hand of the other clenched suddenly around the butt of the revolver on which he had dropped it. Yet he was not quite sure, and he managed a caricature of a laugh. "Sure," he said, "we all could use money. But me . . . I'm a poor man, Swain. You ought to know that about as well as anybody. Ain't your father got one of the mortgages that are killing me?"

"You've got so little money of your own, as a matter of fact," said Jerry, "that you might even think, now and then, of stepping out and getting a little piece of money that belongs to somebody else, eh, Carver?"

Carver turned livid and jerked the gun into his lap. "Now talk out and talk quick," he said. "What are you driving at?"

Jerry Swain, Jr., gave back, pale and trembling himself, but finding his actual fear not altogether unpleasant. He felt himself to be utterly safe, after all. "No use picking up your gun, Carver," he said. "The other man will be back with a wagon. And then . . ."

"Talk out!" gasped Carver. "You talk about me . . . money . . ."

"Carver," Jerry Swain said, "you're The White Mask." He smiled pleasantly as he saw the blow go home and the face of the robber wrinkle. "Though how one like you," Jerry went on smoothly, "can be the father of a sweet little girl like your Mary, I'm hanged if I see. But she's what father would call a sport . . . she's jumped outside of your class. As a matter of fact, I suppose I have to turn you over to the sheriff, eh?"

"You do?" Carver said, grinding his teeth. "When you turn me over, they'll be a pile of dead men turning over in their graves. You rat." He exposed the gun and trained it directly at Jerry.

"Are you crazy?" cried the latter worthy, pale in good earnest. "Don't you know that they'd find my body and . . . and . . ."

"Why not be hanged for killing you, too, so long as I have to swing, anyway?" Carver snarled. "I'll teach you to stand up and pity Mary Carver for her father!"

"Carver," gasped out Jerry Swain, "you're talking too quickly. You don't wait for me to finish. I mean you no harm, if you play the game with me."

Normal color slowly began to return to the face of John Carver. "What game?" he asked sullenly.

"I saw everything from the hill yonder. I saw Tom Keene shoot you, Carver. And then . . . heaven knows why, but I think the fellow's a little wrong in the head . . . he jumped onto your horse and rode off and pulled the hounds after him . . . and saved your skin." He smiled in triumph as he thrust the details into Carver's attention again.

"If you were to tell it," Carver breathed, "nobody would believe you."

"Bah!" Jerry sneered. "Everything is against you. You're exactly the sort of man to be suspected, Carver. You're poor. You're in debt. You have a wife and a child dependent upon you. And if I was willing to go into court against you, don't you suppose that they'd believe me well enough to at

least search your coat pockets and find handfuls of money there?"

John Carver was speechless. All that he dreaded had been revealed. The perspiration rolled down his face and dripped off his chin, and yet the day was not overly hot. "What d'you want, Swain?" he managed to gasp out at length.

"Every cent you have!" exclaimed Jerry.

"What?"

"Isn't your life worth that to you?"

Carver hesitated a fraction of a second. But he had seen enough to convince him that Swain was a coward. Ordinarily he would not even have attempted to argue.

"Look here," he said. "Talk a little sense. D'you suppose I risked my neck for this to give it to you? Man, you make me laugh. You've got something on me, and I've got to buy you off. That's easy. I'm agreeable. But give you all of it? I'd sooner give you a couple of chunks of lead in the head, son, and then take my chances on buying myself off with them that are coming over the hill."

"You can't bluff," Jerry said, but in spite of his smile he was worried.

"Can't I?" cried the robber, thrusting out his jaw. "I'll tell you this, beauty, too. I'm sort of tired of living, anyway. What's a year or two more to live, one way or another? Listen. There's the rattle of the buckboard coming. Swain, talk out sharp. If you want to come to any sort of terms with me, shout out right now. Otherwise, I'll let my gun talk." He changed his voice to a growl: "What d'you want? How much d'you have to have?"

And in spite of himself, though he knew he could just as well have doubled or trebled the sum, the figure that had been forming in his brain and haunting him in his dreams burst from his lips.

"Five hundred dollars, Carver. I've got to have five hundred dollars!" He gritted his teeth and added hastily: "I mean a thousand, Carver, I . . ."

"I know what you mean," Carver said with a sneer. "You need five hundred, but you'd like to have as much as you can get. Well, Swain, I'll give you five hundred. And it sure is easy money for you, that never risked a fingertip to get it. But here you are."

He counted it out of a jumbled mass that he restored to his pocket again, and Jerry Swain watched him with feverish eyes. But, after all, he knew where that money was, and if the fear of being exposed had made the robber pay once, it would make him pay again. In reality, the money he had stolen could be regarded as a sum simply held in trust for Jerry Swain. And a warm feeling of security ran through Jerry. For the first time in his life the grim shadow of financial difficulties promised to be lifted from his path.

Chapter Seventeen

The hounds were speeding far away on the trail of Tom Keene, and the big man felt the blue roan weaken beneath him. The weight of Carver had been wearing out the horse, and now the more ponderous burden of Tom crushed his heart from him. He began to falter at the first long upgrade, and Tom knew that he had not much farther to go. Looking back, he could see his pursuers streaming over a hilltop, only two ranges back.

From the crest where he was at that moment posted, he could survey the possibilities fairly accurately. Turning to the right, he would be entering the ups and downs of mountain work, and the laboring ribs of his horse convinced him that another mile of such running would break him down to a walk. Ahead and below him, a small stream was shooting down a steep channel that no horse in the world could ford.

Striking the level below, the little river disappeared in a long strip of marsh land of no great width. At the far end of the marsh, it formed again and ran on more slowly, bridged where it gathered into a stream. In that direction, then, he should turn his rapidly flagging horse. But, if he did that, he would be cutting across the direction by which the posse approached him, and he would lose vital ground. Indeed, long before he could gain the bridge, he and his faltering blue roan would be within range of the expert riflemen of the pursuit. To avoid that, he must give up the hope of gaining the bridge.

There remained another alternative, a third and last one. If he plunged straight down the slope toward the marsh as fast as his horse could carry him, he would be able to go at a rapid clip, and then, having ridden the roan as far as possible into the morass, he could go on, swimming or running, until he reached the firm ground on the farther side.

There would be this advantage. The hounds would drive straight down the slope, and most likely the posse would rush on in similar manner. In the marsh they would become hopelessly confused. They could not well hope to overtake him, even if they started on foot.

In the meantime, once on the far side of the marsh, he could gain the little farm beyond and, without staying to saddle, fling a bridle over the head of one of the horses in the corral and shoot away toward freedom again.

There were two dangers in this scheme. One was that the farmer might have his courage and his rifle handy and take a shot at the horse thief. The other danger was that part of the posse, the moment they saw the direction of his flight, might not go for the swamp but ride directly for the bridge at the extreme end of the marsh. In that case, they could probably cut around the marsh and reach the farm in time to head him off. In any event, it was a desperate chance, but it seemed the only one worth taking. Otherwise, he was done for.

He shot the roan down the slope at a swift gallop, swung out of the saddle when he saw that the beast would be bogged at once if he were ridden into the water-soaked ground, and then ran on into the marsh. There was water up to his knees almost at once, and then he struck thick mud, which held him back with a grip almost as tenacious as glue. A moment later he was in a tangle of fallen, rotting trees and shrubs. The bark on which he rested his hands came out in molding sections beneath his touch. His feet, which he based on the logs, slipped in the slime, and again and again he was precipitated up to his neck in water. And once the slimy surface closed above his head. So, struggling on in mud, water, and through a hundred obstructions, he pressed to the center of the marsh and there found a small open stretch of water.

Tom was on the verge of diving into this when the cry of the hounds rounded the top of the hill above the marsh. Then he dived and swam as he had never done before. When he came up, chilled and dripping, on the farther side, he shook the water out of his ears and listened again.

Shouts of men were now plainly discernible,

some of them fading away toward the west. In that direction lay the end of the marsh and the bridge. But they were too late, he felt certain. It would be half an hour before they could have rounded the bridge and stormed back up the road toward the farm, and in half of that time he ought to be on the back of a fresh horse. He might even be able to stay and saddle one of the best in the corral.

With freshened vigor, then, he plunged into the heart of the marsh again. Instantly he was sunk to his chest in a quicksand, but he tore himself out with a fierce, soft shout of pleasure as all of his sinewy strength came to bear. Sometimes he tripped and fell headlong. Sometimes his boots were literally stuck in a thick adobe mud, and he had to stop and drag out his feet one at a time.

But—perhaps it was only his fury of impatience to be on the back of a horse again—it seemed to him that he should be already seeing daylight on the thinner, outer edge of the marsh. He stopped and quickly cast his directions again by the hill from which he had entered and the hill toward which he had aimed. And he found that he had been traveling for the past few minutes directly at right angles from the original course he had mapped. That discovery turned him cold. Five minutes were a vital gap. To make up for the loss, he veered and tore ahead in a perfect fury of effort. And so, at length, the trees suddenly thinned out, and his foot struck firm ground.

Just before him was a barbed-wire fence. He leaped it in his running stride, like a practiced hurdler, and dashed across the first narrow field. The trees of the marsh circled in on his left, and therefore he could not tell what might be approaching on the road from the bridge, but, if they had been near, he could have heard the pounding of their horses' hoofs. Another barbed-wire fence. He leaped to clear it, but his foot slipped at the vital moment on a stone, his heel drove into the top strand of the wire, and he pitched forward on his face. The impact stunned him.

When he came out of blackness, so fiercely had his instincts and his subconscious self been fighting to carry him on to his goal that he found he was already on his feet and stumbling blindly ahead. His brain cleared instantly. He raced on for the barn, a hideous spectacle by this time. From where his forehead had struck the ground, a crimson stream was trickling down and clotting in red masses in his great beard. His clothes, ripped to a hundred tatters by the struggle through the marsh, streamed behind his shoulders. His sombrero was long since gone, of course, and his hair, which he habitually wore rather long, now stood on end, stiff with slime and mud.

He had quick reason to discover the effect of his appearance, for now he was among the buildings of the ranch, and a woman, with a pail full of eggs, stepped from the door. She screamed and threw her hand across her eyes at the sight of the monster. Tom saw her collapse against the wall of the barn, and drove on.

Into the right side of that barn he ran, his speed redoubled now, for in the distance he heard the purr of the beating hoofs of many horses sounding loud and clear from a stretch of hard-packed road surface. They were coming fast, and to avoid them would need both a good horse and quick start.

He issued from the barn, with the corral of horses on one side and the house on the other. From the house a middle-aged man and a boy were running in response to the scream of the woman. At sight of Tom Keene, a deep-throated shout and shrill yell arose. He saw the father jerk out a gun, and, whipping forth his own weapon, he fired well into the air. Impulse of self-protection, not fighting heart, had made the former draw his weapon. Now he dropped it and fairly took to his heels, while Tom, running on, snatched from the upper rail of the corral the bridle that had been carelessly thrown there.

His skillful eye swept over the horses in the enclosure. There was only one, to him. It was a fine four-year-old bay, standing an inch, at least, over sixteen hands, and from shoulders to hocks manifestly and expressly designed for the carrying of weight. How such an animal could have come

133

into the possession of such a farmer, Tom did not pause to ask. But now and again mustangs would revert to the true type of that hot-blooded stock from which it had sprung. This must be such a reversion.

Moreover, best of all for his purposes now, the horse was apparently a pet, for, while the other animals crowded away toward the far fence of the corral, the tall bay stood fast, merely tossing up his fine head and looking inquisitively toward the stranger.

Tom vaulted to the top of the fence and looked back. Far away down the road he could see them coming, the men of the posse, a full dozen of them riding as fast as their sweating horses would carry them. And he saw them swing up their quirt-bearing hands at the sight of him and then lower their heads to plunge on. He saw, also, in that backward glance, that the twelve-year-old boy who had run out from the house had not followed the example of his father. Instead of running, he had leaned and swept the fallen revolver from the ground, and now, white-faced and resolute, he faced Tom.

"Don't take the bay," he piped. "Any hoss but the bay, stranger! That's my hoss! Leave Dick alone!"

Tom registered the youngster as a plucky little chap, and the next moment was beside tall Dick. The big horse was gentle as a kitten. He merely snorted a little. Then he allowed the bit to be slipped into his mouth. Tom leaped onto his back.

"No, no, no!" screamed a voice that was partly hoarse with desperation and partly choked with sobbing. "Not Dick . . . my hoss . . . !"

"I'll send him back!" Tom shouted, and he turned the big fellow at the fence. He took it like a bird, though doubtless he had never jumped such an obstacle before with or without a rider. But, as the bay shot into the air, struggled for balance like a feathering oar, and then swooped down on the far side, Tom Keene shouted with triumph, for he knew that he had a horse, indeed.

"Good boy!" he cried. And as the words left his mouth, the revolver spoke behind him, and a bullet whistled above his head. He looked back, his own weapon instinctively poised in his hand. But it was the boy. He stood with desperately twisted face, his feet braced, the revolver extended at arm's length and gripped in both hands. Again the heavy Colt boomed as Tom, with a laugh, dropped his own weapon back into the holster. But this time the bullet did not whistle past. Instead, tall Dick staggered and stumbled.

Something hot gushed across the knee of Tom. He looked down and saw crimson spouting from the shoulder of the horse. An instant more, and the gallant fellow was away again in full stride, only with his ears flattened to give token that he had been injured.

Tom Keene took swift stock of his surroundings. Half a mile away there was a small field with horses in it, which, from the distance at least, looked good enough to be tried even in a great emergency like this. But if he made for them, he would have tall Dick dead before he reached them. No doubt the bay could make the run, even with this wound. But, if he died from it, Tom would never forgive himself.

The revolver was barking again, but, after that luckless shot, none of the bullets came near him. In the meantime, the posse was drumming the road closer and closer. If he stopped the bay, he practically surrendered.

But so be it. It was hard that he could not slip away, disappear, and so give John Carver a chance to play the part of an honest man by himself and his wife and daughter. But the bullet of the boy had cut short the possibility of that. He must stay and tell the truth.

A word and a pull on the reins brought Dick to a halt, and Tom slipped from his back. The boy, who had started wildly and futilely in pursuit after discharging his last bullet, was instantly beside them with a wail of grief as soon as he saw the wound. He threw his arms up, and the big horse, even in his pain, lowered his head, trembling, to the shoulder of the child.

"Oh, Dick!" cried the boy. "Oh, Dick! I've killed you!" And he shouted furiously, through his tears, at Tom: "You'll hang for what you've done! You'll hang for it!"

"Gimme that shirt off your back, son, and stop talking if you want to keep this horse alive. Quick, now. We got work to do, and fast work, at that."

Chapter Eighteen

This was the amazing spectacle that the posse came upon as it stormed around the farmhouse of Pete Chanley. Little Billy Chanley, stripped to the waist and dancing with excitement and eagerness to help, hovered around the mud-clotted form of the man they were pursuing, and that man was working hard to stanch the flow from the wounded shoulder of the big bay horse.

They circled around The White Mask with guns poised, ready to kill. Even in their most optimistic moments they had not the slightest hope of capturing alive a criminal so desperate. But when the sheriff advanced and thrust two guns under the very ear of the big man, Tom Keene merely roared: "Take them gats away! I can't be bothered. Here, buddy, yank out my gun and give it to 'em. I ain't going to put my hands up. I'm busy."

It was not a dignified thing for a sheriff to do, but somehow or other it was impossible to do other than step back and let the fugitive have his way of it. The posse stood back, excited, silent, ready for any sort of trick and a break, but with a growing amazement that there was nothing they could do, and that their notable outlaw had sacrificed himself for the sake of a horse.

When he had done his best, he turned a muddy, wild-bearded face upon them and actually smiled. "Well, boys," he said, "it looks like you have me, eh? And now that you got me, I'm sorry to tell you that I ain't the man you want."

"Maybe not," agreed the smooth-spoken sheriff who saw the greatest feat of his life accomplished on this day, and who believed that he now possessed surety of reëlection so long as he cared to run for office, "maybe not. That ain't the only thing that you'll be wanting to say to the judge. For now, partner, just shove your hands into these, will you?"

His wrists were instantly encircled. "Go as far as you like," said Tom, "but I've got to tell you . . ."

"You know that anything you say is apt to be used against you?"

"Sure." Tom smiled again. "Matter of fact, I don't think I'll do any talking right now."

He had just begun to think of what might happen should John Carver be seized—of the misery and sadness that would be brought into the house. It was better to let matters drag along for a few days, even for a few weeks, until Carver's wound had been healed, and he was equipped for an escape from the country. Then, when he left, he could simply mail from some distant place a confession that would release Tom from all danger of the law. As this idea came to him, he sighed and then lifted his head and smiled through his muddy beard. The sigh was at the thought of the weary days of confinement that lay before him. The smile came when he thought of the bright face of Mary Carver when, on a day, she should learn what he had done.

Back at the farmhouse they reluctantly allowed him to wash himself clean, for they wished to exhibit him to the good people of Porterville as terrific a spectacle as he had made when they ran him to the ground. As it was, the scene was spectacular enough when they rode through the street of the town, with Tom Keene in their midst, bareheaded, with his beard and long hair blowing, and looking more like a giant than ever. His tattered clothes, the ragged and unclosed wound that crossed his forehead, everything about him suggested desperation and desperate strength. Instinctively the men and women who had heard of what was coming, and who had packed into the town to see the sight, looked from the formidable prisoner to the calm-faced sheriff who rode at the side of Tom. And, just as Sheriff Thomas expected, they one and all agreed that he must have their vote so long as he cared to run for office.

As for their comments on the prisoner, they were such as are usually made when a man is arrested for such crimes. In their hearts they half admired and wholly feared the courage with which he must have been endowed even to conceive the things that were attributed to him. For The White Mask was one of those half-legendary figures that grow up on the mountain-desert from time to time. Men had done a hundred many desperate acts, but what little The White Mask had done had served to gather an atmosphere of the mysterious and the awful around him. The figure of Tom Keene, also, fitted in with the conception of great power, though he seemed rather a lion than the fox that The White Mask was reputed to be.

So Tom was brought down the street where he had preached faith and charity. And as the crowd remembered his sermon, the humor of the thing caught them, and a chuckle spread around. There was something intriguing, they felt, in boldness like that of Tom Keene.

He was brought to the little jail. There they searched him again—a mere formality, for he had been relieved of even his matches at the time he was captured. They took down his name and the date of his birth. They asked for a statement, which he refused to make, and then he was brought to his cell. The noises of the little town were shut away. The one stout building in Porterville was this little jail with its walls of thick stone, and when the doors closed and the sheriff alone stood before him, his face checked by the small bars of the door, Tom Keene felt for the first time the full decisiveness of his move. Seen from the outside, the law is a thing that few persons pay much attention to, but, seen from the inside, as Tom was seeing it now, it became vastly changed. It was a great machine. It had long-reaching arms. It had irresistible hands that clutched and crushed whatever came within their grip.

And the little, smooth-spoken sheriff, who had seemed so insignificant to him before, now became a man grim because of what he represented. Now the man of the law raised a cautioning forefinger.

"Keene . . . if that's what you really want us to call you," he said, "I've got one thing to say before I leave you. Nobody has tried to dig through these walls and managed to do it. So long."

And he was gone, whistling lightly as he passed down the corridor. The moment he was alone there came another shock for Tom, and this time he realized with redoubled vividness why men he had known long before—gamblers and their ilk— had dreaded the word *prison*. For, in a breath, his life was shrunk to a space eight feet by six feet, bounded by barriers of iron and stone.

He shrugged his shoulders, however, realizing that it was only a temporary confinement, and lay down on the cot to rest and ponder the sad future of the Carvers. Now, more than ever, they needed him. And he came to the definite conclusion that, as soon as he was out, he would devote himself certainly to their welfare.

What chiefly troubled him was the thought of the panic that would sweep over poor Carver when the robber learned that Tom had been captured. Word must be sent to the man at once, if possible, reassuring him about Tom's attitude, until his shoulder was healed. That, after all, should be a matter of no very long time, because, so far as Tom had been able to make out, the wound was a flesh one only.

Here he shouted loudly until the sheriff appeared again and in haste.

"Sheriff," said Tom, "I need some little things. And Missus Carver is friendly to me. Besides, I want to write out and say a word to her about not knowing who he was when I shot her husband. Can I send out a letter?"

The sheriff paused, then nodded. It was not strictly legal, but the work that he did was rarely circumscribed by legal limitations. He went away and returned with writing materials. "Write as much as you want," he said. "And what you write won't be opened. I'll send it out to Missus Carver myself."

"Matter of fact," Tom said, "I think I'll send it to Carver. I guess that I can't gain anything by entering into a plot with a man I've shot down, can I?"

The sheriff laughed. "I guess not," he said. "You go ahead and write. The letter won't be opened."

Chapter Nineteen

"Here's a letter for you, Carver," said the sheriff, putting the missive into the hand of the wounded man. "It ain't just according to the way things ought to be for me to let a prisoner send out letters that I ain't read. But there's something about this White Mask . . . if that's what he really is . . . that appeals to me. I can't help wishing him luck. Well, so long, Carver. I hope this little accident will teach you to stay put for a while."

He was gone breezily. John Carver heard the man of law speaking to Mrs. Alison, the bent old crone who had come to help while there were two injured people in the house. Elizabeth Carver had gone shopping to town.

Shopping, and gossiping, too, thought her husband. *What would she learn? What must Tom Keene have said in his defense by this time, and how far had the gossips of the village spread the tidings broadcast, labeled with the stamp of their belief?* For the town was filled with people who, he knew, were eager to blacken his name.

And what would his wife think when she heard what Tom must long before this have said with the passion of a desperate man? Carver knew that the love of his wife had long since been dulled by his neglect and his ill use of her. Perhaps this would be the final blow—she would not only believe what the gossips had to say, but she herself would declare against him. And the result of such a declaration would be ruin for him. If she told even a tithe of the things that she knew about him, his reputation would be blasted forever. But perhaps everything was said in this letter, and Tom Keene was holding him up with threats.

Here he tore open the letter, raised it with trembling hands to the level of his eyes, and swept his glance hungrily down to the bottom. Then he dropped the paper with a gasp, raised it again, and repeated the message to himself slowly, stunned by what he saw. The missive read:

Dear Carver: I'm taking a chance on sending this. If it's opened, you're lost. But if I don't send it, you're lost, anyway. This way, I can make sure of you getting away, I think.

This opening paragraph had so staggered the reason of Carver that he could barely make sense of the rest of the letter. It went on:

My idea is this: It will take anywhere from four to six weeks for your wound to heal. And all that time I'll stick out my part here in jail or—if it takes that long—in prison, Carver. But, as soon as you're able to take to the saddle, then start riding, put a lot of miles between you and Porterville, and then mail back a confession that will turn me loose. That ought to be easy for you.

After that, maybe if you leave the country and settle down away off somewhere, your wife and the little girl can be sent after you. If they have no money, I'll work until they're fixed up.

The reason I'm willing to do it, Carver, is because of the little girl. She ought to have a better chance than she'll get if she's raised as the daughter of a jailbird.

Take my advice, Carver. All I ask is that you get well quickly. Because I sure hate life behind the bars. I wasn't cut out for this sort of party. I have to set my teeth to keep going. But I will keep going, and you can lay to that. I'll keep my mouth shut and let them do what they want to do. But, when the time comes, I guess that you'll slide out and leave the confession behind you.

You don't need to worry, about your wife and Mary, because I'll sure do my best to take care of them both.

So long, Carver. Here's wishing you all the luck in the world. You don't need to send me any answer. Just know I've had a sort of a thrill wondering if you'd really write the confession. But I've stopped doubting just about as quick as I began. I know you'll play square on your side, and I'll play square on mine, and so we'll make the best of a bad deal.

Tom Keene

No wonder that, he had to drop the letter twice with a gasp of incredulity, and then raise it again to reread.

After that he lay perfectly still in a sort of happy semi-dream. Under his head was the thick lump of his coat used as a pillow to raise his head upon the couch, and into his trance there passed the blissful knowledge that part of the lump that supported his head was composed of the wallet stuffed thick with the money that was his spoil.

The screen door at the front of the house creaked open. The light, quick step of his wife came tapping down the hall. And not until that moment did he think of concealing the damning letter, or of destroying it. He gripped it to tear it to shreds. But what if the keen ear of his wife should catch the sound? What if she should come running in? Keen with suspicion, what if she should gather up some of the small fragments? He recalled anecdotes of people who had put together just such torn bits of paper and out of them constructed the answer to the riddle.

Accordingly he stuffed the paper hastily under

his coat. But as he did so, he made out that she was not coming directly to him. She went instead into the room of Mary. The doors were open, and he could hear her clearly.

"Is your father asleep?"

"I haven't heard a whisper out of his room. I guess he is."

"Oh, Mary, I'm glad that you weren't in town today to hear what people are saying about Tom Keene."

"I don't care what they say!" Mary exclaimed. "I won't believe any wrong about him."

"Why, Mary, he shot down your own father."

"Maybe Dad was in the wrong."

"Hush."

"But how could he have had time to get so far away and do that robbery that folks talk about?"

John Carver heaved himself up, despite a severe twinge from his wound, and he listened breathlessly. But he relaxed and sank back when he heard his wife replying in a perfectly calm voice: "Why, everyone knows that The White Mask has all the confederates he wants. Distance is nothing to him. He could have relays of horses fixed. Don't you see what was in his head? He showed up here . . . he acted kind to us, the sneak! . . . and all the time he was planning to jump away off south and do that safe blowing. But folks wouldn't believe that it could be he, even if evidence pointed at him, because they would have seen him up here such a little while before."

"I can't talk you down. All I know is that it isn't right for you to turn on him."

"After he's shot down my husband? How you talk, Mary! You're 'most out of your head. Now you go to sleep."

She passed out of the room, and the door clicked behind her. Mary's protesting voice was cut away to nothing, and presently Mrs. Carver tiptoed to the door of her husband's room. He greeted her with a smile. The faith that she had just shown in him had touched his vanity. And her flush of excitement had recalled an almost girlish prettiness to her cheeks. When she saw that he was awake, she came in with a smile and asked how he was.

"I'm doing fine," Carver said, a great reaction sweeping over him. "But gimme a drink, Lizzie."

By his tone there was only one sort of drink conceivable. She would rather have starved thrice over than not have whiskey in the house. Now she brought him the tall bottle and the glass. He filled a big portion and tossed it off raw. Then he lay back with a sigh and a smacking of his lips.

"This pain, it sure wears a man out," he muttered. "What's the news, Lizzie?"

"Oh, I have a whole armful of news. I went right in, and the first person I met was Missus Alice . . . but you can't listen to me in any comfort with that

148

coat all wrinkled up under your head. Wait till I smooth it out. Then I'll tell you all about it."

So saying, she reached for the coat, and in a semi-comatose condition he even partially lifted his head so that she could take it. It was only after she had it in her hands that he recalled what that coat contained, and with a prodigious oath he reached for it.

But lucklessly she had shaken the coat out upside down, and from an inside pocket fell a wallet that thudded softly on the floor at her feet, flopped open, and exposed an interior stuffed full of greenbacks. Moreover, at the same time, from one of the outer pockets of the coat, there slipped a wad of stuff that dissolved in the draft close to the surface of the floor and fluttered softly away—a whole host of greenbacks.

Chapter Twenty

Even when the money fell to the floor, John Carver could have explained, but his nerve left him. For an instant he gazed, his brain swirling with alarm and with the effects of the stupefying slug of whiskey.

"Good Lord!" he breathed, and stared up to Elizabeth, with his guilt making his eyes big.

But her mind grasped at the truth only by dim degrees. She went straight toward the door of discovery. "What . . . money . . . why, John, there are thousands here. Where . . . where did you earn . . . ?" That door to the truth was thrown wide, but she could endure only a glimpse of what was revealed. "John!" she cried. "Tell me that it ain't so! You . . . you . . . oh, my head's spinning."

He was up on his feet. "Stop yelling, you fool!" he gasped. "Stop that racket. Mary'll hear! The brat's been waiting for something to happen, and, if she hears, she'll be telling all that she knows. Stop yelling, I say!"

She caught at him. "The White Mask . . . not you, John!"

She had caught at the arm that hung in the sling, and he tore her away and flung her off with such force that she staggered against the table in the center of the room. It went over with a crash. The whiskey bottle flew clear to the stone hearth and shivered upon it with a loud splintering of glass. And at that moment Mary Carver, white with fear, opened the door and stood before them.

Her father slumped down upon the couch as though this were the death stroke and he no longer had the strength to struggle against fate, but the effect upon his wife was remarkable. From the very depths of hysterical terror and shame and grief she rallied like a flash and turned a pale but laughing face on Mary.

"I slipped and stumbled against the table, honey. That's all."

Mary nodded. "I thought somebody . . . had fallen. . . ." And she closed the door.

John's wife turned away, and he groaned: "Elizabeth, you're wonderful. Just plumb wonderful. How could you face them bright, prying eyes of hers?"

"Stop talking," Mrs. Carver commanded, turning a gray, set face toward him. In that instant she had passed from terror to calm command. "Lie down on the couch."

He obeyed, gaping at her.

"Look quiet. Look cheerful."

"How can I manage to fix the way my face is? I ain't got a mirror, and I ain't an actor."

"You do what I tell you to do," Elizabeth said sternly. With hands moving faster than the picking beaks of starved birds, she was gathering the fallen money from the floor, and now she stuffed it into the bosom of her dress and placed the wallet under her apron.

"If she guesses what's the truth," Elizabeth Carver said, "d'you know what she'll do? She'll run to the town and go through the streets screaming it."

"The little brat!" Carver snarled. "She won't dare. Her own father . . ."

"And a fine father you've been to her," his wife interrupted with a sneer. "You've never come near her except to strike her. You've never petted her or held her in your lap since . . ."

"Since she got old enough to look me in the face," said the father. "Because she had a queer, grown-up look about her. Besides, how much of me shows in her?"

"Little . . . thank heaven. She's your own child, but there's none of your soul in her. But in two minutes, John, she was closer to Tom Keene than to you in twelve years. The very first day, when he brought her up, living, out of the well where she might have died, she lay that night in her bed, with him sitting beside her, and talked her heart out to him. Why, she worships the ground he walks on. And if she finds that she can get him out of jail, I tell you, John, she'd send you behind the bars, and she'd send me with you."

"Us that brought her into the world," whined John Carver. "For a stranger that . . ."

"That saved her from dying out of it," the mother said sternly.

And Carver gasped and was still.

Mrs. Carver sank into a chair and buried her face in her hands, trembling. And John Carver lay on the couch gaping at her. At length he grew restive and managed to say: "Elizabeth, dear, what are . . . ?"

"Don't talk to me," she gasped. "I don't want to hear you talk. I've got to think. I've got to think. Oh, dear heaven, tell me what to do."

John Carver swallowed. "They's only one thing for you to do, and that's to stand by him you swore to stand by through thick and thin when you married him."

"John, John, don't you see it's enough to drag us all down into disgrace and worse if I don't tell the truth?"

"You . . . you don't have to talk at all," he breathed. "That's the thing to do. Don't talk. If they should ask you questions, you just tell 'em what you seen. . . ."

"But I know it as well as if I'd been there."

"What do you know?"

"That what you said you did is just exactly what he did. You're the one that rode the roan over the hill with the mask on, and he's the one that ran and called to you to stop. And you drew your gun and tried to kill him, but he shot you down."

"And little you care, except that you wished my neck had been busted by the fall, eh?"

"And then, like a saint, which he is, when he found out that you were Mary's father, he took your place on the horse and tried to lead them off. They might have killed him." She added in a shrill little moan: "But like as not you'd let him rot in prison in your place."

"But you won't be talking, Lizzie?"

"No, no . . . and when at last it's known . . . Mary, the daughter of a thief . . . a murderer. . . ."

"That's a lie! I never killed a man. I . . ." He caught at one part of her speech. "It never has to be known. Nobody but you and me and him knows of it, Lizzie."

"What?"

The unutterable baseness of his proposal made him cringe as he spoke, but he managed to say distinctly enough: "If he tries to tell the story about what he done and how he took the part of The White Mask, just out of the bigness of his heart and for want of something better to do, nobody'll believe him. They'll laugh at him. I know what they'll do. I can hear the courtroom chuckle when he tries to say that." He chuckled himself.

"Not ever let it be known?" poor Mrs. Carver murmured. "Oh, John, is this the kind of man that you are?"

He blinked at that rebuff, but he went ahead swiftly. "You listen to me. I got close to five thousand left out of the boodle. With that I can make a new start. You know the Miller five hundred acres?"

She nodded. She was only hearing him with half of her attention. With the other half of her mind she was considering sadly the first suggestion he had made.

"He offered to rent the land to me last year," John Carver said. "He ain't so bad, old Miller, if you come right down to it. But I didn't have the teams or the seed to put them five hundred in. But I could do it now. And I could fix up the house so's you'd never know it. And there's more land that I could rent, too, honey. And the first thing you know, that five thousand would grow into twenty thousand. And then . . ."

"Tom Keene would be wearing stripes in a prison."

"Is he a father of a family, I ask you? Ain't a married man got a right to have some sort of exceptions made for him?"

She shuddered. "Don't stop and talk about that. Go on, John. I'm trying to listen, but . . . oh, Lord, I never dreamed that the inside of your mind had things like this in it."

He shrugged that scornful and bitter attack away and went on: "We could get back on our feet. Think of being able to go down into Porterville and look everybody we met in the face and know that we didn't owe a soul a cent. Think of that!"

She gasped. It was, indeed, like the thought of entering heaven.

"And the doctor, and everybody . . . if they looked sharp at us, we could turn right around and look back at them sharp. We could show 'em what it is to be a Carver. And then there's Mary. A fine chance she'd have in the world if folks knew that her father was a jailbird. A fine husband she could get."

Mrs. Carver cried out as though he had struck her. "Don't, John!"

"But ain't it the truth, and don't we have to look the truth in the face?"

"Yes, yes."

"But if you was to forget that you seen anything or guessed anything, honey, Mary could be sent off to school and brought up as fine as the Swain boy . . . much good his books ever done him, the yaller-hearted hound. And when she come back, why, she'll have the pretty face to marry her pick of the country."

He rose to his feet and made a grand gesture. He stalked up and down the room with the future brought upon his once handsome face, and, behold, Elizabeth Carver sat with her work-hardened hands clasped and pressed between her knees while she looked up to her husband with a touch of that old confidence and trust with which she had looked up to him in the days of their courtship.

"Oh, John!" she cried. "She might even marry young Jerry Swain. . . ."

"Him?" snarled the father. "Well," he added, recollecting himself, "she might even do that . . . if you wanted her to. She'll have the face, and I mean that she'll have the education, too. She'll be as good as any, if you stand by me in this, Lizzie."

With the price that must be paid recalled to her, she became white of face at once. But this time she was silent.

Chapter Twenty-One

It takes all kinds to make up a town in the Far West. And Attorney Charles Whitney was one of the oddities. Why he should have left his native New York, could never be understood. And why he should have picked out Porterville, of all other places, for even a temporary place of residence, was indeed a mystery to all who saw him. As a matter of fact, he had a past that might account for a great deal. And he had picked out Porterville on the map as being probably the most obscure place in the country that fell short of being a desert. It was not quite that, but, when he reached it, he thought that he had truly reached the falling off place, for the roar of the elevated trains where they thunder around the last turn off the Bowery was not yet quite out of his ears.

At any rate, here he was in Porterville, and he managed to gain a living. His law practice was not great, but it kept him in cigarettes and neckties of variegated color. Those were his chief necessities. Enough persons came in with small things to be attended to float him along. That they came to see the curiosity did not at all matter to Charlie Whitney. He was used to being stared at, and he rather liked it, in fact. Besides, he had a theory that sooner or later, when he got his fingers well limbered up, he would be able to relieve the rubes of some of the money that they flaunted at the gambling tables in Porterville with such criminal recklessness. To be sure, his fingers had not yet achieved the necessary degree of subtlety. But he was waiting and practicing.

When the judge assigned to him the case of the man who was reputed to be the celebrated White Mask, Charlie Whitney groaned. Of course Tom Keene was penniless, for otherwise he would not have been called at all, which did not make it easier for the lawyer to adjust himself to the work that was given into his hands.

But after the case had begun to develop, although it would not come to trial for some time, it assumed new phases that attracted him. It seemed that Tom Keene was either a simpleton or else a very profound rogue playing a part skillfully. And if he were the latter, it would pay the lawyer to take no chances. He had no desire to risk his neck when the man got out of prison.

That eventuality began to loom large when he learned, through a leak in the district attorney's office, that they were having difficulty in making up their case. The state could show that the bloodhounds had followed a trail during an entire night, but that they might not have crossed scents, could not be proven. Neither could they prove that during the night the rider of that horse might not have dismounted and another taken his place.

And other things troubled them. In the first

place, it was strange that the money had not been found on the person of Tom, if he were indeed The White Mask, who had blown the safe. He had been hunted with sufficient closeness to keep him from finding a secure place of hiding for it. He could only have disposed of it, they felt, by having a confederate in wait for him during the night. That confederate might have changed horses with him. In fact, that confederate might be Tom Keene.

There were people who, during the past years, had seen The White Mask at close hand during the commission of his crimes, and they one and all swore that he seemed inches shorter than the Tom Keene who they saw in the prison. More vital than this, they declared that the voices were different. The enormous voice of Tom Keene was a striking one and not hard to distinguish, but the voice of The White Mask—and they had heard him shout more than once—while it could not have been easily distinguished from the voices of a thousand other men, was at least not at all like that of Tom.

If this had been the testimony of one or two, it would not have been so bad. But half a dozen came forward and volunteered their knowledge. To say the least, it would be puzzling for a jury.

With such information as this to work upon, Charlie Whitney would have had no trouble in working up a story good enough to pass muster and at least hang the verdict of the twelve good men and true—if he could only get Tom Keene to agree to a reasonable story of why he mounted that horse.

The story that Charlie Whitney wanted him to tell was by no means reduced to words; it was only a desire to frame a good-sounding lie. But Tom Keene would not listen to his arguments. Instead, he persisted in vowing that he would tell to the jury a story of how he took the place of The White Mask on purpose and out of the sheer goodness of his heart. It was disgusting to Charlie Whitney to hear that tale.

He went to the jail today for a double purpose. In the first place, he wanted to tell Tom that the trial would have to commence the next day. In the second place, he had to tell him that he had conveyed to John Carver the message requesting him to be present in the jail that day. Indeed, at the door of the jail he found Carver and the sheriff awaiting him. All three went in to the prisoner together.

But just before he opened the inner door, the sheriff asked impulsively: "Whitney, what d'you really think? Is your man going to get off with a free skin?"

"I'll tell you what, pal," said the confidential Whitney, "he's either the greatest bluffing crook in the world, or else he's a simp. I dunno which."

"And how about you, Carver?" asked the

160

sheriff. "You look sort of pale. Put you off your feed to think of meeting up with him? Anyway, hang onto that bulldog temper of yours. It don't pay to fight a man behind the bars."

Carver nodded. He was a far different man from him who had ridden over the hill a month before and exchanged shots with Tom Keene. His hair and mustache were neatly trimmed. His eye was clear. His face was filled, though a little pale. He was, moreover, well-dressed in a new suit of clothes, and his arm, which was still incapacitated for work, was hanging in a sling. Altogether, he made an impressively respectable appearance.

"I don't bear any malice," he assured the sheriff gracefully. "Matter of fact, what would any other man do if he was riding from bloodhounds, and a gent with a gun come across his path? Why, he'd shoot, that's all. And I just happened to be on the receiving end of the slug. I ain't whining about what's happened."

"But why d'you imagine that he's so set on seeing you?"

"I suppose," said John Carver, "that he wants to tell me he's sorry for what's happened. I dunno what else."

And with that, they passed into the corridor that led past the cells. There was no one else confined. And Tom Keene rose at once from his cot where he was seated and hurried to the bars of his cell. The sheriff unlocked the door, and they all entered. It would never have occurred to him to bring the man into his office.

The Tom Keene who they faced now had altered even more greatly than John Carver in the month since his arrest. But, whereas every change in Carver had been for the better, every change in Tom had been for the worse. His cheeks were hollowed. His forehead creased with a deep, perpetual frown. And in every step and gesture he showed a nervousness that had been eating into his peace of mind like an acid.

Shadows of the walls of a prison, indeed, leave a stain where they fall, and never had they struck a more susceptible subject than Tom. He was accustomed to a freedom as great as the freedom of birds, and the constraint was a mortal poison to him.

As they entered, they could see that he was shaking with eagerness while he gave back before them. And, while the sheriff turned and relocked the door, the gaze of Tom was fixed steadily, burningly upon John Carver.

At length, before any of the three could speak, he blurted out: "Carver, I asked you to come down by yourself and see me alone."

Charlie Whitney glanced curiously from one to the other. And he was surprised to see that John Carver had found his way to the farthest corner, and that his hand, moreover, was thrust suspiciously deep in his coat pocket.

"I tried to come down," Carver said faintly. "I tried to come down and find out what you wanted, Keene, because I'm not holding any grudge against you. But they won't let people come in to see you without a witness. Ain't that the way of it, Sheriff?"

"Of course," the sheriff responded. "Got to have witnesses, friend, as you ought to know. First day I let in Missus Carver, but that was all extra."

"Extra," Tom Keene said grimly. "All extra, eh? Well, gents, I got an idea that what you're going to hear now will be a little extra, too."

He turned sharply on John Carver who, it seemed to the watchful Charlie Whitney, shrank from him in an odd fashion. And the hand fumbled at something in his coat pocket.

"Look here, Sheriff," Whitney said. "D'you let people come into your jail carrying their guns?"

"Guns?" asked the sheriff.

"Guns!" insisted Charlie. "Just drop your hand in the coat pocket of my friend yonder."

A savage glare came into the eyes that John Carver turned upon the attorney, a glance so deadly that the man from Manhattan blinked. He had seen more than one yegg and man-killer glare like that in a courtroom.

"I didn't think that there'd be any harm in bringing along a gun," said John Carver, apologizing to the sheriff as the latter approached him. "Besides, you couldn't ask me to stay in the cell here with him, without a gun. I've seen what he'd do once, and I ain't going to take any more chances when I've got a bad arm. Ain't that logic?"

"Logic, sure," said the sheriff, "but poor sense. Gimme your gun."

He took it and stepped back. The center of interest had shifted suddenly to Carver.

"Carver," Tom Keene said, "the thing I'm going to say, I've been holding off with a long time. I don't want to say it now. You know what it is. But first I want to know why Mary or her mother ain't been in? Have you ordered 'em away from the jail?"

Carver saw that the crisis had come, and that he must brave his way out. So he openly sneered and then managed a laugh as he turned to the others. "This gent is sure nutty," he declared. "Does he think my wife and my little girl are going to come in and hang on his neck after he's drove a slug through me?"

"Why, curse you . . . ," began Tom Keene. But as quickly as he had lost control of himself, he regained it. He struck his hand across his forehead heavily and then cried: "I ain't given up hope yet! I've put my trust in him, and I'll keep it to the last gasp. But, Carver, you see where I am. For your sake, I've backed myself right up against the walls of the penitentiary, and now I've either got to tell the truth or else go to prison in your place. Carver,

I give you a last chance. Will you do what you can for me, or do I have to say what I know?"

Carver, sickly white though still sneering, assumed an attitude of careless defiance, but he was a poor actor at that moment.

"Then," Tom cried, "it's on your own head! I've tried patience, and I've tried suffering, until it looks like you're trying to shift the whole load over onto my shoulders. And now, Carver, you'll take what's coming."

And Tom Keene launched into the tale of their meeting, beginning with his walk into the mountains, his return, the encounter on the hillside, the fall of John Carver, and then the strange bargain that he had struck with the robber. And he concluded: "I'd a pile rather have had a couple of slugs of lead drove through me than to say this, Sheriff. But if I didn't tell you the truth now, it'd come out sooner or later and blast the lives of his wife and his little girl. But . . ." He paused, for a faint chuckle was heard.

It came from the lips of his own attorney. The sheriff joined in, and last of all Carver himself. They uttered a mighty, ringing laugh. It seemed that their mirth was inextinguishable. Amazed, confused, he looked from one to the other for an explanation, but, without a return of a word, he saw them leave the cell, staggering with their laughter still, and heard the lock turned. Only his lawyer remained. The other two went off, the sheriff leaning on the shoulder of John Carver, the real White Mask.

Charlie Whitney spoke at length, wiping the tears from his eyes: "What d'you aim to gain by telling a yarn like that, bo? Going to work the crazy stuff? It can't be done. This is too far West to pull the insanity gag, I tell you. Keene, you've only spoiled your game."

"What do you mean?" breathed Tom.

"Mean? Why, it simply means that unless you change your story you go to . . ."

"But I can't change it! Good Lord, man, don't you see that it's true?"

"True? That stuff about shooting a man off his horse and then taking his place? True? Say, bo, what d'you take me for? A simp?"

"Then what does . . . ?"

"It means the pen for you, Tom. That's what it means, unless you change your yarn. But, now that they have this cock-and-bull story of yours, they could wreck our case even if we had a good one. So start thinking, son. Start thinking, or you'll be traveling for the big house. The cell is waiting."

Tom Keene staggered back until his head and broad shoulders crashed against the wall. "They can't put me in the penitentiary!" he thundered suddenly.

"No? Wait and see, Tom. Wait and see. Why can't they put you in?"

166

"Because," thundered Tom, "the Lord won't let 'em!"

His attorney started to laugh again, but perceived that Tom was serious, and changed his mind. He began to back down the corridor with a scared look. And when at the end of the hall he came to the door, he waited there an instant with a gasp of rather horrified astonishment, for there was a jarring sound from the cell, and he saw that Tom had dropped upon his knees and lifted his face and his hands to the stone ceiling above him.

Chapter Twenty-Two

The smile of Warden Tufter was like a ray of sunshine as he greeted his visitor. He would gladly have consigned her to the region of the outer darkness, but the early schooling that he had received as a machine politician was not lost on him. He was known to have a fist as hard as his heart; he could gather his brows until they beetled in a sort of frozen thunder at an offender; he could scare one of his prisoners into a confession in five minutes of silent treatment. But, though he felt like grinding his teeth and snarling at the young lady who sat jabbing a parasol end in a business-like manner at the pattern on the carpet of his office, he managed to convert his anger into rather explosive cordiality.

There was, of course, a reason for his

maneuvering. Women, the year before, had been granted the privilege of voting in that state, and the young lady in the blue hat and the black feather was the daughter of one of its most influential political matrons. Consequently when, as the head of a committee, she came to visit the prison and examine the complaints that occasionally drifted to the public's ear in spite of the thickness of the walls of the prison, the warden had to take heed of himself. He even received from the lieutenant governor a stern admonition to act his best; in fact, that official made a side trip to the prison to prepare the way for the young Miss Ashton. He told the warden in short, curt phrases that Miss Ashton, through her mother's influence, carried some twenty-five thousand votes in the palm of her little gloved hand, and on the result of this visit depended, to a great degree, the side of the scale into which those heavy votes would be dropped. Mrs. Ashton had heard ugly things about the prison—very ugly things—and she was sending her daughter to make sure.

"All because," said the lieutenant governor, "you send your men out of this place in such shape that they raise the devil and try to break into print as soon as they can. Now, in other states that I know of, the crooks would rather lose a leg than appear in a newspaper criticizing the treatment they received in prison, because they could not tell when they would be back in that same prison and have to look that same warden in the eye. This has to be changed, Tufter, and today is the time to do the changing. This Ashton girl has to go out of the prison thinking that everything is so comfortable here that she'd almost like to move in for the summer. You understand?"

The warden made a wry face, but he nodded. He knew that his own political life was hanging by a thread, and that a sword was poised to sever it. The bad opinion of Miss Ashton would be the vital touch of the sword edge. The good opinion of Miss Ashton would convert his precarious position into a place bastioned with impregnable granite. No wonder, therefore, that he was able to smile upon this young lady.

Forty-eight hours before, the prison had thrilled with a sense of change. Even the lifers lifted their heads, and a fire lighted in their eyes as they caught the electric current of the rumor. That rumor could be traced to no source, but it spread wildfire fashion despite walls three feet thick. The exact nature of the rumor was hard to determine, but it was simply a vague report that better times were coming. Moreover, there was a visible and tangible evidence of the change. It came in the form of a cessation of punishments. It came, above all, in greater liberty and in a big improvement of food. The sick ward was suddenly furbished until it shone again. The dark cells were opened and aired and then bolted—with rusty locks. A white spirit of tenderness and mercy seemed to have occupied the relentless bosom of the warden.

And all of this was for the benefit of Miss Ashton. Had they known that the alteration, a matter of a day only, was for the benefit of this girl scarcely entered upon her twenties, how they would have cursed, those hard-faced criminals who were housed under Tufter's regime. But, sitting in a shaft of sunshine that streamed through the wide windows of the warden's office, Miss Ashton looked into the bright, good-natured eyes and the ruddy cheeks of the warden with a feeling that she must have been misinformed. And yet there was a shadowy premonition of evil, so to speak, that dwelt around him and behind him. It was an emotion that was aroused in her by intuition, rather than by anything that she had actually seen. And, when the warden put her to the test with a blunt question, she answered full as bluntly. As a matter of fact, he was too smugly self-satisfied at the end of the tour of inspection. He felt that he had handled fire and laid it aside unburned, so he said cheerfully: "Well, Miss Ashton, what do you think of things up here?"

"Do you really care to know what I am going to tell those who sent me?"

"Of course," the warden said heartily, "of course. My dear Miss Ashton, now that the women of the state have the vote . . . and high time indeed that they should have it . . . they should look a little more closely into the workings of the mechanism of society. This, I suppose, may be called the darker side, eh? Well, dark as it is, I hope that there are some bits of sunshine in my prison." As he spoke, he tilted back his chair so that the sunlight from the window behind him flared and burned across his face and head.

"There are bits of sunshine breaking through, yes," the girl said thoughtfully, and she looked down to the carpet and prodded the pattern again with her parasol end. For she had the feeling that, so long as she looked into the eyes of this cheerful fellow, she could never penetrate to any hidden truth. There was something about him that gathered all of her attention and focused it upon himself like a burning glass. All during her trip of inspection, she felt that she had been seeing Warden Tufter, not his prison. "There are bits of sunshine," she repeated, "but I shall tell those who sent me that I was unable to estimate the importance of what I saw, and that they had better send up an investigating committee of older women."

The floor of the warden's happiness was rent open before him. He felt himself on the verge of ruin. A committee of older women. There was summoned before him a group picture of middle-aged women, their faces squared, the tenderer mists of youth quite vanished from their gleaming eyes, their hands heavier, their fingers blunter of tip, their jaws squared. Such a committee sent to investigate? They would read his secrets stamped in great letters upon his very brow. A committee of fat politicians was one thing. The unofficial visit of this pretty girl had been far more difficult. But a committee of middle-aged women—it was indubitable ruin.

"They'll be welcome," he found himself saying in a lifeless voice. "I wish that the whole world could be invited in to see this prison. I am not ashamed of it. I am proud of it. It is, in a way, my life's work."

The heaviness of his conviction daunted her. And yet she still felt that there was something unsavory behind him and about him. She felt something poisonous floating in the air of the place. It was made up of impressions gathered out of the corners of her eyes, and, when she looked down to the carpet, she was not seeing the pattern upon it at all. Instead, she was visualizing again those little illusory images that she had picked up here and there—a sad face, a suspicious, treacherous side glance, a mouth compressed as though by the endurance of cruel pain. These were the things that she, with a troubled brow, was recalling. And, besides, she was remembering the last thing that her mother had said. "Of course you will miss a great deal, but then you may be able to learn a great deal that a committee would never be able to find. You see, they cannot take you seriously. Your visit will be almost a social call. You must smile at the warden and tell him he is a wonderful man. That will put him off his guard. In the meantime, use your eyes. Yes, my dear, whatever you do, when you are around this warden or any other man, young or old, trust to your eyes, and not to your ears. They talk us into anything. They make fools of us with their words. But behind your eyes, my dear, there is a good, grave judge who may be able to record the facts and put aside the nonsense."

Therefore, Miss Ashton kept thinking to herself: *I must not believe what he tells me. I must only pay attention to what he shows me.*

Certainly her mother, having been thrice married, should know what she was talking about. Yet she faltered before his vast assurance. "You see," she managed to say, "I have an instinctive aversion to heavy punishments. When men were hanged for stealing, theft was much more prevalent than it is now. And that's why dark cells and such things are abhorrent to me. I could never sympathize with your use of them, Mister Tufter."

The warden groaned aloud. He converted the sound into a clearing of his throat, but, nevertheless, he groaned. He had heard this argument so many times before that the mere repetition of it unnerved him. Did he have to attempt to justify cruelty to this bright-faced, tender-voiced girl?

He swung himself forward in his chair, determined to make the attempt.

"Suppose," he said, "that I were to show you a man who was cured of the most terrible criminal impulses by cruel punishments . . . that is to say"—he corrected himself quickly—"punishments that will, I am afraid, seem cruel to you."

The girl started. This was exactly what she wanted. It seemed too good to be true. She wanted this concrete evidence on which to hang her favorable report.

"Can you do that?"

"Yes, if you are willing to believe your eyes and your ears."

She signaled her eager assent, and the warden rose from his chair.

"Come with me," he said. "What I'm going to show you isn't the rule, I'll admit, but, if punishment can produce one example such as this in the way of a result, there must be some good in punishment, I think you'll agree."

He led the way from his office and down a short hall that terminated in a pair of swinging doors, the upper halves of which were glass. Through that glass she could see the thick ranges of books along the walls of the room.

"That's the library," the warden explained unnecessarily as they came down the hall. "We'll stop at the doors, and then I want you to look through the glass and take notice of the man at the desk in the center of the room. That's the librarian. He's the man I want you to notice. After you've had a look, we'll go inside."

She nodded, breathless with her excitement. At the doors she paused, on tiptoe, with stealthy caution. She felt that she was about to peep into the truth about prisons.

What she saw was a great dark room paneled in bookshelves, with partitions built out into the room to accommodate still more volumes. Those volumes had an indescribably battered look, all the reds and yellows and vivid greens of the bindings having been dimmed as with a dust by long time and long usage. For these were the collections from a thousand sources, outworn books for which the owners had no use, and that were sent to the prison rather than to the junk pile.

Just in the middle of this space, where the light from the narrow and distant windows reached so faintly that the electric hanging lamp above the desk was always lighted, sat a great-shouldered man with close-cropped gray hair, an inscrutable face of the prison pallor, and a huge, powerful body encased in the striped suit.

There was something in the picture so over-powering that the girl gave back from the door with a gasp, cast a somewhat frightened glance over her shoulder at the warden, and then peeked again. Her attention concentrated on three things: the pale face, with its deeply carved, strangely attractive features, the book on which he was intent, and the immense hands that supported the volume.

The hands in particular fascinated her, for they were hands suggestive of the most unmeasured power. They were young, mighty hands. They were hands not only of strength, but of agility, for the fingers were not blunt and misshapen from labor, but smooth and shapely. Yet the hands represented animal strength; the face was stamped unutterably with the symbols of pain, and the book in that tremendous grasp was an anomaly. He should have had a battle axe in his fingers, or some skull-shattering mace. Never a book.

"Well?" the warden murmured. "Shall we go inside?"

She hesitated. She was quite pale with excitement. "I . . . I . . . don't know," she said. "Do . . . do I look all right?"

"What do you mean?"

"Do I look calm?"

"Not very," admitted the warden with a smile. "But that's the way he affects people. He's not a common man."

"Of course not. And I mustn't walk in staring at him as though he were an animal." She took a hasty turn up and down the hall. Then she faced the warden in a calmer mood. "I'm all right now," she said. "We can go in together."

He nodded, pressed the door open, then followed

in behind her. The man at the desk looked up without putting down his book, and by that, for some reason, she knew how deeply he had been absorbed in his reading.

"Miss Ashton," the warden said, "this is Tom Keene."

Chapter Twenty-Three

It seemed to her that he would never finish rising. At length he stood to his full height above her and bowed. She was abashed. If he had been a judge upon his bench, he could not have been more imposing to her. There flooded about her a profound bass voice that was acknowledging the introduction. And then she found that she had to fight herself to keep looking him in the face.

She strove to read in him what her mother had told her to hunt for in the faces of the criminals—malignant secrecy, hardened hatred of society as represented by anyone they encountered. But she found neither of these things in Tom Keene. He seemed much younger, hardly more than early middle aged, now that she was close to him and had heard him speak—this in spite of the solid silver gray of his hair. His glance dwelt upon her as steadily as light dwells on a steel bar. And, although there was about his face a battered and worn look, there was none of the cruel cunning for which her mother had told her to look. But in every respect he impressed her with great size, not only of body, but of spirit. She wanted to draw back and view him in greater perspective, both in a physical and mental sense.

The warden was saying something beside her. She did not hear more than the murmur of the words. Yet it was a jest, it seemed, for now the room was filled and quivering with the great, booming laughter of Tom Keene. It made him seem younger still.

"I wanted to see the library," she managed to say. "I didn't dream that it could be so large."

"Big as it is," the warden said, "Tom has read about every book that's in it. Haven't you, Tom?"

"No, no," protested the gigantic librarian. "By no means."

"You ought to have gone through them by this time, though," said the warden. "You've been five years without a book leaving your hand, I might say."

Then he heeded the signal from the girl and started back for the door, but Miss Ashton, as she turned, let her glance trail down and across the back of the book that Tom had been reading and she saw the name Thucydides stamped in black upon the red leather. She felt it was too much. There must be a fake in this. What if Tom Keene had been simply planted here with book to impose upon her with his melancholy face and his musical voice and his quiet manner?

She and the warden were hardly back in the office again before she made his smile vanish by exclaiming: "Do you really think that he reads Thucydides for his own pleasure?"

"Does he read . . . which?" the warden asked anxiously. "I don't know. But I'll tell you that I've never seen a man who wades through books as he does. He'll make his mark on something when he gets out. Thucydides? I don't know that writer. But if Tom has tackled him, he knows what's in the book. The minister used to think it was a bluff and so he started giving Tom examinations. After a while he stopped. He made up his mind that he didn't know enough to ask the right questions, I guess." And he laughed heartily at the very thought. "You should have asked some questions yourself," he said. "If you want to, we can find some sort of excuse for going back . . . though I don't like to."

"Ah?" she cried suspiciously. "You don't?"

"I'll tell you why. He has the pride of the very devil. He doesn't want to be showed off. He prefers to sit by himself in his library and dive through books the way I might dive through water. Not that he ever says anything, and not that anybody can ever read anything more than he wants you to read in his face . . . but I've just guessed at what goes on inside that big head of his. It cuts him up a good deal to be stared at. He's as sensitive as a girl . . . under the skin."

All of this agreed so thoroughly with what she had felt when she first looked at the big man that she began to be ashamed of her doubts.

"And," said the warden, "suppose I tell you how he came to be the way he is now . . . and what he was when I got him?"

"Yes, yes!"

"Well, to begin with, he was The White Mask."

She gasped a little at the mysterious name, but she shook her head. "I never have heard of that person before," she said.

"Naturally. You wouldn't have," said the warden. "Fact is, you were pretty small when he was stirring up the West with doings. He's been here with me for eight years."

"Eight years," she echoed in horror at the thought. "Such a man as that for eight years?"

"Maybe for life. He's got enough hanging over him."

She gasped.

"Let me explain. The White Mask was a desperado of the old school. Men are quickly forgotten as a rule. Eight years would be enough to blot out the names of most of us. But The White Mask will be remembered for a long time, and you can depend upon it. Men were killed, trains were robbed, people were held up on the highway . . . all by the man who wore a white mask."

"Men were killed by him?" the girl murmured, her cheeks blanching.

"A dozen of 'em," said the other calmly. "And look at him now."

"It can't be," she answered stubbornly. "No matter what has happened, he couldn't have changed so much."

"There's been no mistake," said the warden. "Not a bit of it. I tell you, he came in here full of the devil . . . excuse the expression . . . and I took the devil out of him."

Her eyes widened; that was her only comment.

"I'm going to prove to you that sometimes there are bad men who have to be treated in a bad way. Tom Keene was one of them. I'm going to tell you about him in detail. I saw you look at the dark cells. And I know that you've heard stories about men who were badly treated in this prison. Well, Miss Ashton, some of those stories are true." He made the admission with a reckless extravagance of spirit, as one whose case is so good that it can be safely made less good by admitting some points upon the opposite side. "Men have been cruelly treated inside these walls," he said. "In this very room, seated in this very chair, I have made some men tremble by the sentences I have given them. But I simply warn you of this . . . every story that you hear is exaggerated tenfold. I'm now going to tell you the truth about Tom Keene." He lit a cigarette, puffed a blue-brown mist into the air, and talked behind it with the greatest animation.

"When Keene came to me, he was a great, black-bearded brute twenty-seven years old. . . ."

"And he's been eight years here. . . . Do you mean to say he is only thirty-five now?"

"You think of him as being older, but that's because of his hair. But you think back to his face, and you'll see that he's no older than that. If you could see him stripped for boxing or wrestling . . . we have games now and then on Saturday night . . . you'd realize that he's not so old. He's still a young athlete. Looks a little bulky and heavy in his clothes, but peel those off, and you get at the kernel of the man. He's a great tiger. He moves like oil on the top of running water. His grip, when he wrestles, simply turns the flesh of another man into pulp. And when he strikes, he sends the other fellow down for keeps."

The warden so far forgot himself as to chuckle in soft exultation at the memory and clench his own hard fist. The girl looked upon him as from a great distance, but still she was intensely interested.

"He's young," went on the warden, "and you saw his shoulders for yourself. Well, when he came into this prison, he was a madman as well as a giant. At least, he acted like a madman. He kept swearing that he was innocent, though as a matter of fact he had been caught red-handed. He was put into one of the old cells. He tore the bars out as though they were wheat stalks and broke into the yard. He was climbing a wall when the guard shot him. . . ."

"Oh!" cried the girl.

"Would you have had me send some of the guards at him with their bare fists? Madam, he would have wrung their necks as fast as they got up to him and crashed in their skulls like eggshells. I would as soon stand in the path of an elephant as in the path of Tom Keene when he's angry!"

"I believe it," said the girl, shuddering as she remembered the size of those hands and the intolerable brightness of the steady eyes.

"He got over the bullet wound quickly," said the warden. "And by that time he had changed his mood. He didn't try to tear the prison down with his hands, but he was still vicious. One of the guards disciplined an obstinate prisoner in the shoe shop. Tom Keene took that guard and threw him through the window. And the guard is still only half a man."

"But what happened to Tom Keene?" asked the girl.

"Dark cell," snapped the warden.

"Did he have no defense to offer?"

The warden laughed. "Sure. He said that the prisoner the guard was disciplining hadn't done a thing. The prisoner was sickly, so he said. But he had crazier ideas than that. Seems that when he first came to prison, he thought that he had struck up a bargain with the Lord, and he used to make speeches, telling the Lord that He had fallen down on His share of the contract. That's about what it amounted to. Used to make me laugh to hear his ravings."

"Poor man," she said, and sighed. "How awful."

"But I gave him the dark cell," the warden continued, "until he came out raving worse than ever. I had trimmed it down fine. That was a large dose of the silent treatment, but it did a fine job with Tom Keene. It started him thinking that there might be something better than going against authority. That wasn't the end of the battle. Not by any means. The guards here will tell you how I fought Tom Keene for three years. And he was a handful. Before those three years ended, Tom Keene had white hair . . . white hair at thirty."

"White hair at thirty," repeated the girl. "How can you smile when you tell of such a thing?"

"Because you don't know what's coming. In time he learned his lesson. He decided that there was no use in battering his head against a stone wall. He gave up. And, after he gave up fighting, he came around mighty quick. The first crazy idea he had was that the Lord had broken a promise with him, you see? The second was that not only was *he* being oppressed, but that all of his fellow prisoners were being oppressed. And he decided that he would fight their battles for them. And when both of these crazy ideas had been worked out of his head, three years had gone by, as I said before, and his hair was white. By the Lord, I've lain awake half of a night thinking of new things to do to Tom Keene. I've tried things with falling water . . . drop by drop . . . that have been forgotten since the days when the Spaniards were working their Inquisition. Because I knew from the first that the way to fight him was with pain. And with pain I broke him."

"Broke him?" cried the girl. "No, he would rather die than surrender."

But a malignant light played in the eyes of the warden, and he had to look down for fear that she might see it. "I mean what I said. He told me that he saw the light. He was through with the fight. He gave up!" His voice rose in the exultant memory of that scene. "And the minute he said that, d'you know what I did?"

"What?" asked the girl.

"I shoved my hand through the bars and shook hands with him. Which was taking more of a chance than any guard in the prison would ever have taken, because with that grip of his he could have smashed the bones. But I shook hands with him. 'Tom,' I said, 'as long as you wanted to fight, I fought you. But, now that you've come to your senses, you'll find me different. You're a man after my own heart . . . a strong man. And I'll show you that I know how a strong man ought to be treated.' And I kept my word." He leaned back and slapped the fat palm of his hand upon the nearby desk. "In one month he was the librarian . . . the best post this prison has to offer to a man in stripes."

Miss Ashton had actually risen from her chair in her excitement. The warden rose, also.

"Go on," she urged him. "Don't stop there. I want to know a thousand other things about him."

"I could talk all day about him," the warden said. "There's enough things to say."

Chapter Twenty-Four

It was a full two hours later that the warden, a weary but a happy man, rushed into the library, the doors hurtling wide and crashing against the walls on either side as he entered. Dashing to the side of big Tom Keene, he smote the giant a resounding thump on the shoulder.

"She's gone!" he cried. "She's gone, Tom! And she's gone away swearing that, if she had a son or a brother that she wanted to have disciplined, she'd send them to me first off."

Tom Keene smiled.

"It's you, Tom!" cried the joyous warden. "It's you that have done it!" He strode rapidly up and down and at length came to a halt in front of his librarian. "I had an idea," he said, "that this was the beginning of the end. I thought that the women would kick our party out of office and me along

186

with it. But, by the Lord, if they want votes from women, let 'em send delegations down to visit our prison."

He broke into uproarious laughter as he said this, and again he clapped Tom on the shoulder. The latter closed the book, marking the place carefully.

"And it's going to be a great day for you, Tom, too," Tufter said. "Boy, I've planned to do something for you before I was through, and now I've made up my mind. Why, that laugh you turned in for the benefit of the Ashton girl was as good as a year's salary to me. She's going to leave this prison spreading a report that I'm the greatest reformer of characters that ever held down the job."

The laughter broke through his talk again. Then he became sober. The elements of the brute that he had carefully masked while the girl was with him now came to the surface. But withal there was a certain honest revealing of himself, and he looked with a real kindness upon Tom Keene.

"Keene," he said, "I've fought you, and, I don't mind saying, I've beaten you. But that's forgotten. Now I'm your friend, and I'm going to show you what a friend I can be. Tom, what's your sentence worked up to now, after all your tries at jail breaking?"

"Twenty years from next Tuesday," Tom answered. "That's all I have left to serve," and he laughed softly.

"Twenty years, eh? You have the iron nerve with you, Keene if you can laugh at that. But suppose I were to write to the governor and tell him that you're a cured case . . . that it would do me good as a warden to have you out spreading the word around that I'm a white man, and that it would do the whole party good if we can find something to balance against the talk they're starting about that rat-faced dago that died here last year, and some of the others. Tom, what if I write in to the governor and make out a good case for you? Would you be my friend the rest of your life?"

"Your friend? What do you think?" Tom asked, and he smiled frankly at the warden.

The latter shook his head. "Sometimes I don't know," he said. "Sometimes I think that you've never got over hating me for what I did those first three years."

"That's five years old," Tom Keene said.

"Five years . . . I know. And I've sure treated you white in these five years, Tom, haven't I? D'you know, though, that I used to lose sleep at first, wondering what would happen to me if you ever got out of prison and came across me?" He sighed at the memory, and then added more cheerily: "But I'll take that chance, now."

And he was as good as his word. That night the mails hurried a long report to the governor, covering the case of Tom Keene in full, detailing the three years of battle that had commenced his term, and that had brought a number of sentences heaped upon his head, which practically amounted to a life term.

One week later came the pardon. Yes, seven days to an hour after the advent of pretty little Miss Ashton in the prison, Tom Keene stepped out of his prison garb and thrust his long limbs into civilian clothes. He had been allowed, in various ways, to pick up small bits of money during the past five years. He had made lariats, and small toys out of horsehair, and from the sale of these he had saved a little store of coin. With this he was able to buy the outfit he needed. And when Tufter came to see him, he found the big man luxuriating in the full cowpuncher regalia, and rolling a cigarette.

Tufter regarded him with a critical eye. There was only one fault to be found, and that was because his face was so pale. No cowpuncher could have ridden into the wind for any length of time without being sun- and wind-burned to a deeper tan. However, a long illness might account for that defect. Then the eye of the warden fell to another thing, and he started a little.

"A gun, too?" he said. "You've even got a gun?"

Tom Keene moved his hand. Into the palm, with an oiled and frictionless speed, came a heavy Colt revolver.

"It's my old gat," he said gently. "It's been lying up in the armory all the time. I got it out this morning. And there she lies as snug as ever."

He put the weapon away. He handled that rather clumsy weight as though it were a sentient thing that he simply wished into place and it obeyed him. And the warden noted his movements with a touch of awe. If he had been kindly in his attitude toward Tom before, he now became almost whiningly subservient.

"You don't seem to have lost the knack of making your gun jump when you talk to it, Tom," he said.

"No," said Tom. "I've never stopped practicing."

"What?"

"I fixed up a cloth holster. I got a lead pipe to do for the revolver and bent it into shape. I've been slinging that regularly and pointing with it at marks. Not bad practice, either."

"Even when you had twenty years hanging over you . . . you did that every day?"

"Every day . . . for the past five years," Tom said. "A man never stops hoping, Tufter."

There was a certain brusqueness about this speech that jerked the mind of the warden violently back through five or six years to certain scenes of brutal violence during which Tom Keene had learned how heavily the hand of the law may fall upon its chosen victims. And out of those gruesome recollections the warden stared sharply at Tom Keene. Had he loosed from the prison a man who might . . . ? He dared not finish his thought. And there was no need to complete it, he told himself, for in a moment Tom Keene was smiling upon him with the most equable gentleness.

"But now tell me, man to man," the warden said with great heartiness, "is there anything more that I can do for you?"

"There's one favor," said Tom.

"Name it, man."

"I'd like to talk to Johnson."

"The cripple?"

"Yes."

The warden hesitated, and then reached for a bell and pressed it. "That's the man that you first put up the fight for in the shoe shop?" he muttered slowly. "Is that the man, Tom?"

"That's he," said Tom.

"*H-m-m,*" said the warden, but, as the trusty entered at this moment, he snapped an order over his shoulder that Johnson should be brought up at once. "Has he been riding in your mind all these years?" the warden asked.

"More or less," answered Tom.

"You're a queer fellow," the warden said. "You're a mighty queer fellow. I'd have thought that you'd be so glad to get shut of the prison yourself that you wouldn't waste time thinking about others. But I guess that the chaplain is right. You've got a big heart in you, Tom. You want to remember that you owe him something. He was always interested in you from the first."

"I'll remember him," Tom said. "I have a pretty good memory."

And again there was a quality in his voice that made the warden start, but on his face there remained only an inscrutable smile. Two pairs of feet approached the door. Johnson appeared, and the warden took his leave.

"It isn't regular for you to be alone with him," he said, "but this isn't the first irregular thing that I've done, eh?"

"No," Tom said, and this time with an unmistakable dryness.

The warden turned a frightened glance toward him from the door, seemed about to speak, changed his mind, and went out.

Chapter Twenty-Five

One savage outburst of temper had placed Johnson in the prison. He had struck a single thoughtless blow that ruined his life. For the term of his imprisonment was endless, and the cause of his imprisonment was murder.

Yet he was the mildest of men in appearances. Indeed, he was mild of heart, also, but he had given way to one of those savage bursts of temper that rise in any man. He had turned the corner in one wild instant. And, after that, he could never regain his old place in the world. Society banished him.

He was a cripple. His left leg and his left arm were withered, not so that they were completely helpless, but so that his strength was eaten away at the root. Habitually he carried his left hand high upon his chest as though to keep it from striking against anything. It must have been a form of paralysis that afflicted him, for the left side of his face, also, was slightly drawn. It was not a great contracting of the muscles, but it was sufficient to exert a pull on the corner of the eye and the mouth, so that a faint and inexpressibly disdainful leer was his usual expression. And because of this, the warden hated him and had broken him in body and soul.

He was well past forty now. He had been ten years in the prison. He had perhaps three years of life left to him, and he knew that his remaining term was short. Perhaps it was for this reason that his good humor increased instead of diminishing in the prison. Besides, the warden had always felt that it was impossible truly to torture the man. He who is walled in with fire, does not fear flame, and little Henry Johnson, constantly tormented by the separation from his family, that was forced to drag out a laborious and bitter existence as well as it could, felt the worst torments of the prison life as only dim and secondary pain.

This was the man who presented himself before Tom Keene. He greeted the big man with a silent nod, and, in return to Tom's gesture toward a chair, he crossed the room with his twisting, labored gait and sank down upon the edge of the chair with his eyes fixed on the floor.

To him Tom Keene addressed a hard-toned speech. "Johnson," he said, "eight years ago, when I entered the prison, I attempted to keep a guard from bullying you. I was thrown into the dark cell for it and left there until I went almost mad. But, while I was in that cell, I swore to myself that someday I would do something for you. Eight years have gone by, and I haven't fulfilled that promise to myself. Now I'm leaving the stripes behind. Tell me something you want me to do . . . something that I can do."

The head of Johnson jerked up. "Keene . . . ," he began in a trembling voice.

But Tom Keene interrupted him by holding up a forbidding hand. "No use in talking like that," he said, "I'm not doing this for your sake. I'm doing it because I made the promise to myself, and I keep my promises. Tell me what you want."

Little Johnson shrank from the big man, examining his face with incredulous eyes. It did not seem possible that that smooth, deep voice could come from a heart as matter-of-fact and cold as this. Then he nodded.

"It's true, then," he said at length. "They've killed the heart in you, Keene. That's what the boys have been telling me, and what I couldn't believe, that . . . that . . ."

"Look here, Johnson," Tom Keene said, "I've come to make a fair proposition to you. If you wish to accept it, do so. If you want to deliver a lecture, find another audience. Is that all clear to you?"

"It's clear," Johnson said sadly. And he waited, his glance on the floor.

There was no sign of impatience from Tom Keene, but after a considerable wait he said: "Well, are you going to talk?"

Johnson looked up with a faint smile. "Don't you suppose I know that you and the warden are working hand in glove?" he said. "Good Lord, Keene, what an awful fool you must think I am."

Keene leaned forward. "Johnson," he said, "make up your mind. I'm not going to stay for you to think twice. What's the thing you want most in the world? Tell me that, and I'll try to get it for you when I'm out. But tell me quick. I've got business ahead of me . . . big business. I can't wait for you to think."

That direct challenge caused the other to come out of his chair, and he came hobbling to Tom, his left leg pulling his body halfway around. He laid a hand on the shoulder of Tom. "Keene," he whispered, "you mean it? You mean it?" He was on fire with sudden enthusiasm. "Keene, if I tell you a thing that'll make us both rich, can I trust you?"

Tom sighed. He knew of other men in whose

195

minds these hallucinations had grown up while they were in prison—strange dreams that, once they were free, they could find a treasure in coin out of their freedom.

"I'm asking what I can give you," he said, "and not what I can take from you."

"I know . . . I know. Oh, Lord, can I trust you?" He wrung his feeble hands.

"Talk soft," Tom said, "or you'll have to be trusting the whole prison. Understand?"

The other gasped and made a sign of assent. "It's a whole ledge of gold," he said, "and . . ."

Tom stopped him again with a quiet, almost pitying protest. "Think that over before you ask me to believe it, Johnson. You say you know where there's a whole ledge of gold. If that's true, why haven't you let your family know about it years ago? Why haven't you written to them?"

"Write to them?" sneered Johnson. "Why, my letter would never get to them until it had been opened by the warden. And why should I make him a rich man? Blast him."

The truth of this staggered Tom.

"That's been the worst of it," Johnson said. "I've had a million . . . more'n a million . . . under my hand, you might say. But I haven't been able to use it. Lord knows what's become of the wife and the kids. And . . ." He broke down into horrible choking sobs.

Tom Keene rose and placed himself at a

window, totally unconcerned. He was even humming a tune when he faced Johnson again. Apparently that indifference made Johnson feel that he must prove the truth of what he had been saying. Also, it assured him that Tom was not attempting to draw a secret from him. And under the double stimulus he told his strange tale.

Ten long years ago he had been prospecting in a country that, a generation before, had been thoroughly combed—as what stretch of Rocky Mountain land has not been examined at one time or another by seekers after precious metals? But, with an amateur's delight and an amateur's disbelief in the results, he had come upon a mountain side that had been recently gouged to the bedrock by a great landslide. And here it was that he made his strike.

He lingered in detail over the beauties of that ore until Tom shut off the flow of words with a weary request that the directions to the spot be given him. He would keep his promise and go to the place.

"But how do you know," he said to Johnson, "that I'll give you the mine if I locate it?"

"Half of it," Johnson said eagerly. "That's all that I ask. There's enough for ten. More than enough for two. But for heaven's sake, hurry now, Keene. Trust you? Why, I've got to take the chance now or never. You reached your hand into the fire to try to help me once . . . and now pray

197

the Lord we can help each other." Quickly he sketched the site, and so he left him.

Tom Keene went on to the warden. "I'm through, Tufter," he said. "I know what Johnson wants, and, when I've done what he asks, I'm held back from the prison by only one thread."

"And that's me," remarked the warden, swelling a little with self-satisfaction. "That's me, Keene, eh? Well, friendships have started in even stranger ways than ours."

"Friendship?" Tom said, grown cold. "Who spoke of friendship?"

The warden was not a very tall man, but he was compactly, almost roundly, built. Yet his rotundity did not keep him from literally fading to the far side of the room where he jerked a drawer open and gripped the revolver that was thereby exposed to his hand. And still Tom Keene leaned against the door, rolling his cigarette and smiling in the same deadly manner toward him.

"It's you that have acted the fool and driveled all the nonsense about friendship," said the cowpuncher. He placed his sombrero on his head, and, although they were still within the prison walls, that act seemed to break down the bounds and place them out under the free sweep of the sky and wind. The warden moistened his white lips and waited. It was worse than death, this delay.

"You're going down," Tom Keene said. "I'm not fool enough to lay a hand on you while you're in the prison, Tufter. That would be playing your own game. But, as soon as the election comes around next month, you'll find your party out, and you'll be out with them. And about the same time, Tufter I'm going to start looking for you. When I find you, I'm going to step on you, partner. Remember that. Why, you fool, don't you see that I've been playing a game? I saw I could not beat you by force, so I played your own game, and, though it took five years, I've beaten you. Good bye, Tufter. And remember, Tufter, remember how I told you, when they took me down toward the dark cell the second day, that I would be even with you? Remember, that? This is only eight years later."

Chapter Twenty-Six

There was to be no money wasted on railroad fares on his journey from prison. Tom Keene rode the rods as far as the main-line trains would take him and then traveled into the hills on a branch road. When he tumbled off that train, Crystal Mountain was a huge blue triangle splitting the sky fifty miles to the north. And Crystal Mountain was his goal. On its side, according to Johnson, was the rich ore that the landslide had exposed.

His survey of the mountain was interrupted by two hostile brakemen. They had been trying for the space of several stations to get him off the train, but always he had evaded them. Now they decided to swoop down upon him from either side and annihilate him.

"But," one exclaimed as Tom took off his hat, "he's an old man!"

"Old nothing," said the other shack. "A hobo never gets old. He ought to know better, anyway."

And they tackled him from behind. What followed was afterward described by the fireman who sat on the steps of the cab, filling his pipe.

"They hit the old boy at the same time, like they was bucking the line on a football team. But it seemed like they had bucked into a wall. He didn't budge, but they sort of caved back. He opened up his arms and fell on 'em. There was some squirming, but it didn't last long. The cloud of dust blowed away.

" 'Well, boys,' says the hobo, 'you picked out a hot day for your little joke.'

"He sat on 'em till he'd rolled a cigarette. Then he got up. He was about a mile high and all man. He looked old, but he sure dropped twenty years when he got into action. I went down the line and picked up them two shacks. They were just beginning to breathe and think.

" 'He hit me with a blackjack,' says one of 'em.

" 'He slammed me with a gun butt,' says the other. 'Where is he?'

"But he was too dizzy to see the big, white-haired hobo walking twenty steps away."

Such was the manner of Tom Keene's reëntry to

his own country. He walked up the street of the little town with a tingle still in his fingertips, where his great grip had crunched into the flesh and bone of the brakemen. And there was a growing satisfaction in him. The shadow of the prison, he felt, had not yet been worn away. He was still not accustomed to the bite of the sunshine. The world as he found it again was harder than ever—burning hot from the sun and icy cold from the calloused cruelty of men.

He felt that a veil had been torn from that world. He had practiced in the prison in his new effort to pierce to the truth about men. He had learned there, he felt, that no such thing as generosity or good will existed. But now he had a wider field in which to exercise his faculties in the scientific inquiries.

All that he had seen since leaving the prison was an addition to the old story. Sometimes he laughed bitterly at himself to think of that large-hearted credulity with which he had begun his pilgrimage as a preacher of brother love and of faith in one another. At least he had recovered from that illusion while there still remained to him time that he could remedy the mistake and show the world the hardness of his fist before he was through.

In a way, he was grateful to the warden for the completeness of the lesson that had been taught him. The tortures of those first three years would never, of course, be wholly forgotten. The wounds might close, but there remained the scar tissue in his consciousness.

The first year had been a time of animal fury, of wild moments when he reproached heaven for having betrayed him with lies written into the book of books. In the second year, he had forgotten all about heaven in the intensity of the passion with which he devoted himself to the hatred of men. And all through these three years he had made attempts—first to break from the prison, and then to injure the guards of the prison, particularly to get at the throat of Warden Tufter.

But at the end of the third year the great light of a higher knowledge had come to him. He knew that, huge and powerful as he was, he made no match, in sheer strength, for the powers of banded society. If he wished to strike them hard, his way must be to use cunning.

So it was that he had conceived the great idea of pretending a change in mind and spirit. So cleverly had he done it that he made no overnight attempt, but for a month he deftly schooled himself and prepared himself by mentally smiling upon his guards even while they were cursing him and dreading him. And when he had made sure that he could control himself, and that the savagery that was buried in the core of his nature would not break out, taking him by surprise— then, and then only, did he allow the guards to become slowly aware of the change in him. But even then he did not make any avowal in words. He worked up toward it so slowly that when, on a day, they heard him singing, they did not gape and gasp, but they summoned one another to listen. The beast, it seemed, was dead in him, or dying, and a kindly man was taking its place.

And the warden had fallen instantly into the trap. He had carried matters so very far in his persecution of this singular giant that he was quite willing to make an about-face. So soon as Tom Keene gave him an opening, the warden, for the sake of dear life, changed, also. He knew that one could never tell. There were ways and ways for prisoners to be freed from their sentences. Suppose, for instance, that someone should rake over the old evidence against The White Mask and discover, as the warden himself had done, that it was entirely founded upon flimsy hearsay. Suppose a pardon should be based upon these discoveries. Then what would happen between the big man and himself? There would simply be a murder. The devil that he had so often seen rising into the eyes of Tom Keene would take possession of the man, and he, Warden Tufter, would be caught and killed with a slow relish.

The prospect had given him some nightmare hours and wakened him out of his deepest sleeps with a choking and gasping. And now he bent himself to the task of bringing happiness into the life of the big man. He had succeeded, he felt, wonderfully. To the very day of Tom's delivery, he felt that he had done a truly great work in regenerating a savage soul. He had looked on—somewhat from the distance—while Tom pursued his labors in books. How could he have known that this bookishness was only a part of Tom's plan to gain freedom, a plan worked out with the most consummate patience and devotion? For Tom had consulted his own mind, and, in looking for that thing which, in his own judgment, made a man least dangerous in appearance, he had picked upon the love of books at once.

So he had forced himself mightily into the subject. For five years, he had spent many hours every day bent over turning pages. At first it had been torture, but gradually he acquired a taste for the very thing that had been a torment. Suddenly he found himself looking forward to his work of the day in the library. For three years since that date, he had devoured books, reading not according to any plan, but anything and everything as it came into his path.

And as he strode up the street of the town, he was surprised to find that the only warm spot that remained in his heart was that dark library room in the prison itself. Yes, his spirit turned back toward that place as toward a home.

He stopped in front of the blacksmith shop. "Where's there a good bunch of saddle stock around here?" he asked.

The blacksmith whipped the sweat off his brow and looked sidewise up from the hoof that was twisted across his knee.

"Pop Sherman," he said, and turned with a curse to the hoof again.

"Where's Pop Sherman's place?" Tom asked at the next corner.

"Right out on the edge of town. You can't miss it. He's got his corrals plumb full of new stock. He's going to start shipping 'em north to fatten 'em up."

There was little exaggeration in that description. He found the corrals alive with twisting, lashing bodies, thinly veiled with clouds of dust of their own raising. They were packed in well-nigh as thick as fish in the bottom of a weir when the tide runs out.

Tom found Pop Sherman sitting on a fence post talking to three or four prospective purchasers, for the ranchers were coming in for miles to look over the horses and pick out one, here and there, for their own uses before the herd was sent to the cars. And at Pop's orders, two or three horse wranglers were expertly sifting the horses through the corral, stringing them out from one enclosure to the other, so that they could be reviewed in detail. And yet they were careful not to give them so much exercise in a day that flesh would be worn from their already bony sides.

On joining them, Tom waved to the others, was

greeted as negligently himself, and then mounted on a second rail, the better to view the milling crowd. He could feel, the moment he gave his attention to the herd, that the eyes of the others were drawing covertly toward him. It was always this way. Men could not pass by that pale, worn face without turning for a second glance. And in his bitter heart, Tom Keene cursed them for their curiosity. He had seen the eyes of women soften because of the story of pain that they read. And he had hated them for their pity.

Now, sweeping the crowd of horses, he dismissed the greater portion of them abruptly from his attention. It took a horse of parts to bear the crushing impost of his weight. No doubt he would never again find a weight carrier like the black. But, if he expected to put a single respectable day's journey behind him while he was in the saddle, he must choose with the very greatest care.

"Your horses seem to run to the runty kind," he remarked coldly to Pop Sherman. "You don't happen to have any real horseflesh out yonder, do you?"

Pop Sherman snapped his teeth together. "I don't keep no horseflesh on my place," he said pointedly. "I keep horses, though, son."

"You treat all your horses as tender and kind as that, do you?" Tom said.

"I do," Pop Sherman said coldly. "What's more,

I don't sell to no man that aims to turn a horse into a machine. That's final, stranger."

He was a savage old fighter, was Pop Sherman. And now he sat on the top of his fence post with his lower jaw thrusting out, staring straight before him, after the fashion of a man who is ready to whirl and rend the nearest enemy at the first excuse. The others, who knew him well, exchanged quick glances and covert grins. They did not approve of the supercilious fashion in which the stranger had looked down upon the horses of that district. And they were intensely pleased because Pop was calling him.

But the big man neither smiled to ingratiate the fierce horse seller, nor did he attempt to turn the subject upon other threads of conversation. He merely turned and looked steadily upon Pop, and without emotion.

"I've come to buy a horse," he said slowly. "After I've finished looking over what you have, I'll start talking with you . . . talking or whatever else you have a mind for."

The stiff lips of the old man parted readily enough to snap a savage return that might have led to instant action, but, before he could speak, the big man had turned his shoulder. And, having turned his shoulder, he began to sing softly to himself in a mighty though controlled bass voice while he looked over the swirling masses of horses.

Chapter Twenty-Seven

Pop Sherman so far forgot himself that he dropped his cigarette. And the smiles of satisfaction disappeared from the faces of the ranchers, for, though many men sing or hum to cover their nervousness when they are confronted with a crisis, he who truly sings, because his spirit is singing within him in the imminent danger of battle, is one to be avoided.

As for Pop himself, he would not by any means have sat quietly under the imputation of having taken water in the slightest degree from the huge stranger. But he contented himself with a sort of oblique, or left-handed, invitation to the big man to take another step and cross the line before he fought.

"If it's just plain meanness under the saddle that you're looking for to exercise on," he suggested, "take a slant at one of them hunchbacked roans over yonder . . . them six or eight that runs in a bunch most of the time. They'll kick up enough dust to satisfy even a particular gent like yourself, I'd say."

But Tom Keene shook his head. "They have no underpinning," he said. "I want something that has legs. I'm not a bantamweight. If they have some fight in them . . . why, that can be taken out."

"Maybe," suggested one of the bystanders, all of whose sympathies turned toward the venerable and dreaded Pop Sherman, "he'd like to take a turn with Christmas."

The suggestion brought an ugly gleam in the little eyes of Pop. He slid from his post, with a single glance at his neighbors that warned them that there was excitement to be had in the immediate future. "I got a horse," he said, "that ain't particular much to look at. But maybe you'd like to see him. His legs are strong enough, I guess, to suit even you, stranger."

This brought a smother of laughter from the others. But the big man seemed quite oblivious of the whole scene.

"Lead me to that horse," Tom said. "I'll take my chances with him."

He was taken to a shed, and there, in the midst of the wreckage of several stalls that had apparently fallen under the flying heels of the animal, stood an immense gelding of a dirty cream color. It was one of the largest horses that Tom Keene had ever seen, and one of the ugliest. That is to say, he was built on the typical lines of the mustang cow pony, with rather heavy legs, even for his bulk, ewe neck, roach back, ragged bit of a tail, and huge, lumpish head, given significance by the great Roman nose from time immemorial the token of a stubborn and war-like horse. He turned a little as Tom looked in, and regarded him out of a little bright, bloodshot eye indicative of a treacherous nature.

"There he is," said the elder man. "There's old Christmas. He ain't what he used to be, but still he's got . . . strong legs."

Tom Keene turned and regarded the owner with a smile. "That's an outlaw," he said quietly. "That horse has never been ridden."

"Sure he ain't," said the other, "but, as I said before, he's got legs enough, and legs was all that you was asking for. But, if you was to ride him . . . which that saddle and bridle hanging in there ain't to hold you back none . . . why, you could take old Christmas along with you for a gift."

There was a brief roar of laughter from the others.

But Tom merely tightened his belt. "Legs, as you say, was all I asked for," he remarked. "So, if I may use that rope yonder . . ."

"Go as far as you like," said Pop Sherman.

The rope, accordingly, was scooped up, and Tom advanced into the shed. Old Christmas did not need to be told through an interpreter what the designs of the man might be. He took one look at the rope, another at the man who held it, and then planted his forehoofs firmly, hunched forward, whirled with great dexterity, and let loose a volley of kicks that would have torn the head from Tom's wide shoulders had the least of them landed.

But Tom had leaped back to a corner of the

enclosure, his agility bringing a shout of mingled amusement and approbation from the excited spectators. In another moment the rope left his hand. It tangled those mighty rear legs of the cream-colored horse, but thereat, instead of venturing the kick that would have thrown him helplessly to the ground, he changed his tactics to meet the assault. He turned again, and this time he presented his gaping mouth and lunged with flattened ears at his tormentor.

"Get out, you fool!" shouted Pop Sherman. "He ain't no common horse. He's a killer!"

The last word rose up the scale to a shrill scream, for, as Christmas plunged, the man suddenly plunged straight at Christmas with a shout so savage and so fiercely joyous at once, that it curdled the veins of the spectators.

Madness seemed to have swept the giant off his feet. But there was a cunning mind directing his attack. At the last instant, when he seemed rushing into the teeth of destruction, he veered far to the side, at the same time curling a twist into the rope that spun at the head of Christmas and whipped around his face. The great horse had reared to smash the enemy with his forehoofs and rend him with the gaping teeth at the same instant. But just under the downsweep of those great hoofs slid the big man and at the same time brought all of his lunging weight against the rope.

He had turned as he lunged, digging in his heels,

but now the shock staggered him and brought him lurching forward. The effect upon Christmas, however, was even greater, for, taken unguarded by that heavy wrench to the side, the horse swung over in mid-leap and crashed heavily upon his side. The fall stunned him. Before he recovered his senses, he was blindfolded with a sack, and, when at length he rose, he stood with legs braced as though expecting to receive another fall as mysterious as the first.

The onlookers regarded these maneuvers with undisguised admiration and wonder.

"I'd've hated to try that in a forty-acre lot, let alone in a little box like this," Pop Sherman said, summing up the opinion of all.

And then, having saddled the quivering but motionless gelding, Tom led him through the door and into the open. He swung into the stirrups, jerked off the blindfold, and, with a wicked slash of the spurs, bade Christmas start his battle.

Christmas needed no second bidding. As Pop Sherman declared afterward: "The air was plumb full of Christmas. I looked for the stranger to begin to shake down in bits."

But he would not shake down. Huge Christmas fought like a great cat, vengefully, and with a practiced skill that had made him the terror of bucking contests throughout the state. But for every squeal of rage that he uttered, there was a shout of savage delight and exultation from the giant rider. And for every maneuver in which he indulged himself, maneuvers that had made other riders pull leather desperately, he simply received fresh goading from the spurs, fresh cutting with the heavy quirt.

In the meantime, the intelligence that had made him so successful as a bucker now operated to warn him that he had met his match, and that continued battle simply meant continued pain. Therefore, as suddenly as he had begun, he stopped, sidled toward a bunch of dead grass, thrust down his cut mouth, and began to crop the grass with a foolish pretense that he had never intended anything but play from the first. But the red, vicious eyes and the heaving sides told a different story, and Pop Sherman paid Tom a generous tribute.

"The best piece of nerve that I ever seen," he declared, and the others shared the opinion.

Tom merely shrugged his shoulders, and, swinging down from the horse, he took the reins over the crook of his arm and approached Pop Sherman to set a price on the outfit, actually turning his back upon the man-killer. They arrived at an agreement quickly enough, for the saddle and the bridle were old, and Christmas was a gift won in the riding of him. In five minutes, big Tom Keene was ready to depart. He left behind him a group won over from hostility to frank good-fellowship, and Pop Sherman said, as he shook hands: "Partner, what name am I going to jot down in the books to remember you by?"

"Timothy Kenyon," Tom said. "That's my name." And so he rode off toward the trail up Crystal Mountain.

He found beneath him a gait that was racking and pounding even at a canter, but he also found that there was no wearing out of Christmas. All day the cream-colored gelding could stick doggedly to his work, even with such a bulk as that of Tom on his back, and the rider remorselessly urged him on through the hills and then up the long trail on the mountain side.

All the way he blessed the rugged strength of Christmas, for it meant that this detour would not so vitally affect him. He could swing back at once toward his true destination and, rushing Christmas through the hills, strike down at John Carver and his treacherous wife. In the meantime, he must keep his word to poor Johnson and complete the journey.

In the early afternoon he was so far up that he could sight across the two peaks to the northwest on a line with which, Johnson had said, the exposed ore lay. It was a full hour later, however, before he reached the designated spot and saw, with a gasp of astonishment, that the little cripple was right—the whole side of the mountain had been gouged bare by a great landslide. He swung out of the saddle, secured the gelding, and then began hurriedly examining the rocks until the stroke of his hammer cracked off a fragment and . . .

He threw up a great, brandished fist. "Gold!" shouted Tom Keene. "Gold!" He began striking right and left, and at every stroke on that narrow, outcropping ledge, the dull, weathered, outer layer of stone chipped off and exposed the rich, rich ore—such ore as Tom had never dreamed of.

Then he stopped abruptly. Eight years before, if that had happened, he would have fallen upon his knees and given thanks to heaven. But now he turned from the mountain side, each hand weighted down by a heavy chunk of ore, and peered into the distance where the smoke columns of a mountain village were twisting lazily into the blue of the sky. And he scowled at them with a savage satisfaction. For this gold was power, a greater power than sheer muscle could ever be. It was in itself a weapon and the arm that swings the weapon.

And now let heaven pity his enemies, for he, Tom Keene, would not.

Chapter Twenty-Eight

In order to be perfected, vengeance must wait. He delivered up a prayer that the gold-bearing ledge not be discovered in the interim, rushed for the county seat to file his claim, and then rode even staunch Christmas well-nigh into the ground in his burst for the railroad. Thence he headed for Denver with his specimens of ore and returned a week later with experts. A fortnight afterward a small cow town was startled by the appearance of a gigantic horse and a gigantic rider who stormed down the main street, paused to ask a single question at the store, and then continued to the lower end of the town.

There, on her doorstep, her face supported in her work-knotted, work-reddened hands, with clamor of three children sweeping about her in the yard of the little shack, sat a middle-aged woman. The arduous labor needed to raise three children by the strength of her hands had bowed her body and, perhaps, broken her heart long since, but still she had never yet failed in the battle. Only the spark and the spring were gone from her, and it was a dead-gray eye that looked up to Tom Keene.

"Are you Missus Johnson?" he asked.

"That's me."

"Are you the one whose husband is . . . ?"

He hesitated, but she brought out in a hard, unshaken voice: "Whose husband is in prison for murder? Aye, I'm her that married the worthless rat. I'm her that have worn myself to the bone raising his brats. And what are you to ask? Are you one of the worthless good-for-nothings that used to take him out of his home?"

But Tom Keene shrugged his shoulders. He looked at her curiously. In the old days, he would have felt a pang of pity, and there would have been a great outgoing of the spirit in his desire to help her. But now she was something so detached from him that he felt she must even be of a different species. For what was her pain to the agony that he had passed through—three years of mental and physical torture and five years of torment of the spirit, which had whitened his hair?

"I'm a friend of Johnson's," he admitted coldly. "I've come here to tell you that it was only bad luck that put him in prison. And good luck may get him out again."

"That's the way they all talk . . . all the old friends," the woman said bitterly. "They talk about luck, but what I talk about and what I feel is the work and the pain of work. What fault was it of mine that he killed a man? But all on account of him the curse of Adam is put on me."

"Suppose it were taken off again by him?"

"Suppose . . . ?" She started up and stared at Tom, then shook her head, the fire dying from her face. "What good is there in supposing fool things like that?" she asked.

"Listen to me," Tom said. "You're wrong to accuse him, and you were wrong to give him up as soon as he was sent to prison. But that's the way of it with people. Presumption of innocence? *Bah!* But let me tell you that that night, ten years ago, Johnson had come down out of the mountains to celebrate because he felt that he had the resources of a rich man under his thumb to tap when he pleased. That very night he had the fight and struck the blow that killed a man. That blow sent him to jail to await his trial. He wrote to you, telling you about the location of the gold ledge. But you were through with him as soon as you heard about his arrest. You returned his letter unopened. Johnson was furious. He decided that he would take his secret to prison with him. Well, Missus Johnson, after he was in the prison, he changed his mind again and wanted to let you know, but he could not write a letter without having its contents pass under the eye of the warden, and that would have meant simply putting his secret in the hands of Warden Tufter. So he could do nothing. He had a fortune waiting for him in the hills, and with that fortune he could reopen his case and fight for a new trial . . . anything was possible."

"Why are you telling me all this?" the woman asked harshly. "What good does it do me?"

"It does you this good," the big man said cruelly. "It shows you that, if you had stayed with your husband when he was arrested, and if you'd been willing to fight for him, you and your youngsters would have spent ten years of comfort instead of ten years of slavery."

And he watched her with a contemptuous smile while she gasped, her eyes rolling at the thought.

"It ain't the first time that men have talked about

a fortune that they had . . . in the ground," she declared. "But that's no part of my life. I'd like to see a grain of gold dust out of it. Then I'd begin to think that I'd missed something. But I know that Johnson was always no good. I was a fool to marry him. I was a double fool to have three babies. And I was more fool still to wear out my life working for his children. But who sent you here? Who sent you here to tell lies for my husband?"

In response, Tom drew out his wallet, sifted forth a thin packet of bills, folded them, and passed them to the woman. "Here's that grain of gold dust you were asking for," he said. "Buy tickets to Denver. Go there with your children. Go to this address." Here he handed her a card. "You will find out things which it is to your interest to know."

She flipped up the corners of the bills, saw their denominations, and uttered a faint moan. She pressed the money to her heart and stared timidly at Tom.

"In the meantime," he said, still cold as stone, "get down on your knees and beg your children to forgive you for the ten years of poverty you've condemned them to because you had no trust in . . ." Here he paused as though the words choked him, turned Christmas away, and sent the big horse in a thundering gallop down the street.

He had found himself talking of trust. Some of

his old roadside sermons came dimly back to his mind, with the memories of the prison years like whiplashes barring those thoughts. Far south lay Porterville and the old Carver Ranch and the Carver family on the road just outside the village. Having once known them, how could he be so mad as to use the word trust ever again? He could only pray, then, that John Carver had indeed reformed as he had sworn to Tom that he would do that day when he lay wounded on the hillside. For if Carver had turned the leaf and become an industrious citizen, then Tom could strike with redoubled purposefulness.

After that, there was no mercy shown to Christmas. The great ugly horse was driven remorselessly down the south trail. So, weary days later, he was forced up the slopes of a mountain range and at length checked for an instant on the brow of an eminence while Tom Keene searched the familiar land below.

Yonder, out of sight and too far away for even smoke to betray its presence, was Porterville. But closer at hand were the trees and the buildings of old Carver Ranch, a faint blur. Closer still, and he saw the very dale where he had changed places with John Carver on that luckless day that had brought him, for his whole-hearted generosity, eight years of bitter penance.

It was for only a brief view that he paused. His very heart was burning up with a desire to come closer. Down the slope he pushed Christmas until the big horse trotted, frothing and spuming, into the hollow. But, as he turned the corner of the hillside, he saw that he was not the only visitor to the place on this day.

He heard a volley of shouts—a man and a girl, calling sharply to racing horses, the drumming of whose hoofs was muffled on the brown turf. Then, over the brow of that hill where The White Mask had appeared to him, shot Jerry Swain. Jr., on a flying chestnut mare that was straightened to full speed—her head, snaky with its flattened ears, poking eagerly before her. It was a beautiful animal. Breeding showed in its every line and in its every movement. There was red earnest in its eye as it raced, and Jerry Swain, with a sort of laughing dread, urged the fine animal ahead.

There was an immediate explanation of his haste, for now over the hilltop plunged a black-haired, black-eyed girl on an immense stallion blacker than her own shining hair. How fresh and beautiful she was, and, in contrast, how terrible the strength of the horse. And the heart of Tom Keene for the moment forgot its sternness and melted at the sight of great Major, seen for the first time in eight years.

He did not seem to have aged a day, and he rushed in pursuit of the chestnut mare with a speed whose edge had not been dulled by passage of time. Who was she who sat on his back, neatly turned out in a riding dress with a white blouse and a high white collar and gleaming boots? There was loveliness in her such as Tom had never seen before, and there was something familiar, also. It needed only an instant of reflection, and then he knew. It was dark-dark-eyed Mary, Elizabeth Carver's girl, grown into a twenty-year-old beauty.

With a rush of new interest he studied her. Yes, unquestionably John Carver had turned over a leaf and had brought prosperity to his family. The quality of her clothes meant money; her very carefree attitude meant that she had never been bowed by the necessity of labor.

Tom turned attention to another thing, and that was the consummate ease with which she handled Major. The great horse who refused obedience to any except one master, now answered every whim of the girl. It was plain to see that at any instant she could turn loose a hurricane of speed that would sweep her past the chestnut mare. The latter could not live for a moment beside the great, striding stallion. But the girl held Major in, checking him closely and playing with her antagonist. The goal was apparently a brace of small pines a little distance ahead. For this they rushed, Jerry Swain beginning to quirt and spur at the same time to lift his mount forward.

But there came a short, thrilling shout from the girl. She bent over into the position of a jockey, the long, blue-black mane of the stallion flying in her face, and in a trice, unspurred and unwhipped, Major was at the side of the mare and had shot past her. A good length in the lead, he went by the pines. Jerry Swain brought up his mare with an exclamation of rage, sawed violently at her head, and then spurred and cut her with the quirt, so that she leaped high into the air.

It made Tom Keene set his teeth. Plainly Jerry Swain was as viciously worthless now as he had been eight years before. Time had altered his character no more, it seemed, than it had altered his face, which was the same smoothly handsome countenance that Tom remembered. But the girl now cried out: "Shame, Jerry! Shame! She did her honest best, poor girl! You mustn't beat her!"

"She's no good!" Jerry cried savagely, though he desisted from the punishment. "I'll tell the governor that he was done brown when he bought this nag. Thoroughbred? *Bah!* She's not even a half-breed. That black plow horse simply walked by me."

"He's walked by better horses than the chestnut mare," the girl said proudly. "Good old Major . . . he has the feet of the wind when he wants to run."

"But the black devil wants to run for nobody but you."

"You hate him because he threw you two years ago. That's small-spirited Jerry. I'm ashamed of you. You wore spurs. I told you that Major wouldn't stand them."

They dipped out of sight beyond the next hill, the chestnut still foaming and prancing, and Major jogging softly on with his head a little turned to listen to his rider, just as in the old days he used to listen to Tom Keene. It sent a thrill of jealous anger through him.

Then he started on toward the high road. There were many deductions to be drawn from what he had just seen. Jerry Swain, it seemed, was back in the good graces of his father. And the girl had not only been happily raised, to make up for the miseries of her childhood, but she had been sent off to a school, to judge by the manner of her talk. If all were as it struck the observant mind of Tom, then might it not be that the daughter of the newly prosperous Carver and the son of rich Jerry Swain were about to marry to unite the fortunes?

He pushed ahead to the road. There he found that Mary Carver and Jerry Swain, Jr., had arrived before him, but they were proceeding at a laggard pace, the shoulders of their horses almost rubbing as they talked in the most animated fashion. And it seemed that Jerry was pressing an argument of some sort upon the girl, an argument to which she listened seriously but without acquiescence. Was their debate on the subject of love and wedlock?

Tom Keene smiled with a gloomy content. This would be a fitting end for the daughter of the traitor.

He pressed past them, Christmas dripping with

sweat but full of energy and viciousness again after the brief breathing space among the hills. But the sight of the foaming horse drew an exclamation from the girl and from Jerry Swain: "Blasted outrage!"

Tom took off his hat. "I beg your pardon," he said politely, like one hard of hearing. "Did you speak to me?"

The sound of his great, rich, bass voice had a peculiar effect upon both Jerry and his companion, for they started and glanced rather wildly at the stranger. But then their attention was held by the shining silver hair that he had exposed for the moment as he removed the hat to honor the girl. This observation, as a matter of fact, seemed to encourage Jerry Swain to follow up the protestation that he had muttered as Tom rode the foaming horse by them.

"I spoke not to you," Jerry said, swelling with virtuous indignation, and very conscious of the presence of the girl as an applauding witness, "but about the horse. It looks to me as though you've ridden your horse to the dropping point, sir." This severe remark concluded, he turned a side glance to note the approval of the girl, and, receiving a faint smile and a nod of encouragement from her, he turned again upon Tom with redoubled wrath. "Men like you," he said, "are the ones who make it necessary for us to have societies for the prevention of cruelty to animals. And . . ."

Tom smiled mirthlessly on the other. "My white hair," he said, "is what gives you courage, but I'm younger than I look, my friend, and quite young enough to wring the neck of a knave."

So saying, he swung the terrible, foaming Christmas in toward Jerry Swain. The latter, with a gasp, reined the mare away and reached for his revolver—only to find that he had ridden out without it. At the same time, the chestnut struck the black stallion, who reared, and the trio were suddenly in the greatest confusion.

Here Tom at once drew the gelding back, bestowed a contemptuous smile upon Swain, and continued at a leisurely pace down the road. He heard Swain exclaiming behind him: "If it weren't that the mare is so restless, confound her, I'd give that horse killer a lesson in spite of his gray hair."

"Jerry," returned the grave voice of the girl, "I think you'd better keep away from him. He looks like a fighter. And he reminded me of some-one . . ."

"He reminded me, too. Who the devil is he?"

Thus far, a fall of the wind had allowed the words to come distinctly to the ear of Tom, but now it rose again and drowned the conversation behind him. He roused Christmas to a gallop with relentless spur.

Chapter Twenty-Nine

The talk that Tom had observed between the girl and young Jerry Swain had been of exactly the nature that he surmised. Jerry was pressing for an engagement, and the girl had been of another mind. It was all revealed that night in the library of the rich cattleman's house. He welcomed the chance to escape for a few moments from the weary volumes. Above all, he was glad of the opportunity to talk of Mary Carver, it seemed.

In the shadowy corner at the far side of the big room was the intellectual preceptor of the rancher, quite lost in the dark, indistinct as a ghost. The only reality about him was the glowing of lamplight across the page of the yellow tome that he was perusing. Though he had bought largely for the rancher, he had used the latter's money to buy still more largely for himself, and now, as he bent over the book, his hanging white beard was a bit of mist and the book was held open by spirit hands. There was no need of sending him from the room. No matter how private the conversation, he would not hear and retain a word that was spoken.

"I talked as I never talked before," Jerry said to his father. "And she listened, but she wouldn't be persuaded."

"*Bah!*" snapped the older man. "The best you could do in the line of talking would be shabby work. But she's a sensible girl as well as a lovely one, Jerry. If you put the point directly to her, I'll wager that she would be reasonable enough."

"But I did that very thing," said poor Jerry, Jr. "I told her pointblank that, if she cared much for her father's happiness, she'd better marry me."

"And she . . . ?"

"She had tears in her eyes. But still she managed to shake her head."

"And with the sheriff's sale tomorrow. Did she shake her head, anyway? Well, then, she has a harder heart than I ever imagined."

"No, you don't know her," the son said. "She's as hard as flint under the surface. I even told her that Major would be sold as well as the roof over their heads. Major means more to her than all the rest of the place. And the tears ran down her face when she answered me, but still all she would say was . . . 'But I don't love you, Jerry. I don't love you, and therefore it's a sin for me even to think of marrying you.'"

Jerry Swain, Sr., exploded. "There's nothing like one of these stubborn girls!" he shouted. "Still you must have her, Jerry. By the Lord, she's got to be your wife. Mind what I said before. If you win her, then I forget all that has happened between us. I'll see that you have money enough. I'll see that you have a house . . . this very house we're in now, if you want it . . . and I'll give you an income that will be big enough, you can be sure."

The son writhed in his anguish. But still he protested that he had talked as he never talked before, and she persisted in being adamant. In the midst of it there had come an unlucky interruption in the form of a stranger on an immense and ugly horse who rode past them and picked a quarrel with Jerry. And, if she had been cool before, she was veritable ice thereafter. To this the father listened with a sudden concern. That his son was a coward, he sometimes guessed, but he could never be sure. And it seemed impossible that the girl could have thought it of Jerry because he had not flown at the throat of the elderly stranger.

"He had white hair, Dad," said Jerry, Jr. "How could I knock an old fellow like that off his horse?"

And his father, of course, agreed. Then he laid down his ultimatum. "You're going tomorrow to that sale," he said. "If you had come home tonight and told me that you were engaged to Mary Carver, I intended to give John enough money to pull him through. But, as it is, I'm going to save money by buying him in. At that, I think I'd rather own his place and him outright than simply be his creditor. He owes a flat thirty thousand dollars, and his place won't bring in more than twenty thousand as it stands. But . . ."

"Thirty thousand?" exclaimed the son.

"You wonder how he happens to owe that much?" asked the father. "I've wondered the same thing. There's a mystery about it. He's been a perfect demon for work this past eight years . . . ever since he was shot by The White Mask, in fact. And everything that he's turned his hand to has prospered. And yet, in spite of that, he's in debt . . . thirty thousand dollars in debt."

"He spent a lot of money educating Mary, for one thing," suggested Jerry, Jr. "And he's spent a good many thousands in repairing the fences and buildings on the old ranch."

"I've counted all that in," his father said, "but, in spite of those items, he ought to be well ahead. In the past eight years, about twenty or twenty-five thousand dollars has simply dropped out of sight on that ranch. What's happened to it? Where's the leak? Where's the hole down which John Carver pours his profits? Well, that's an ended matter. Tomorrow night will see me the owner of old Carver Ranch, and then perhaps Mary Carver will look at things in a different light. What could she do for a living?"

"Teach."

"Stuff and nonsense! One term of teaching, and then you'll see her ready to fall into your arms. Tomorrow you go to that sale and bid on the old place no more than twenty-five thousand dollars. Probably you can get it for twenty thousand. Chances are that nobody will buck you up higher than that."

"But suppose that somebody should go up

230

higher than twenty-five thousand?" asked the son.

"Suppose the moon were made of green cheese," the father responded. "I tell you, I know what the ranch is worth, and what every man in this neighborhood is qualified to bid on it. As for strangers, there is nothing about it to attract them to the sale."

To this, Jerry, Jr., returned no answer. But he took the first opportunity to leave the room and go up to his own chamber. He had many reasons to wish to be alone. It seemed that, after all, it made no great difference what happened. If his father became the eventual owner of the Carver land, all would be well yet, he promised himself.

He lit the lamp in his bedchamber and had turned to take a cigarette from the box on the table when he saw a dim form in the corner of the room, a form that immediately slid from the gloom and took shape as a man. Jerry had been caught once that day without a gun in time of need. This would not happen twice. And as he dexterously put a table between himself and the other, he brought his Colt into his hand and directed it steadily enough at the intruder.

But the other continued to approach, with no gleam of answering metal in his hand, until he stepped into the circle of the lamplight, which shone upon the rugged features of John Carver. He was much altered by the eight years. Not only were his features heavily lined, but his hair was turned to a rough and patchy gray. His body was changed, too, having lost much of its original, bulky strength. His step was slouching. His head thrust forward with a chin protruded by weariness rather than pugnacity. His big hands dangled loosely at his sides. Altogether, he gave, as he stepped into the light, a very picture of weariness too great to fear danger. A wave of his hand literally brushed the gun away.

Jerry Swain, with a gasp of relief, lowered the weapon and said softly: "You, Carver? I thought for a minute that . . . no matter what. But I'm glad to see you."

"That's more," Carver said, "than I can say for you. Heaven curse the day that I first laid eyes on you. You leech!"

"This is a queer way to talk," Jerry said. "What's wrong, Carver?"

"Everything's wrong. The fool girl's gone mad."

"You talked to her, and she wouldn't listen?"

"Aye! I talked . . . her mother talked. She done nothing but sit and fold her hands and look out the window and mumble like an idiot . . . 'I don't love him. How can I marry him?' I went near mad. But nothing can be done with her."

"I'm sorry," Jerry said. "You're a witness that I did all I could to help. But when a man is refused by . . ."

"You failed once," Carver said doggedly. "That

means that you got to start in again. Find another way for me. Try again."

Jerry Swain flinched and changed color a little. "Look here," he said. "I want to help you out. But this is your fight, you know. It isn't mine."

"Ain't it? I'll show you where you're wrong. Who's pulled me down? Who's been the leech all these years? You, Swain . . . you . . . you hound! You've squeezed me white. I've kept the accounting. Twenty-eight thousand five hundred is what I've dumped into your pockets these past eight years. If I had that, d'you think I'd be afraid of bankruptcy? No! And where has the coin gone? It's gone across the gambling table, where you're too big a fool to win . . . and you're too weak to keep away from the game. I owe the world about thirty thousand dollars. But you owe me twenty-eight thousand five hundred. My money is due tomorrow . . . your money is due to me tonight. Swain, come across!"

Jerry Swain had backed away until his shoulders were wedged into a corner of the wall during this speech, every word of which seemed to push him away like a jerk from a hand. Now he managed by a desperate effort to step forward again and speak with some show of self-control. "Someday I'll pay you," he declared. "You know that."

"I know nothing about you except that you're a rat," said John Carver. "I know that, and I know it makes me plumb sick to think of you marrying

Mary. Why, she's got more man in her little finger than you have in your whole body."

"Talk low," muttered the other, half frightened and half savage, but excited by the fear of discovery rather than by the insults that were being showered upon him.

"I'm tired of talking low," Carver said. "I've a mind to begin talking out loud. I've a mind to break up this eight-year-old silence and begin letting the world know what I know about you, Swain!"

"Suppose I were to do the same thing, Carver? You'd go to prison fast enough."

"And you'd go to Hades," Carver replied.

"I'd risk that. But what's the use of this sort of talk? The point of it all is that we need each other. Now listen to the latest. Father will buy you in tomorrow. There's no fear of anything else. Father will buy the ranch in."

"What good does that do me?"

"It does you every good if you'll open your eyes. It means that you'll keep right on living on the ranch, and that Mary'll have more time to come to her senses. When she sees that the right thing is for her to marry me, then there'll be no more trouble. You understand?"

"Aye." The rancher nodded, and his lips trembled with weariness and grief as he spoke. "Aye, old Jerry Swain ever had an eye for something with value. And that's why he wants to buy my girl in for you . . . buy her in just the same as if she were a horse or a cow."

"What other way is there?" asked Jerry.

John Carver glowered at the younger man. "Mark this, son," he said heavily at length. "I'm a calm man and a peaceful man, but there's one thing that I'm going to stand on . . . if there's any slip or mix-up in the business tomorrow, I'm going to have your life. Mind that! If you don't buy me in, I'm coming straight for you with a gun."

He made a half-completed gesture that revealed more clearly than words the position of the heavy revolver that he carried. And all at once, in the eyes of frightened Jerry Swain, he ceased to be the father of Mary Carver, the patient rancher who during the past eight years had labored so ceaselessly, so bitterly to help his family up. He became, in a trice, the savage manhunter and robber, The White Mask.

"There'll be no need of that," said Jerry. "You go home and stop worrying."

Chapter Thirty

It was the first large business transaction that had ever been entrusted to the hands of Jerry Swain by his father. And accordingly he swelled with pride. There were only fifty or sixty persons in the room, most of them men. They sat at the desks, their knees depressed and cramped in spaces intended for children. But the demeanor of each man was solemn. In a way, they were attending the obsequies of a comrade. They were sitting at the burial of the last of the once great Carver estate.

And it seemed to Jerry that in this manner he was stepping up and assuming a proper place among the men of the community. They had long paid the proper respect to his father; it was now high time that they should pay the proper respect to Jerry himself. Looking carefully over the faces in that room, he was aware that the most prominent members of the community were around him. Few had come to bid, it turned out when the bidding commenced, but they had come to listen and to take notes.

It was John Castor who, when the bids were first called for, began with the ridiculous sum of $5,000.

"Not that I figure on five thousand pulling down the plum," he had assured the auctioneer with a broad grin, "but because I like to start in easy."

"Six thousand!" sang out Jeff Crothers from the other side of the room. "Not that I figure on six thousand pulling down the plum, but because six thousand looks to me a sight better than five thousand!"

But, though this remark brought a laugh, it was plain, before long, that both Castor and Crothers were in earnest and were going to make a serious battle for the ranch. At once they jumped up to $15,000 and thereby shut out all the other contestants, for several had come with a hope that the ranch might be knocked down at some lucky and low figure.

From $15,000 to $18,000 the bids climbed by $500 a time. Plainly Castor and Crothers wanted that ranch, but it was equally plain that they hated to push up the bidding.

At $18,000 there was a momentary pause, and the auctioneer seemed about to knock the ranch down to Crothers at that sum, before Castor boosted $100. And the progression up the ladder was commenced again by hundreds, a slow and yet an eminently thrilling process.

And all the while Jerry Swain sat back in his chair and spun around his forefinger his gold chain weighted with a knife. He was waiting until the favorable opportunity came when he would, as the saying went "knock them out of their chairs."

The time came.

"Nineteen thousand four hundred and fifty!" sang out Castor.

Crothers, with a black face, made no answering bid. He had come in hopes of a bargain. But now he began to see that he would have to calculate values closely if he wished to get more than a hundred cents for every dollar.

An electric quality hung in the air. Men began to

center their attention upon Castor as the probable winner.

"Twenty thousand," Jerry Swain said calmly.

He had succeeded better than he had dreamed. Heads jerked around in his direction as though a string were attached to their chins and he had pulled it.

"Twenty thousand!" cried the auctioneer, taking a new lease on life at the prospect of three bidding one another up to the skies. And he turned a broad, kindly smile upon poor John Carver. Perhaps, despite all expectations, John would get enough, not only to clear away the debts, but also have a little left for himself.

Such hopes died at once, however, for no sooner had that $20,000 been bid and the bidder located definitely as no less a person than the son of the richest man in the community than Castor and Crothers both gave up the battle and sat back in their chairs with disgusted looks. By waiting until the last moment, Jerry Swain had as effectually knocked the wind out of their sails as his shrewd father could ever have done.

At $20,000 the bid died an abrupt death. If Jerry Swain actually wanted the ranch, who in the world could keep him from taking it? Certainly he had a wealth at command that defied competition.

The joy faded from the face of the auctioneer. But John Carver, with a look of relief, began to roll a cigarette. The boy had kept his word, after all. And now the crowd began to understand. The love of Jerry Swain for Mary Carver was an old story. It was taken for granted that Jerry would buy the ranch, let Carver pay what he could on his debts with the purchase price, and then deed the ranch back to its original owner.

It was a fine thought. Though the auctioneer, disappointed in his hope of further battle, registered gloom, there was a deep-throated mutter of content that passed around the rest of the room. This pleased the stern cattlemen. This was an exhibition of sentiment in the form of dollars and cents that they could fully appreciate.

"Going to Mister Swain at twenty thousand," the auctioneer announced. "Going . . ."

"Twenty-one thousand," said another voice.

It was a huge bass voice that flooded through the room, and the little crowd turned and saw that the doorway was filled by the form of a very tall, very heavily built man who was smoking a cigarette, and who now, stepping into the interior, removed his hat and exposed a mop of silver, shining hair.

He was so big, when he stepped into the room, that the rectangle of the lighted doorway was just of sufficient size to outline him. And Jerry Swain recognized, with a peculiar sinking of the heart, the big man who he had encountered on the road the previous day.

"Twenty-one thousand," repeated the big man, for the silence that greeted him was so profound that he might well have been forgiven for feeling that his first call had not been heard.

"Twenty-one thousand! You hear it, gentlemen?" cried the auctioneer. "You hear him calling it? Twenty-one thousand? Who makes it twenty-two?"

Jerry Swain glared at the big stranger. There was nothing in the make-up of the man to suggest wealth. He was plainly, even roughly dressed. A rough shirt of gray flannel, heavy ready-made boots, great buckskin gloves, a worn and floppy sombrero—in all of these particulars, he was the type of the ordinary cowpuncher.

Yet, when he inhaled a great cloud of cigarette smoke and then blew it toward the ceiling, there was no one to dispute the fact that he was full of potentialities. His ease, his careless manner as he leaned against the wall and looked the crowd over in detail, gave the feeling that he was sure of himself, that he had ten times the power necessary to live up to his words.

Jerry Swain rose to his feet. The limit that his father had set was still $4,000 away, but it was probable that, when the big stranger realized who it was he opposed, he would cease bidding. For though, in his ignorance of the identity of Jerry Swain's son, he might have been blustering and bold on the road the day before, it stood to reason that he could not have remained in Porterville overnight without learning the truth about the county's richest man. Therefore it was that Jerry rose and faced squarely toward the intruder while he announced his next bid in a defiant voice.

"Twenty-one thousand five hundred!" And he waited for the announcement to take effect.

Indeed, the big man turned a little away—it was only to scratch a match on the wall—and as he faced the auctioneer again he said "Twenty-five thousand."

A haze of darkness spun before the eyes of poor Jerry Swain. He saw his hopes of Mary Carver fade into a thin mist. He saw the danger of terrible John Carver looming, close and grim, John Carver changed to his old identity—The White Mask! He must bid higher for the ranch. If only his father had not set that limitation.

"Let me have half an hour's time to reach my father!" Jerry cried to the auctioneer. "He may sanction a higher bid and . . ."

By that confession he had delivered himself into the hands of the enemy, and he was at once made aware of the fact by the jarring, booming laughter of Tom Keene as the latter gave way to his mirth beside the door.

But John Carver, in the far corner, devoured with hope as he saw the bidding leap to $25,000, now rose and seconded the appeal of Jerry Swain.

"Bill," he called to the auctioneer, "it ain't right to knock the place down unless everybody that wants to bid on it has a chance to bid all he can!

Give young Swain a chance to talk to his father."

The auctioneer wavered. It was not exactly legal, this suggested delay, but on the one hand he would be injuring a stranger, and on the other hand he was being urged on by two neighbors. He actually stood with parted lips, unable to speak, while Jerry Swain started hastily for the door, calling over his shoulder: "It'll be less than half an hour! I . . . I'll run the horse all the way. I'll be back in fifteen minutes!"

But now the floor of the room quivered under a heavy tread, and Tom Keene strode to the center down the main aisle. "Everybody around this town," he declared, "has had a chance to think over the amount of money he could pay for old Carver Ranch. Swain, Senior thought it over. He decided that twenty-five thousand was his limit. He told his son to come in and bid as high as that and no higher. Well, Mister Auctioneer, he turned out to have guessed wrong. Is he going to have a chance for a second guess? Is this an auction sale or a bargain shop? Do your advertisements mean anything, or is it just a little town deal of the kind you permit in Porterville?"

As he spoke, he looked about him at every face. Suddenly they were aware that he was scoffing at them, challenging the manhood of the entire town with his mirth, as it were. But with an equal suddenness they felt that he was changed. His gray hair, which had been branding him with the helpless sluggishness of age, now became an inconsiderable object. Instead, their attention was centered upon the square outlines of the face, outlines of bony strength to resist shocks. And they saw the dark, beetling brows that gathered above the eyes, and they saw the huge hands that were raised with the thumbs hooked inside the cartridge belt. At the same time, they became aware of the Colt revolver that had been hanging in the holster at his thigh, but which now received a singular prominence. In spite of themselves all of those hardy fellows were abashed. They resolved, in their heart of hearts, upon a fixed hatred of the big man, but at the same time they felt that their like or dislike would mean absolutely nothing to him, and that, against men who have this attitude, society has no weapon except downright force.

The effect on Jerry Swain was immediate. He had felt that, once outside the door, they would not dare conclude the sale behind his back until he had a chance to bid again. But now he dared not leave, so he swung nervously around to watch. And he was in time to see the auctioneer succumb. Not only physical power but legal right was on the side of Tom Keene.

"What's your name, stranger?" asked Bill, the auctioneer, in a crisp tone that was intended to cover whatever shame there might be in the surrender that was to follow.

"Timothy Kenyon," Tom said instantly.

"Then, Mister Kenyon, I got to say that you're certainly speaking inside of your rights. If there's any bidding to be done beside what's been done, let me hear 'em speak up. This sale has been advertised. As Mister Kenyon says, it ain't a bargain counter."

He had adopted the attitude of the just, the scrupulously law-abiding man, and there was no resisting him. The protest of Jerry Swain was a mere wail of despair as he disappeared through the doorway. "I'm going to break this sale. It isn't legal. It's a crooked deal. . . ."

His heels crashed down the front steps, then the rattle of his horse's hoofs passed away. The broad hand of the auctioneer descended upon the teacher's desk with a bang. The Carver Ranch thereby was sold to Tom Keene.

In the stir and confusion of the succeeding moments, with everyone rising from their places, the auctioneer approached Tom to learn what payment he wished to make to bind the deal.

"Twenty-five thousand dollars cash," Tom said, "is the way I intend to bind the deal."

The auctioneer blinked. It was a good round sum even in a district where good round sums were not unknown. He took Tom Keene to the corner of the room, where a condoling group of men surrounded the haggard-faced Carver as the latter attempted to smile and shrug their

244

consolation away. There they were introduced, and there Tom shook hands with Carver and smiled upon him.

And it seemed to Tom that the sweetness of revenge was like an intoxicating wine. His brain whirled with it.

Chapter Thirty-One

They waited in the front room of the house, the three of them—Elizabeth Carver with her patient, troubled eyes never moving from the face of her husband, and John Carver staring steadfastly at the floor. Plainly he was broken. In his effort to reform, to make himself a new place in the world during the past eight years, he had poured too much of his energy. Now he had no power left. He was only saying to himself that he would wait for the time when he could strike down the leech who had stolen the fruit of his labors—Jerry Swain. After that they would jail him if they could catch him. Yes, he would not even attempt to flee. Let the law end a useless life, a failure, with a rope around his neck.

These thoughts were moving solemnly, fiercely through his brain as he sat there with his shoulders slumped forward, his hands falling on his knees with the palms turned up. He heard the voice of his daughter like the voice of a brook in the distance. It was a pleasant sound, but it conveyed no meaning to him. It was only a cheerful pattering of sound against which the black gloom of his inward thoughts became more and more solemn.

"He'd ought to be here," said the wife. "I told Jeff that we'd be wanting to get out of here early. He promised to be here by eight-thirty at the latest. I don't know what can be keeping him. Maybe his rig broke down."

"Maybe," John Carver said automatically.

He had not heard a word that she said; at least, he had not heard it in his conscious mind. It would not be work for a gun, he was deciding—the proper end for Jerry Swain. No, the right thing would be for him to get the throat of the younger man inside of his hands, and then, with a great pressure, thrusting his thumbs into the flesh . . .

The effort of that thought jerked him up in his chair. He heard Mary Carver clearly for the first time.

"It isn't going to be a tragedy," she was saying. "You've worked for me long enough, Dad and Mother dear. Now it's time for me to work for you while you rest."

He looked wonderingly at her. His relation toward her was more singular than ever. He had kept the promise that his wife extorted from him as the price of her silence eight years before. He had sent the girl to school in the East. And, when she returned home during vacation times, he had felt a pride in her. But always she had grown more and more a stranger, and he never could feel that she was his own. Even her mother had less and less claim upon her as the years rolled by. Now it was typical that she sat on the sill of the open window, swinging one foot unconcernedly, with her hands dipped into the pockets of her tweed coat.

She did not wear clothes like other girls in the neighborhood of Porterville. She wore them, indeed, like no one that he had ever seen. Perhaps they taught her how to do such things at the school. But, sitting there in the window, with the bright morning light bringing a glow upon her cheek, she seemed more aloof than ever, and she seemed more distantly beautiful, also. Sometimes he wondered how his wife could maintain such a possessive manner when she was around the girl. It seemed more natural that she should always be as she was this morning—off by herself, independent of them, stronger than both of them put together.

"There are all sorts of openings, too," she went on. "I can get work as a secretary, you know. I understand shorthand and typewriting. And a good secretary gets . . . well, ever so much. Someone told me about a girl who started working for some railroad president. She started at ten dollars a week, and inside of twelve years she was getting fifty! Why, in twelve years I'd be only thirty-two and . . ."

But here the voice trailed out of the hearing of the father. He turned back to the all-absorbing topic, the killing of the traitor. He had promised the purchase of the ranch. And certainly it was in his power to buy if he really wanted to buy. No, there had been treachery somewhere. Just where and why, he was too weary in the brain to figure out. But he was done with thinking. Hereafter, he would confine himself to action. In the old days, he had shown the world action enough.

He raised his head again, and this time with a faint smile, for far away he was seeing some of the exploits of The White Mask. Suppose he should step back behind the mask? He was a little slower, a little less agile, but he was stronger in body, and he would be steadier in nerve, he assured himself.

"Why doesn't Jeff come?"

This time the shrill, angry voice of his wife roused John Carver. Yes, Jeff was very late. There was nothing on the ranch that they now owned. House, land, stock—all were the possessions of Timothy Kenyon. They did not own even a horse and buckboard to take them and their clothes to town. Jeff had promised to call for them, but now he was so late that it seemed they could not avoid seeing Timothy Kenyon arrive and take possession of the old home.

"But I want to see him!" said the girl.

"You want to?" Elizabeth Carver cried. "Oh,

Mary, have you no heart? Do you want to . . . ?" She choked and could not finish the sentence, but Mary ran to comfort her.

"I only want to stay and offer to buy Major from him."

"Major? Are you thinking of horses on a day like this?" wailed the mother. "Besides, you have no money. Not a cent!"

"At least, I can give him my note, payable in a year. Major is twelve years old. If I can't make enough money to buy him in a year . . ."

"Hush! What's that?" Mrs. Carver ran to the window, and then shrank from it with a cry, and, when the others looked out, they saw a huge rider on a huge horse of a dirty-cream color thundering down the road and coming to a halt in front of their hitching rack. They saw Timothy Kenyon swing down out of the saddle. Christmas edged clumsily toward him. A fierce jolt in the ribs from the master's elbow made him jump away with a grunt.

"Oh, what a brute of a man!" gasped Mary. "How can he treat a horse like that?"

"He's a bad man to have trouble with," was all that John Carver said. "I can see that. I'd dislike crossing him."

Then, as the stranger approached the house, he was lost to view. His heavy footfall went up the steps, sounded loudly and hollowly on the porch, and then he smote the door with his fist. Mrs.

Carver and her husband could not stir. But Mary ran to let the big man in.

It seemed to her, as she stepped back and swung the door wide, that he was not quite so formidable at close range as he was at a little distance. It was the presence of pain in his face—pain and unsuspected youth—that made him seem less terrible. Neither was he so overmastering in size.

"We'll be gone in a moment," she told him. "We're just waiting for the rig to take us to town."

He took off his hat, pushed his thick fingers through the unwieldy growth of gray hair, and answered nothing. He merely stared at her. She must not let him come into the presence of her parents. It would madden her father, and it would break her mother's heart. So she held him in the little room to the right of the hall. The first founder of the Carver fortune had planned that room as a little reception hall. Now it was serving its original purpose, but there was only one rickety chair in it. That was all the furniture.

"We'll be gone in a minute," she repeated. "Won't you sit down here and wait?"

"Thank you," said the big man, but he made no move toward the chair. He stood impassively, with his fists dropped upon his hips, his singularly white face expressive of no emotion whatever.

And Mary strove to fill in the awkward pause. She pointed out the window to black Major standing in his corral alone, for his tyrannical disposition made it impossible for him to be kept with other horses.

"I want to talk to you about that horse," she said. "I was riding him yesterday, you may remember."

He nodded.

"That's Major. I've had him for eight years."

"You raised him here?"

"No, he was four years old when he came. You'd never guess who brought him. It was The White Mask!"

"The White Mask?" he said, and lifted his brows.

"Yes, The White Mask. He came pretending to be a wandering preacher. Imagine that! I remember him as though it were yesterday." She had interested him beyond her hopes. "He was a giant among men," she went on. "Yes, he must have been at least four or five inches taller than you are. And he had a great black beard that flowed down over his chest. Your voice is heavy, but his was like thunder. I can remember him still, laughing." She shivered at the thought and then raised her eyes, still full of the strange memory. "But, no matter what they say of him, he had some good in him. He saved me out of the well. That's one reason I think there was some good in him. Besides, he talked with such a fire that he must have meant a little part of what he said."

"He's dead now, I imagine," suggested Timothy Kenyon. "I haven't heard of him since he was sent to prison."

"Worse than dead. He's in prison for life. But I want to talk to you about Major. That horse has been almost like a chum with me. No one else can ride him, but I used to climb onto his bare back when I was too small for him to suspect me. That's how I learned to manage him. You see? And I want to know, Mister Kenyon, if I can hope to buy him with a note. If you'll take my note for a year, I . . ."

"He looks big enough to carry me. And, if he's strong enough for that, I won't sell him."

"But no one can ride him, you see."

He turned squarely to her with a faint smile that made her flesh creep. "I guess I can manage that," he said. "Now let me see your father."

She stared at him. It was incomprehensible that a man who seemed to possess some shreds of culture should have, at the same time, so very little tact. But there was nothing she could do, since he asked so bluntly, except take him into the other room. And, with a lugubrious look, she conducted him out, talking loudly at the same time, so that the others might be prepared. But before they reached the doorway, she heard her mother—most welcome sound—start out of her chair exclaiming: "There's Jeff at last, thank heaven! Come along, John!"

And both of them were started for the door when Mary came before them with Timothy Kenyon.

He greeted the pair he was dispossessing

without the slightest embarrassment. Indeed, there was even a great cheerfulness in his voice. "Wait half a minute," he said. "I hear that you're starting for town, but what are you going to do there, Carver? These are hard times for men without money."

"Money or no money," growled Carver, "I'll get on in my own way, no doubt."

"You'd better get on in my way," said the new owner. "Stay here. There's work that has to be done on the ranch. Why not do it? I've no wish to turn you loose on the world. I'm not as hard-hearted as that, man."

In a trice, Jeff and his waiting and his long-expected buckboard were forgotten. Suitcases were dropped out of hands. They sat down in the parlor to discuss possibilities. And in five minutes all chance of removal was ended. In fact, the eagerness with which her parents fell in with the proposals of Kenyon proved conclusively to the girl that it would have been a tragedy had they moved away. They were rooted too deeply in their attachment to the old home. It would have broken the hearts of both of them to go.

So she waited quietly in the background, watching her poor mother dab furtively at the tears of joy that ran down her face while she nodded and smiled at every suggestion the big stranger made.

With dazzling swiftness, it was all settled. Mr.

and Mrs. Carver and Mary were to live in the little cottage behind the big house as soon as the smaller building was placed in a state of sufficient repair. Carver could have a steady job on the ranch as foreman. His daughter could eke out the wages of the family and increase their savings working as cook and general housekeeper for the new owner. At that idea Mary hotly revolted, but a moment of reflection showed her that it was for the best.

It had been all a pleasant dream, that thought of moving away from the ranch and living else-where. But penniless and without work, the most they could do, at least until they had accumulated enough funds to take them to some city would be to work as hired hands on one of the neighboring ranches. And, bitter though it might be to step into that capacity on the old home place, it would be still more bitter to do the same work on strange land.

So it was all settled quickly. There was an immense kindliness in the manner of Timothy Kenyon. To be sure, now and again one might run into a certain hardness. But this happened only now and again, as when she tried to buy Major. But what difference did that make, now that he assured her that she could ride the black stallion as much as she pleased while she stayed on the ranch? Moreover, though he did not express the sentiment in exactly these words, there was an air about Timothy Kenyon that seemed to say: *Trust all this to me.*

Tom Keene almost forgot those eight terrible years in the vista that was opening before him.

Chapter Thirty-Two

It was a joyous month that began at old Carver Ranch. The hope with which the Carver family looked upon Tom, turned into a golden opinion before that month ended. He was better than all his spoken and unspoken promises. The cottage he fitted up with comfortable and solid furniture, even appearing to bestow more attention upon it than he paid heed to the care of the big house itself. And, although he reserved the main building for his own uses, Mrs. Carver declared with a covert smile of great insight that before long he would tire of the loneliness of the house.

"He ain't so old as he looks," she said. "And he'll be hankering for company one of these days. Those rooms will look every one as big as barns to him. Wouldn't be surprised if he cleaned out everything that he's put into the cottage . . . including us . . . and move it all back to the big house."

This was also the true opinion of the girl, and of her father as well. As for John Carver, he began to thank heaven for the day when Timothy Kenyon arrived and ended the long persecution that he had undergone at the hands of Jerry Swain. There was less dignity, to be sure, in his position as foreman of the ranch than there had been when he was owner. But, for all that, he had more real comfort and power joined. The new owner seemed to care little what was done on the ranch. He left it all to Carver, giving him a free hand to spend as he pleased in the repairing of sheds and barns or the replacing of outworn fencing. Neither did he examine the receipts for expenditures with too close an eye, and Carver found increasing opportunities to line his pockets.

Mrs. Carver, for her part, was only too delighted by the returning good nature of her husband, and by the entirely unexpected ease with which he bore the blow that had fallen upon him. She had been prepared for a sorrow and a despair that would weigh her husband to the grave. But, instead, he began to show better spirits than she had known him to be in for years. He began to show for what he really was—a stalwart fellow in his forties with the constitution of an ox and the ability to live through well-nigh as many years in the future as he had in the past.

Moreover, Mary Carver was far better off than anyone could have expected. She had undertaken the work of the house and the cooking for the master with a fine spirit of cheerfulness, gritting her teeth and forcing herself through many an unpleasant task. But, if she showed an ideal spirit for a servant, Timothy Kenyon showed an even more perfect spirit as a master. There was nothing that could upset his equilibrium. If the soup were burned, he shrugged his shoulders. If the pie crust was of a leathery consistency, he shrugged his shoulders again. He seemed oblivious to faults, and yet he was instantly and keenly appreciative of all her successes. It became a strangely fascinating game for her to play. A month was not a long time, but before that month was ended, what with her own eager efforts and her mother's patient instruction, she was doing very well, indeed. She had forgotten the prospective secretaryship to a railroad president at the end of twelve years. She had banished, with astonishing ease, so it seemed to her mother, all the high hopes and ambitions that had been nurtured by her schooling. Behold, she sang in the kitchen, and she sang as she scrubbed the floor.

"Why," she cried to her mother as she sat in the cottage in the middle of the afternoon with the sun spilling into the room through the leaves of the climbing vine, "I've never been truly happy before in all my life, and the reason is simply that I've never really worked! It's as though he paid me for being happy."

The cause of that remark was the monthly pay that she held in her hand, examining each bill with a smile of pleasure before she handed the whole to her mother. At this rate, they decided, it would not be long before they could go to the city, should they so desire. In the meantime, all was well on the ranch, and they were saving money much faster than they could ever hope to in a town where Mary might work as a clerk, at the best.

There was not even the strain of feeling that they were shamed in the eyes of their neighbors by their work as servants. Indeed, with the fine and truly Western spirit, the ranchers and their families made a point of going out of their way to prove to the Carvers that, although fallen in fortune, they were not despised. Mrs. Carver was the recipient of more calls than she had ever been in a similar period before. And the hearty good humor with which the whole Carver family met the new turn in their affairs only called forth the unstinted praise of man and woman throughout the mountains.

"The long and short of it is," Mrs. Carver said on this afternoon, "that Timothy Kenyon is a good man as well as a rich man. And if you're going to keep on being foolish and turning up your nose at Jerry Swain and his millions, there is no man in the world I'd rather see you marry than just such a man as Timothy Kenyon."

At this Mary Carver clasped her hands. "Good heavens, Mother dear!" she cried. "Good heavens!" And she turned a delightful pink from her forehead to her throat. "Why, he's old enough to be my father."

"Father, fiddlesticks!" said Mrs. Carver. "He's not more than thirty-five or thirty-six, if he's a day. His hair is white, but what of that?"

"Why," cried Mary again, "I wouldn't dream of such a thing! Why . . ."

"Humph!" her mother said with a shrewd look. Then she turned and pointed through a window on the other side of the room. "There he is now with Major."

"With Major," Mary repeated. "Oh, he's trying to steal my horse from me."

For Tom—now Timothy Kenyon—was standing by the corral feeding wisps of hay and wheat heads to the great black horse. Presently he left the stallion, walked to the far side of the enclosure, and whistled. Through the open window the notes fell faintly upon the ears of the listeners. The call brought Major whirling around on his hind legs, rearing in order to swerve the more quickly. And he rushed for the big man, halted as though his eyes gave other evidence than his ears, and then advanced and thrust out a nose that the new owner patted.

"Why," Mrs. Carver murmured, "doesn't that beat all? I never saw Major act as friendly as that with anyone other than you, Mary."

But here she found that Mary was sitting bolt erect with a face as white as it had been pink the moment before. "Oh," she whispered. "Who can it be? Who can it be?"

"What do you mean, silly girl? It's Timothy Kenyon. Who else? Mary, you'd make a mystery out of one-two-three. He's heard the whistle you learned from that terrible Tom Keene, that's all. He's heard you use that whistle, and now he's trying it himself."

Mary Carver sank back in her chair, but still she stared, fascinated. "I suppose that's it," she whispered, "and yet . . . look at Major now."

The great black horse had reached out with such deftness that he caught the sombrero from the head of the man, and now he tossed it and pretended to be on the verge of trampling it under foot as he galloped about the corral, but he ended by stopping in front of the man and letting him take the hat again. Mary Carver rose, crossed the room, and resolutely closed the window and drew the curtain.

"I know I'm foolish," she said, "but I . . . it's like seeing a ghost."

"A ghost of whom?" her mother cried sternly now. "A ghost of that Tom Keene . . . simply because a man has a bass voice and whistles to a horse? Besides, Mary, you have to stop remembering The White Mask, murderer and robber that he was. He carried you out of a well. Heaven bless him for that. But what other man wouldn't have tried to do as much?"

"I never speak of him," Mary said. "I haven't spoken of him for years."

"That's because you think of him the more and keep your thoughts to yourself, you strange girl."

But here Mary, her lips compressed, bowed her head and made no answer.

No matter what the courtesies that Timothy Kenyon had extended to his family of hired hands, he had not yet invited them to come into the big house to spend the evening with him. And it was on this very day that he broke the precedent, not by calling in the entire family, but by asking John Carver alone. Mrs. Carver prepared her husband for the eventful occasion.

"It means a lot, John," she assured him as she brushed his clothes. "It means that, if everything goes well, he may want us to move back into the old house. And then . . ."

"And then what?"

"And then if Mary and him . . ."

"What the devil do you mean, Lizzie?"

"Nothing," she said, smiling. And they looked at each other with infinite understanding.

Five minutes later, John Carver was seated opposite Kenyon at a table in the parlor of the ranch house, and he was shuffling the pack of cards that the rancher had pushed toward him. It had been almost too good to be true, the sight of those cards. In his day, John Carver had been a very good gambler, and, though he had never neglected his main trade of yegg and stick-up man, he had nevertheless turned some pretty deals. And at the sight of the pasteboards, even now his blood quickened, and the hands, which eight years of steady labor had stiffened, were suddenly made deft and limber.

Why should he not do a great deed this evening? Why should he not, if all went well, lift several cold thousand out of the swollen bank account of the rancher and transfer them to his own? At least he would make the effort. The game was of his own choosing—stud poker. At that game he was a master, and before midnight he had piled up $500 worth of chips on his side of the board.

After that, the rancher grew suddenly careless. He was becoming bored with the game, perhaps. There was too much effort for too little return. At any rate, he made a large bet against which John had to stake his winnings and month's pay in order to see the cards, and, when those cards were exposed, the card in the hole, which Carver could have sworn was a jack, turned out to be a ten, and a miserable two pair was thus converted into a full house. How it had happened that he made this mistake, John Carver could not see.

Carver left the table and excused himself while he went after more money. And on the way he decided that, after all, it was a good thing. Following this victory, the rancher would have a taste for the game. He could be drained far dryer than if he did nothing but lose.

In the cottage, he stole into his bedroom and

deftly, noiselessly extracted from the top bureau drawer the money that his wife had placed there—all his daughter's pay for the month, and all of the money that he himself had made, by small peculation here and there while handling the funds for the repair work on the ranch. It made no difference. In the morning the store would not only be replaced, it would be redoubled and more than redoubled.

When he returned to the ranch house, he found Kenyon yawning and talking of bed, and it required great dexterity for him to lead the rancher back to the game. In that, however, he succeeded, and luck, of course, again favored him. The money flowed smoothly into his hands, its steady course only halting infrequently, when Kenyon was dealing. An hour passed in this fashion before the big man became nervous again. And now, as before, he wagered the entire sum that Carver could muster.

This time there could be no mistake. That deck was a perfectly stacked one. He knew where every card lay. And the buried card of Kenyon's hand was a queen of hearts. In addition, there were exposed in that hand a king of clubs, a king of spades, a nine and a seven of diamonds. His own hand consisted of an ace in the hole and an ace exposed, with nothing else of the slightest value. But, when he called the big bet that Kenyon shoved to the center of the table, the buried card had been mysteriously altered from a queen of hearts to a king of the same suit—and three of a kind certainly beat a pair.

For a time he leaned staring at the result of the hand, utterly baffled. There was only one way in which that card could have been changed, and that was by the most consummate dexterity in palming. He raised his glance to the face of his host and stared fixedly. Had he been tricked and duped by a cardsharper? It seemed impossible. The whole course of the evening's play went to show that the rancher was utterly indifferent to victory or defeat, so far as the money was concerned. It was only the thrill of the playing of the hands that amused him. A rich man, decided John Carver, could well enjoy that thrill. Yes, impossible though it seemed, it must be that his eye had simply failed him. The queen of hearts had not fallen. It had been the king instead, just as it had been exposed. The certain proof that there had been no crookedness lay in the calm ease and steadiness with which the winner met his eye.

Afterward, when he had managed to mutter a half-stifled good night, and had escaped from the big house, John Carver paused with the cool of the night air against his face and attempted to see a way out of the dilemma. His wife must not waken in the morning and find their hoard gone. That much was plain. But how could he replace what he had lost?

Chapter Twenty-Three

It was the endeavor to answer that problem that brought him, hardly a half hour later, to the house of Jerry Swain. Once before, he had entered that house by stealth and at night. Now he entered again and, as before, went straight up to the room of Jerry, Jr.

A shaft of pale moon shine struck across from the window and fell upon the bed of the sleeper. John Carver wakened his man by touching his foot and stifled the exclamation with which Jerry wakened by presenting a revolver under his nose.

"Maybe you think," he began bluntly, "that I've forgot how you lied to me and fell down on me a month back at the sale. But I ain't forgot. I've come now to remind you."

It was a moment before the sleep cleared from the brain of Jerry, and the hysteria, also. He managed to stammer: "I . . . I've been wanting to explain ever since."

"And why haven't you?" asked John Carver. He eyed the other with cold displeasure. Only the fact that the past month had been the happiest one in years had kept him from acting upon his hatred for Jerry, Jr. And now he regarded Jerry with the roving glance of one who seeks out the place where he will strike the blow.

"I was afraid," Jerry said, trembling visibly, "that if I came to talk to you, you'd . . ."

"I'd start making a gun talk, instead, eh? And maybe I would've . . . and that's what I ought to do now. But the matter of fact is that I've made up my mind to change things around, Swain. Instead of you blackmailing me, I'm going to stick you up for a little hard cash. Swain, I'm not going to drain you dry the way that you've done me more'n once. I'm only going to ask you for a hundred and forty-five dollars. That's what I've got to have, and that's what I'm going to get out of you."

Jerry Swain swallowed twice. Then he managed to gasp: "John, I swear to heaven I haven't that much money."

"Then get it from your father."

"From my father!" His voice raised. It seemed that his hair stood up at the very thought. "Why, he'd kill me if he found me out trying to steal."

"Would he? Then he'd save me a job that I'm apt to have on my hands. And, whether he'd kill you or not, Swain, I'll have that money, or else you'll talk to me right here and now."

He was in a black fury. It set his voice shaking and quavering. And the eyes of Jerry rolled back in his head in his anguish of fear.

"I've got twenty dollars, Carver," he gasped. "That's all I've got. There's no way I can get any more unless I have the key to my father's safe downstairs. And I can't get that. He keeps it with him day and night."

"Gimme the twenty," commanded Carver.

Jerry climbed from the bed, produced the money, and handed it over.

"It was the limit that my father put on the bidding that kept me from buying the place. You got to know that I'm telling you the truth when I tell you that, Carver. Besides, you're not such a fool as to get me out of the way. If I'm gone, your last chance to have enough money to retire on is gone, because Mary will have to marry some poor man."

"Is Timothy Kenyon poor?" asked the other.

There was a gasp and a start from Jerry Swain. Only the day before his father had told him with bitter and biting scorn that some other man would win Mary Carver unless he acted quickly. And, in spite of his dread of the girl's father, he had come within an ace of riding over to the familiar place.

"What do you mean by that?" he asked.

"I mean what I say. He's acting mighty kind and smooth to all of us, Jerry. What's the reason for it? No reason that we can figure out except that he's made up his mind that he wants to marry our girl."

"It can't . . . how does she like him?" muttered the wretched Jerry.

"She sure likes him fine . . . a thousand times better than she ever liked you, Swain. He's a man, and she likes him for that." He continued, after a moment's pause to allow his contempt to sink into the other: "I'm going back now, Swain. I see it ain't any use trying to get you to squeeze money out of your old man, because, even if you're afraid of death . . . and the Lord knows I never seen one that was more afraid . . . you're worse afraid of him. I'm not going to waste time trying to collect back the thousands that you owe me. But one of these days, Jerry, we're sure going to have an accounting, unless you and Mary should happen to hook up together. You write that down inside that head of yours and keep thinking about it until I see you again. So long."

It was the sight of the $20 in his hand that changed the mind of John Carver, so that he began to think to himself: *There is still a way out before I collect in full from Jerry Swain.* To that thought, and to the feeling that, after all, Jerry might be destined to marry Mary Carver and bring prosperity to the family, the rich rancher's son owed his life.

The destination of Carver, as he rode hastily from the Swain house, was Porterville, and in Porterville he went to the gambling house of Will Jackson. On lucky evenings he had made $20, ere this, grow into far more than $150. But this night all luck was against him. The losses that he had sustained in his play against Kenyon, he never for a moment attributed to the dexterity of his opponent, but rather to a display of blind chance. But the losses that he met in Will Jackson's were unquestionably due to the manipulations of a sharper more skillful than he, for, with unspeakable bad fortune, the man who he picked as a gull who might be easily trimmed, turned out to be an expert dauber who dispatched John Carver's wretched $20 in five minutes' play.

A muttered curse was all that the loser could invest further in that game. He hastily left the table and mingled in the crowd around the roulette wheel as though about to wager there. As a matter of fact, he was only lingering in the gambling house until he could make sure who had won heavily during the night.

The scrupulous honesty that he had built up during his eight years of patient labor and suffering had completely broken down under the shocks of this single evening's misfortunes. He had determined to step definitely back into his rôle of The White Mask—for that night at least—and so regain what he had lost to Timothy Kenyon and enable himself to face his wife in the morning. His victim it was not hard to select. Just as every ball will, as a rule, show its belle, so every evening in a gambling hall is apt to produce one favorite of fortune who, so it seems, cannot lose. For one bright and brilliant evening he startles his fellows with a spectacular series of successes. Cards, roulette, faro—it makes no difference to what he turns his hand, he is invariably successful.

The thrill of that evening plants in him the germs of a lasting fever from which he can never free himself so long as he lives, and the view of his performances inspires every onlooker with the hope that he, too, will someday have just such a run of luck and make his clean-up.

On this occasion, in Will Jackson's gambling house at Porterville, the favorite of fortune was a stalwart young rancher, no native of the district, but a stranger from the south, whose winnings were all the more stinging because the chances were small that he would give Porterville an opportunity to win back from him what it had lost. Carver waited until he had printed in his mind all the necessary means of identifying his man, not only through his features, but by the outlines of his body, which was even more important on a moonlight night.

At length he left the hall and crossed the street, where he waited in the shadow of a wall until—for it was now 3:00 a.m. and even the most resolute gamblers were being worn out—the winner of the evening stepped out from the door of Will Jackson's, followed by a shout of farewell that was half envious cordiality and half a groan.

He took the saddle on a cow pony that stood under the shed to the left of the house, and trotted off down the street, to be quickly lost to view around the first turn. Then Carver ran to his own horse, mounted in haste, and pushed on in the same direction. He took a moderate pace until he was well out of Porterville, but then he spurred on at a sharp gallop, until the moon haze before him divided and the black form of the horseman he followed began to show through. The latter, as though feeling that the pursuer might be from Jackson's with either a message or else something that he had forgotten, turned his horse halfway around and waited for Carver to come up as soon as his ear caught the rapid poundings of the horse in his rear.

Carver had prepared his mask before. He now waited until he was comparatively close before he reached up under his hat and jerked loose the white handkerchief with great gaping eyeholes cut in it. At the same time, he saw that both hands of the winner of the evening were engaged, the one in holding his reins, the other in waving good naturedly to the approaching messenger. He saw the white mask too late. His startled cry had hardly left his lips, and his hand no more than started to dart back for his gun, when Carver was drawing rein in a pungent cloud of dust beside him, and the long blue barrel of the robber's gun was directed at him.

He had little fighting spirit. Up went his hands. In a few seconds he was stripped of all plunderable property, and he submitted with only stifled curses while Carver tied his hands securely behind his back, made him dismount, secured his feet in the same fashion, and left him, gagged and helpless, by the roadside. In the morning he would be found, unless a stray and hungry wolf happened upon the victim. But Carver needed peace and quiet in which to go back to the ranch.

He drove the horse of his victim far down the road. Then he turned in the opposite direction so that, if the plundered man had sat up to watch the direction of his flight, he would be able to draw no true deduction. Cutting across the fields, he struck back squarely toward the ranch.

It had all been so ridiculously easy—it had all been so perfectly safe—that he found himself chuckling and shaking his head in wonder to think of the wretched years that he had spent in poverty and honesty. This was not only the way out of his present small dilemma; it was also the way in which he could start to build a comfortable small fortune. No one would ever suspect the honest laborer whose eight years of patient work in the immediate past had guaranteed him. No one would suspect him, and in the meantime he could slip out at night—not too often, not more often than once a month, say—and strike down a carefully chosen victim. Within a few years he would be a comparatively rich man. And then he might be able to buy the improved ranch from kindly Timothy Kenyon. Or, at the least, he could buy a partnership with the latter. So old Carver Ranch would be once more established in the family.

He reached this point in his reflections and the home place at the same time. He had cut in from behind the house, and now he turned his mount loose, watched the cow pony obliterate all saddle marks with a luxurious, wallowing roll in the dust, and then started for the barn, carrying the saddle over his arm.

Only one more thing he had to do, and that was to get quietly into his bed without attracting the attention of his wife. But, even if she wakened, he could simply explain that he had been up with an attack of insomnia. Meanwhile, he could safely count his spoils.

Having hung the saddle on its peg, he sat down on his heels near the wall, spread the wallet upon his knee, and lit a match. The bills were laid out in a neat pile, packing the wallet thickly. Holding the match in his right hand, with the forefinger of his left he drew back the edges of the bills and counted. There was a $1,000—no, closer to $2,000! It was a better haul than he had dared to hope. The second match burned out. He would wait for daylight before he made an exact count. He would only take the $140 that he needed to replace his and his wife's savings. He reached out a third match to scratch it against the board, and, as he did so, something like a shadow fell across him—if there could be such a thing as a shadow in the complete darkness. Or rather, it was a chill that struck out at him like a breath of cold wind that went through and through his spirit. And he knew that someone was standing directly behind him, and had been standing there watching his count of the money.

Chapter Thirty-Four

Never before had his mind traveled so swiftly through so short a space of time. If he did not scratch the match, the man behind him would guess that he was discovered and would attack to kill, no doubt. If he did scratch the match, he would be furnishing the light by which he might be shot. He decided on a compromise. He scratched the match, but, as it flared into light, he allowed it to tumble from his fingertips, and then he put it out on the ground by fumbling for it— cursing softly as though in vexation. All this was to throw the watcher off guard and make him wait for the lighting of the next match.

But, the moment the match went out, the robber whirled and flattened himself sidewise along the floor, at the same time reaching for his gun. As he twisted to the side, he saw a huge indistinct form take shape in the darkness and fall from above him. The revolver came smoothly forth into his hand, but, before he could twitch the muzzle up, the body above him struck. A great weight knocked the breath from his lungs. Then tearing hands, with a force such as seemed hardly human, caught at him. One ground into his throat and throttled him. Another seized his right wrist and, having crushed it in a pressure like a twisted vise, turned and seemed to be burning the flesh loose from the bones.

The revolver slid out of his numbed fingers. There was a savage grunt of satisfaction above him, and then he was jerked to his feet. This time he could measure the height of his assailant. He was half paralyzed by the attack, but, as the hand relaxed from his throat and he was simply crushed back against the wall of the barn, an over-mastering horror swept across his brain. The rumbling voice that snarled at him, the immense bulk and strength of the attacker—all pointed far back in his memory to a man who would be quite capable of a brute ferocity such as this, and who would also have a motive for such an attack.

"Tom Keene!" he stammered. "Tom Keene . . . good Lord!"

"Yes," gasped the conqueror, "Tom Keene."

After that, stout John Carver was wet clay to be molded as Tom wished. The conviction of Tom Keene as The White Mask had been sufficient to put a headline in every paper in the state. But eight years was a long time, and the news of the pardon was carried only in small items that were not copied as yet in the little Porterville weekly sheet. To Carver, the big man was presented as one who had escaped from prison. If so, he would be careless of life and death, and, if he did not kill instantly, it was because he wished to torment his victim before the end.

A twist of rope, handled with wonderful dexterity, considering the dark, had rendered the hands of Carver helpless. Now a match was scratched, and, shielded in two huge hands, the light was thrown in a bright focus upon the face of the cringing rancher. Then a lantern was picked from the wall and lit. No sooner had the flame steadied in the chimney and the wide circle of light struck out around it, than Carver groaned in wonder and in dismay, for he saw before him not the handsome, black-bearded face of Tom Keene, but the white and worn features of Timothy Kenyon. And the whole strange truth burst upon the brain of Carver.

"I thought they'd strung it out . . . almost to a life sentence," he gasped.

"They did. But then I was pardoned. You should follow the newspapers more closely, Carver."

"I've been blind . . . blind," murmured Carver. And he watched Tom Keene scoop up the fallen wallet and the scattered bills. The big fingers of the man crushed home on the handful of money.

"Look here. I've got you as sure as I've got this money, Carver. Do you see?"

Carver nodded. It was beginning to dawn upon him that his life was not immediately threatened. He caught at the fresh hope silently. Or was it the prison that Keene was threatening? That must be it.

"I'm going to take this wallet and all that's in it into the house," he said. "There I'm going to write out a full statement of everything that's happened this evening. Then I shall seal the wallet with my statement and send it to my lawyer. With it go instructions to open the wallet if I should die in the near future. You understand, Carver? I'm not going to use this to put you in jail. It's simply a club that hangs over your head if you displease me. And, if you attempt to get rid of the danger by simply putting me out of the way, then you cut the string that drops the club on your head. Is that clear?"

Carver nodded. But still his eye was wild and wandering. "It's the same voice . . . and the same bulk . . . but you talk different. You talk like a schooled man, Keene."

"I've been schooled," Tom said, "in a place where one remembers one's lessons for a long time. But if you doubt that I'm Tom Keene, I'll tell you about the hillside where you lay after I shot you off the horse and . . ."

Carver put up his hand, and his tormented glance wandered from side to side, dreading that he might be overheard. "But you can't keep the money, Keene," he protested. "If you do, it makes you a partner in the crime. . . ."

"I'll find out tomorrow who you robbed, and I'll send him the exact amount he lost in fresh new bills. That clears me. In the meantime, Carver, you're my man. I've waited a month for this. I've managed to smile in your dog's face while I waited. But tonight the chance came. Did you think it was luck that changed the queen of hearts into the king of that suit? *Bah,* you fool. Your hands were so stiff that a child could have followed your tricks. And when I cleaned you out, do you think it was because I wanted the miserable money? No. It was to make you do exactly what you did . . . go out to take the coin at the point of a gun."

Carver turned livid with fear and hatred, but he could not speak. He saw with what far-sighted ease he had been trapped, and the more clearly he saw it, the more he dreaded the man he had injured so profoundly.

"I've told you what I want to tell you," said Tom. "Now you're free to go back to your bed. But mind you, Carver, I'm keeping this blow ready to drop. If you please me, you may go along pretty much the way you have been going. If you displease me, I send you up for robbery on the highway. And, to a man of your age, that means life. Now get out of my sight."

The other felt the touch of the knife that severed the ropes that bound his hands, and then he turned and stumbled for the door of the barn. Once in the outer night, the touch of the cooling wind struck his face like an inspiration. He hesitated, on the verge of turning to attack the big man even with his bare hands. But a moment of afterthought, and the burning of the bruised flesh on his wrist where the grip of Tom Keene had lain, made him change his mind. He continued toward the cottage, with the soft, deep laughter of Tom Keene mocking him from the darkness.

Carver knew not what lay before him. There were a thousand possibilities of torment with which the big man could make his days an agony. So full was he of the dread of the future that all smaller fears were as nothing.

He stumbled into his room. Instantly his wife was awake, and she turned up the flame of the night lamp that burned near the head of her bed. It showed her the face of her husband obscured by a gray mask of fear, his eyes glaring, his mouth compressed with his anguish.

"John, dear," she breathed. "What in heaven . . . why, John . . . ?"

The tenderness and the fear in her voice melted the last particle of his self-restraint. He dropped on his knees beside the bed and buried his face in the work-worn hands that she held out to pity him. "Lizzie," he said, "I got to talk. I got to talk. The whole truth is out. The whole truth."

"What?"

She started to a sitting posture on the edge of the bed, and she forced him to look up at her. So intent were they in their agony that they did not see the white-shrouded form of Mary coming to the door, for she had been roused by the noisy entrance of her father. She would have drawn back at once, but, as she turned away, she heard the next speech of her father, and it froze her where she stood.

It was impossible for Carver to tell the story slowly. It had to burst out in one heart-tearing sentence: "I lost all we made last month to Kenyon at cards, because that devil cheated . . . and then I went out and robbed a man to get it back, and, when I come home, Kenyon seen me with the money, and he has it now."

Mary Carver leaned against the wall, her head swimming.

"This Kenyon, he's been laying for us," went on John Carver. "He hates us, Lizzie. And he's been waiting till he could get me in his hand. You'll see a change in him tomorrow. He knows that he can send me up for the rest of my life. And you'll see a change in him. He can treat us like dogs from now on and . . . Lizzie, ain't you going to even look at me?"

"Oh, Lord," moaned the poor woman, "what have I done to deserve all this?"

Mary Carver stole away to her own room and sank on the floor where the moon shine fell through her window and there she prayed. She did not hear the answer of her father to Elizabeth Carver.

"It's a curse come on us," John Carver said, "for what we done to Keene."

The wife shrank away as though the words stung her to the quick.

"What has he to do with it?" she demanded fiercely. "And why d'you have to stir up all the torment in our lives and make us look at it this night? Ain't what you've just told me enough? But it makes my head go around like a windmill. The Lord alone knows what he gains by being able to keep the whip hand over you. D'you mean, John, that he's been kind to us all this month only waiting to . . . ?"

"He's Tom Keene," the husband said heavily.

"Who is Tom Keene? John, what's happened to you? Are your wits all gone? Who is Tom Keene?" She had risen now. She leaned above him and clutched his shoulders, shaking him as a teacher shakes a small boy to rouse his brain.

"It's Kenyon, don't you see?" he answered. He staggered to his feet and clumped over to sit inertly in a chair. "Don't you foller it, mother? Tom Keene . . . Timothy Kenyon? He got that white hair in the prison, and then he was pardoned."

A shrill moan from Elizabeth Carver stopped him. She had collapsed upon the bed with her face buried in her arms. And in this fashion and without changing their positions they lay and waited and waited while the night grew old and the deadly dawn light began to grow beyond the eastern windows.

Chapter Thirty-Five

There was one part of his bargain upon which Tom Keene had not counted, and this was revealed to him in the morning. His sleep had been short but unutterably sweet during the close of that eventful night, and he wakened to the daylight realization that the man and woman who had sent him to prison were now in the hollow of his hand. Just how he should dispose of them, he did not know. What immediately confronted him as a problem was the best method of extracting the maximum pain from them. With this in his mind, he bathed and dressed slowly.

But when he went downstairs, his brow still puckered in thought, he was greeted by an unexpected voice.

"Breakfast is ready," Mary Carver was saying. "It is waiting for you, Mister Kenyon."

Then he jerked up his big head and stared at her. She was an encumbrance, decidedly. His quarrel was with the mother and the father, and he had nothing to do with the offspring. He must get her out of the house in some manner. He had hardly noticed her during the month when he was laying his traps, but, now that he was ready to strike, he must have her gone. He studied her carefully. She was a trifle pale this morning, he thought. And there was a singular air of sadness about her.

Doubtless Carver had told his wife and daughter all that had happened. In such case, let it stand as it was. He would crush out the last feeling of pity that might linger in his heart for her. Because, after all, she was the daughter of the mother and the father who had conspired against him. She came of an evil line, and therefore she herself must be evil. Appearances were shallow; they amounted to nothing.

So he hardened his heart as he went into the dining room. And, as he began to eat, he was aware of her out of the corner of his eye where she waited in the shadow near the kitchen door. At first, she had taken up a white apron and her part as a servant with a sort of joyous enthusiasm as a new experience. And she had always appeared to Tom like an actress in a part—a $1,000-a-week actress in the part of a $5-a-week servant. There was an element of the ridiculous in the affair.

But this morning she fitted perfectly into her place. There was no longer any playing of a rôle. When he looked directly at her, he found her staring with wide, sad eyes straight before her. In spite of himself, that expression surprised him with a pain of misgiving. But he forced the emotion out of his head. What had he to do with the troubles of a girl? His business in life was to extract from a mature man and woman the same amount of pain that had been extracted from him by the professional methods of the prison. Then a great thought came to him. How could he better torment the parents than through the child?

He dropped his knife with a clatter and leaned back in his chair, full of a savage satisfaction. She had started forward a step at the clatter of the knife. Now, before she could retreat again, he summoned her by merely crooking his finger, not looking at her at all.

She came slowly before him and stood with her hands in front of her, the fingers interlaced gracefully, her eyes quietly upon him.

"Last night," said Tom, "your father talked to you?"

That question banished whatever color remained in her face. But still she did not flinch. He expected her voice to tremble. But it was perfectly even and smooth.

"No," she answered.

"What?"

She flinched now, but it was only from the sudden explosiveness of the word. "No," she said.

"Then what's the matter with you?" Tom Keene asked, pushing straight for the heart of the matter. "What's in your face? What's in your eyes?"

"I am sorry," said the girl. "If there's anything wrong with me, I'm sorry."

"There is," he declared, frowning. "There's enough trouble around without finding it on faces. Smiles are what I like to see. Will you remember?"

"Yes."

"Now tell me again. Your father didn't talk with you?"

"No. I overheard him . . . a little."

"Ah?" He struck his fist on the table. "I see that breeding will tell in one shape or another. Eavesdropping on your own father, eh? Because he came in late?"

She flushed with anger, then changed to wonder, as though she could not believe what her senses were telling her of this man who had been, for a whole month, so kind a master. But suddenly she controlled herself. She was as calm and grave as he had ever seen her.

She did not answer the insult directly, and he felt a pang of shame at his own brutality, but that feeling was quickly banished. "Go on," he said, "tell me what you heard. You've got a dead eye and a white skin. I want to know what you heard."

She winced and set her teeth. But still she made no audible protest. Only she passed through a silent moment of nerving herself before she could speak. When she managed it, she spoke very softly. "I heard him say," she said, "that he had . . . robbed a man . . . and that you knew about it . . . that you had taken what he . . . stole."

"That's all he said?"

She started and looked wildly up at him. "Is there more than that to know?"

He knew, at once, that the parents had decided

that she must not know more of the disgraceful truth than was unavoidable. Tom Keene smiled in his self-content. This was better and better. It was another whip with which he threatened the Carvers. If they offended in a small way, he would let the whole grisly story of betrayal be told. If they offended in a large way, it would be jail and disgrace in the eyes of the world for the man.

"That's enough, I guess." Tom nodded. "And what does that make you plan?"

"I don't understand."

"When, I say, are you going to leave them?"

"Leave them? Now that they need me?"

Tom considered her with mock enthusiasm. "That's good enough to have come out of a copybook," he said. "But don't lie to me. I want to know how long it will be before you leave this place and go off to change your name and forget the disgrace."

"I'll stay here," she said. "No matter what he's done, he's my father. No matter what others say, I'm not ashamed of him."

"No?" Tom said, fiercely disappointed as a hound is when the hare doubles back to a momentary safety through his very teeth. "No? That's more copybook talk. But what the devil good will you be to him?"

"I'll be one person who still trusts in him. That is a great deal."

"*Bah!* Comfort John Carver . . . you?"

"Yes, I."

"Well, that's charity. Charity and duty mixed up together, I suppose."

"No, no. It's love, Mister Kenyon. And if I put my trust in him, he surely will be happier. Don't you think so?"

It startled him so that he half rose from his chair, and then, settling suddenly into it, he ground it back a little from the table. "Don't ask me about it. But you're babbling Bible talk at me. Bible talk!" His tremendous laughter crowded the room. The morning light in the water in his glass trembled. Then he cleared his eyes to look at her again. Would she be indignant at his scoffing, or would she be filled with the holy zeal to convert him?

She was neither; she simply stood back a little into the shadowy corner and watched him quietly.

"Am I lost for laughing at the Bible?" he asked her.

"I hope not."

"Come, come. Hereafter I want smiles. But for one moment each day I'll let you tell me the truth. Tell the truth now. You hate me, eh? You wish me damned as black as coal."

But she only smiled and shook her head. And all at once he felt foolishly as if she had escaped from him, and as though his reach did not quite extend to her. He fell back upon another method.

"Go tell your father," he said, "that I want Major

saddled. Tell him I want the horse brought around to the front of the house at once."

"I'll saddle him myself. It's dangerous for anyone else to come near him with a saddle."

"You'll saddle him? You'll do what I tell you to do, if you please. Send your father . . . and then come back here. I may have need of you."

He lowered his eyes to his plate, prepared for the tremulous voice of protest and weeping. But, to his unutterable astonishment, she simply paused for an instant, and then went with a quiet step from the room.

Tom was so amazed that he waited a moment, thinking that she surely must come back, and, when she failed to do so, he rose from the table and stepped hastily to the window. And there he saw her already disappearing into the cottage. There was only a moment's pause. Then she came out again and walked slowly back toward the big house. An instant later her father appeared, whiter than death, and faced toward the corral where the great Major stood, shimmering and beautiful and terrible in his strength.

He had barely time to resume his place at the table when she was back with him in the room. He went on eating, humming to himself in his great bass voice. Truly this was a moment such as he could not have planned in detail. It was the result of an inspiration. Yonder at the corral, John Carver was about to risk his life saddling the great black stallion. At the cottage stood his wife with the horror of his danger striking her dumb. And here in the room with the tyrant who had brought all this danger on the head of Carver was the daughter, serving him and standing at the window through which she could see the peril of her father.

No wonder that Tom Keene smiled to himself and could not keep from humming. And across his mind there flashed a picture out of the past—how he had been locked in a small cell, a murderously small cell in which he could neither stand up nor stretch out on the floor, but in a wretched cramped position had to endure the hours of the torture on one scant portion of bread and water each twenty-four, and how, thrice daily, the crafty warden had had the great trays of food borne steaming past the prisoner.

That had been a torment such as he thought it must have been past the ingenuity of man to surpass. And yet he had a shrewd faith that the torture that he himself had contrived on this bright morning was not falling far short of the other. And his voice swelled in volume as he hummed, until it was like the murmur of a whole hive of prodigious, rumbling bees at work in the sunshine. But sometimes even a perfect thing can be made more perfect. In the parlor, in view through the opened sliding doors, he saw the piano.

"You play the piano?" he queried. Mary did not

answer for a moment. "I've heard your father say that you do. . . ."

"Yes," she breathed. "I play it sometimes."

"Let's have a tune now, if you please."

"I . . . if . . . ," she began, stammering.

"You're too modest," said Tom easily. "I'll wager you can sing, too, and accompany yourself. And what's a better way of beginning the day than with a song? Let's have a song, please, Miss Carver."

She hesitated for a bitter moment, and he turned in his chair. Her glance was out the window and fixed on some far-off subject with such desperate fear that it well-nigh drew Tom from his chair to run and look. But in a moment she was aware that he watched her expectantly, and she started toward the parlor.

And he saw, as she went past him, that there was no anger or revolt in her expression, but only profound pain and fear. He wondered at that. But now she was opening the piano—and now she sat at it. She was so tensed that even in this distance he could see her hand trembling upon the white keys.

"What shall I sing?"

"Anything," Tom said, and to himself he thought: *By the Lord, she's going through with it.*

An instant later a tremulous voice rose, quavered, and then steadied desperately into an air to which she kept a soft accompaniment stirring on the piano. It was a Scotch song; he had never heard it before. He could not have remembered a moment later what the words or the tune were, so great was his excitement. He simply knew that she was singing at his command while her father braved the stallion in the corral. Yes, if she turned her head, she would be able to look across the house, and through the dining room window she could catch at least a glimpse of the struggle.

Then, through singing, there broke the sharp, tearing sound of a horse's squeal of rage and fear. A stifled cry came from the girl as she rose from the piano. From the outside the scream of a woman was thin and small.

"Sit down!" commanded Tom sternly. "Sit down and keep on with the song!"

And then, like an answer to the girl's prayer, the shout of John Carver was heard, clear and strong, rolling through the open window. To Tom's own bewilderment, she sank back onto the bench before the piano and began again to play. Her voice quavered and struggled weakly, but at length she managed to strike the true note where her song had been interrupted. And she kept on to the end of the verse.

The song was hardly terminated when the snort and the stamping of a horse in front of the house announced that Major had been successfully saddled and was now waiting for the master. And there was a sob of relief in the stifled sigh of the girl.

"What shall I sing next?" she asked. "Or is that enough?"

"Enough?" Tom Keene said as he rose from the table and kicked his chair clear. "It's only a beginning. It's only a small beginning."

She winced away from him, but he strode on toward the door with a chuckle. At the hitching rack he found Major, stamping and frothing already from the excitement, and nearby was John Carver still shaking from his close call.

"Thanks," Tom said as he swung into the saddle. "I see that you and Major are going to get on."

He received only a glance of rage and terror from poor Carver. Then, as he turned toward the house, he saw Mary Carver stepping away from the window from which she had been watching him mount the stallion.

Chapter Thirty-Six

"Speaking of women," said Jerry Swain, Sr., at the breakfast table just one day later, "a woman waited for is a woman lost, I believe. Which reminds me that I haven't heard you speaking of Mary Carver lately. Not for a whole month, Jerry. And that means that you haven't been near her."

"How is that?" queried the son, not unwilling to

put off the embarrassing question for a moment while he combed his wits for an excuse.

"Why," said the father, "there are some women who drive a man to cursing, and the best we can do by most of them is to be silent . . . but now and then there is one who makes us talk . . . turns us into poets. They are few and far between, but they shine like stars at night, Lord bless 'em. And such a one is Mary Carver. When you have been to see her, you come home raving. You find her face in the fire. You draw it in the empty air." He dropped down from this rather elevated strain with a sigh and a frown. "And I wonder, Jerry, why in blazes you don't keep on in the only business that you and I agree upon? You can break your heart for the sake of a gambling table, and you can groan for the sake . . ."

"No gambling to amount to anything for a long time, you know," protested Jerry, Jr., anxiously.

"Don't lie to me," he father answered a little wearily. "I have to watch you, Jerry, and I know that you've played off and on pretty steadily during the past seven years or more. And I also know that you've lost pretty steadily. Where you've got the money to pay your debts, I don't know, unless you've persuaded your friends to wait for the old man to pass on."

"Father!" cried the son in righteous horror.

"Bah!" snorted Jerry, Sr. "If they wait for that, they'll wait a long, ripe time! But we'll skip over

that. We'll come back, if you please, to lovely Mary Carver. Why haven't you been near her all these days?"

"I've been busy," Jerry, Jr., said. "Ever since you gave me that southwest section to farm I . . ."

"Blast the half-section! If farming interferes with the only good job you're ever apt to do in your entire lifetime, I'll sell the place. No, Jerry, my boy, why she will look at you twice, I can't tell. But, if she'll tolerate you, you may consider that as an entering wedge to be followed up by assiduous pounding. Yes, sir, constant attention is what wins 'em, unless you have the brains for a sudden flash of fire and enthusiasm that will carry them off their feet. And you and I both know that you haven't the brains for that, so why waste time talking about it? Come, come, why aren't you at the Carver place every day of your life?"

The half-contemptuous, half-patronizing tone that the stern old fellow adopted toward his son was the one, after all, which Jerry, Jr., was glad to hear. He knew that the rest of the rancher's scale embraced invective and terrible sarcasm, and that these weapons were ever sharp and in store for use.

He had intended, however, to go back to the pursuit of Mary Carver on that very day, and he had only been held back by the constant fear of John Carver. For, when the report went the rounds of the countryside that a heavy winner at the gambling hall in Porterville had been robbed on the road just outside of the town by a man wearing a white mask, he guessed at once that Carver had done the work to gain the money for which he had asked Jerry previously on that very night.

He assured his father, therefore, that this very day would see his return to the courting of Mary, and he had no doubt that he would soon be able to press the matter through to a satisfactory conclusion. When he had finished his little speech, the rancher continued: "Because, if you take much longer, Jerry, we'll have to look elsewhere."

"Elsewhere?" exclaimed Jerry in the greatest alarm.

"I'm getting along in years," the father said. "As a matter of fact, I'm failing rapidly. I have three diseases, the least of which would kill me within three years, my boy."

"The devil!" gasped Jerry.

The old man stiffened and regarded his son with fiery eyes. "Your heart is pained for me, I see," he said dryly. "But no matter for that, Jerry. The point is that I have not long to overlook your affairs and mine, and I shall certainly see you married to a wife you'll stick to before I die. And I intend to see that you'll stick to her by settling half of the estate on your first born. So, in short, we'll give you ten days from this morning for winning the promise of Mary. Ten days from this morning, and not a day longer. After that, we'll ask Colonel

Winwood and his daughter Estelle to spend a month with us. Mary Carver would be a glorious victory, but Estelle would be well enough as a match."

Jerry, Jr., remembering the withered face and the oversweet smile of Estelle Winwood, sighed. He pondered over an answer, a plea for more time, but he knew that his father, having announced a decision, would abide by it at all costs. That was his way. What he said with a smile, he abided by to the end of time. In short, that little quiet speech was nothing more or less than an ultimatum. Within ten days he should bring back the promise of the girl to marry him, or else he must take as a wife a girl who he detested.

That danger sent him into the saddle as soon as the breakfast was over, and at a hard gallop he went toward the Carver Ranch. He reached there before midmorning and went at once to the cottage behind the main house, for, though he had been very little around Carver Ranch during the last month, he had heard of the change in quarters.

But he was by no means prepared for the change that confronted him in Mrs. Carver as she answered his knock. Twenty-four hours had sufficed to plant a ghostly look of dread in her eyes. Her color was altered. Her very carriage was bowed. Her step, when she moved back to permit him to enter, was faltering and uncertain, and in her movements and her looks she was the very picture of one who has been recently unnerved by some horror.

So greatly was Jerry Swain impressed by this that he even forgot for a moment his own motives and reasons for coming. He was genuinely concerned.

"What on earth has happened?" he asked. The answer struck him dumb.

"He knows everything. Timothy Kenyon is Tom Keene."

When he could speak, he answered: "Does Mary know?"

"No, thank heaven for that. All she knows is that poor John held up young Crofton."

"It was Carver, then?"

"Aye. He had to have the money. Tom Keene had tricked him out of our savings of the month. And now he has John at his mercy, and he's torturing us, all three."

"All three?"

"Mary, too."

"The devil!"

"He's a devil, a cold, calculating devil. He'll kill John with the dread and the worry inside of a month. Look at him now."

There was a sound of a foot crunching in the gravel of the path around the cottage. John Carver appeared, gave only a sullen glance to the younger man, then pushed past into the house.

"He ain't closed his eyes for a wink of sleep. He's sure going mad," said the poor wife. "Not even Mary can get a smile out of him. Oh, Jerry Swain, in the name of heaven, what can we do?"

A great light fell upon the brain of Jerry Swain. It caused him actually to spread his feet farther apart and thrust his hands deep into his pockets and fight to restrain a smile. "Missus Carver," he said, "there is one way to reach any man in the world."

"How is that?"

"Every man has his price."

"But Tom Keene is rich now. No one knows where he got the money, but money he has to burn."

"He was pardoned?"

"Yes. Maybe he bought them off."

"Rich or poor . . . every man has his price. And there is one way that price can be offered to Tom Keene. . . ."

"But I tell you, money won't do. He wants to grind us down. He wants to make us pay in suffering for his time in the prison. He has no heart. We showed him no mercy when he was here before. Now he'll show us none."

"Still you're wrong," said Jerry Swain. "I'm not speaking of a few thousand. I'm speaking of enough money to offer such a price for the ranch that he'd have to take it and move away and leave you here unexposed. And there's only one person in the country rich enough to offer the money. That's my father."

"No good for us. He has no use for John."

"But he has for Mary . . . he'd pay high if I could marry Mary. I'll tell you, Missus Carver, the thing would be for me to marry her, and then let him know afterward the scrape that John is in. That would make him curse, but, when he got through cursing, he'd bring out his checkbook and start signing checks. I know him. There's no quitter about him."

"Jerry . . . Jerry Swain . . . oh, are you speaking truth to me?"

"I tell you, there's only one thing in the way, and that's Mary's consent. I'm going to get onto my horse again and ride up the road. You send for Mary. Tell her the truth. Tell her how fond of her I am. I know she doesn't love me, but I think she likes me well enough, and I can make that grow into a real love one of these days if I have a chance. Tell her these things but, first and last and all the time, make her understand that, if this doesn't happen, there's no way to save her father. You see, Missus Carver," he added with an attempt at humility that was entirely graceless, "I know that it's wrong to force her into a wedding in this fashion. But in the end, also, I know that she'll be happier."

"You really think Tom Keene would give up . . . ?"

"Give up his chance of tormenting you and

Carver? Of course he would. For a clear profit of twenty or thirty thousand dollars, such a man would give up anything. Isn't that true?"

The great sum dazed her. "Would your father pay as much as that to get rid of him?"

"Twice as much as that, if he had to. Now get Mary and tell her what I've told you. I'm not going to stay here to bargain. But I'll come back in half an hour for her answer."

He went out to his horse and, a moment later, had cantered out of view around the next hillside. No sooner was he gone than Mrs. Carver rushed for the house. There, in the kitchen, she found Mary busy scrubbing pots and pans. She dragged her daughter to the window, a trembling hand on either shoulder of the girl, and held her so that the light flooded upon her face.

"Mary, Mary, Mary," she whispered. "There's a chance in your hands to save your father . . . to save all of us from shame. Oh, child, listen to this word from heaven . . . it's no less than that."

And she stammered out, in short and confused sentences, all the plan as Jerry Swain had laid it before her. Not until she had ended did Mary speak, and then it was a low-voiced wail of despair rather than a refusal.

"But I don't love him, Mother. I never can."

"Love?" her mother cried fiercely. "Is this a time to be talking about such foolishness? It's the life and the death of your father that I'm asking you to think about. Mary, will you mind that and stop thinking only of yourself? Oh, if ever you want my blessing, and if ever there's a reward coming to me for bringing you into the world, Mary, tell me now like a good girl that you'll do this."

Poor Mary, beset in such a way she could not turn, raised her head and looked out through the window. Far away she saw the towering outline of black Major, with the new master passing over a hill. She watched him out of sight.

"I have to say yes," she said. "Heaven forgive me for it."

"Heaven forgive you?" exclaimed her mother. "Heaven will reward you for it."

"You don't understand," answered the girl sadly. "You can't understand. But . . . I'll do it, and that's enough. When . . . when do I have to see him?"

Chapter Thirty-Seven

Astonished, Tom Keene drew rein, and Major came to a jog trot. It was the sound of a man's voice singing in the cottage near the big ranch house that had startled him. It could not be, he told himself, that John Carver was actually singing on this day of all days. But, listening for a moment, full recognition of the voice came to him.

With an oath, anger and bewilderment alive within him, he sent Major on at full speed again.

Crossing in front of the cottage, he struck the butt of his quirt heavily against one of the pillars of the little porch.

"Carver!" he called.

The singing ceased. Presently steps hurried to the door, which was opened by Carver himself, a rather dim figure in the gathering hour of the dusk.

"You're feeling better today, Carver, eh?" asked Tom.

"I was singing an old song my wife used to like," Carver muttered in answer.

Tom swung to the ground and tossed the reins to the other. "Take Major and put him up. Maybe you'll feel like singing to him. What the devil has happened to you? Have you found or inherited a fortune?"

"Is there anything wrong in singing?" Carver asked, half sullenly and half in fear. As he spoke, he gingerly fixed his grip on the reins and regarded the great stallion in dread.

Tom Keene watched him for a moment, then turned and strode for the house. He rounded the corner in time to see the kitchen door open and Jerry Swain, Jr., come out of the door and down the steps from the rear verandah to the ground, whistling and swinging the riding crop that he affected instead of the usual quirt used in that cow country. Tom regarded him with a start of surprise and detestation. From the day of his first encounter with the fellow over eight years before until now, he had heard no good of him. The narrow, handsome face and the small eyes, set close together and giving a fox-like look to his countenance, were indelibly connected, in Tom's recollection, with the hold-up after his first winning in the gambling house of Will Jackson at Porterville. As he hailed him now, he thought of the mingled knavery and cowardice that Swain had shown on that occasion.

At the sound of his voice, Swain whirled sharply on his heel and even jerked back his right hand in a gesture that unmistakably showed that he was carrying a concealed weapon on his hip. Plainly he was not expected back until dark. In fact, he had announced when he left at noon that he would be late on the road and had left orders for a dinner served accordingly. That was the reason he had overheard Carver's song, that was the reason he now saw Swain leave the house.

The smaller man waited uneasily, not at all sure of the reception that he would receive. But Tom put him instantly at ease with a cordial handshake.

"The first time we met," he said, "we were taking opposite sides of a question. I hope we'll get on better now."

Jerry Swain hoped that they would. He wished that everything might prosper with Mister Kenyon. In the meantime, he would be late home unless hurried.

"But why hurry?" asked Tom. "Dinner will be

ready here in half an hour. And I see that you've been with Mary, peeking at her dishes, no doubt before they were cooked. But if you've seen them already in the oven, wait to see them again on the table."

Jerry Swain hesitated, glaring anxiously at his formidable host as though he wanted to escape, but also as though he felt that he must curry the favor of the big man.

"The only place I could see Mary was in the kitchen," he declared, "she was so busy there. As for staying . . ."

The suspicions of Tom were instantly sharpened. "Tush," he said, "you must stay. I have grown lonely here for an entire month. Come in. Besides, I have some old whiskey left over in a corner of the cellar from a better day."

His joviality had already produced a mellowing effect. But the mention of the liquor was a conclusive point. And up the steps they went, chatting like the best of friends. In five minutes they were safely established with glasses and a black bottle, and at the second drink Jerry Swain's tongue was loosened, exactly as Tom had known it would be.

The air of constraint vanished, and they sat in an atmosphere of good fellowship. It was agreed that Jerry was to stay for dinner. The moment that agreement was reached, Tom called for Mary, and she came in to them.

"Another place for tonight at the table," he requested. "Mister Swain is staying."

Mary turned with a wan, joyless smile toward Jerry Swain. And after that acknowledgment of his coming, she looked back to Tom with lackluster eyes. The big man studied her keenly. He had seen her in the bitterest trouble for the past month, and yet he had never seen an expression of such suffering in her face. He could not avoid connecting her sadness with the coming of Swain.

When she was gone, he turned the talk, however, on other subjects, and he began to ply Jerry with liquor. It was not raw-edged moonshine, but old stuff as smooth as oil and of a deceptive strength. Jerry was decidedly mellow before they sat down at the table, and throughout the meal Tom plied him with well-regulated care. He was drinking himself, and an equal amount, but his mind was working ceaselessly, and the alcohol had no apparent effect.

It was necessary that he draw out the truth about Jerry Swain's visit to Mary Carver. He waited until the soup that began the meal was gone, and until the slender white hands of Mary had brought the meat. The edge of Jerry's appetite was gone by that time, and he was ready for words. Tom opened the subject deftly.

"A good cook," he declared, "is like a good artist . . . she's born, not made. There's Mary Carver, now, for an example. So far as I can make out, she was raised to be the lady of the family, but, when the pinch came, see what she's done."

It needed no more than that to tap the floodgates of Jerry Swain's emotions. "Cook?" he exclaimed. "Mister Kenyon, when you speak of her, you speak of my future wife!"

And the last words fell upon the ears of Mary as she entered from the kitchen bearing another dish. Such was the alcoholic enthusiasm of Jerry Swain that he would have started up from the table with a fervent address had not the gloomy look of Tom Keene held him a little in check. When she had passed out again, he resumed his eloquent praise of her.

She possessed, he declared, every virtue. Her loveliness was beyond compare. And upon this subject he quoted a man who he vowed to be always infernally right, namely his own father.

"But," interrupted Tom, "I fail to see, Mister Swain, how you are entitled to such a wife as she."

"Entitled to her?" Swain said, almost sobbing with self-denunciatory enthusiasm. "Why, I'm not entitled to a single smile from her. I'm not worthy of looking at her. But luck is behind me . . . luck and the old man. And the old man always has his way. The devil and the deep sea combined couldn't beat him. He's a known man, is old Jerry Swain. A dozen of the hardest have tried to down him one time and another, but he's always come back to the top like a cork, and they're the ones who have gone down in the end. Well, sir, it's he who wants me to marry Mary Carver now, and, because he wants it, it has to happen. He's succeeded in everything else he's ever undertaken, and now he says that the rest of his life will be failure unless he gets me married to please himself. You understand?"

Only too well the big man understood. His prey was about to slip through his fingers. The marriage of Mary would withdraw her, and at the same time it would put in her hands an enormous weapon to use for the benefit of her parents. Money, Tom knew only too distinctly, was a power that could evade danger of a thousand sorts. His own fortune had taught him that. But what was his own fortune compared to the great wealth of Jerry Swain? It was a mere nothing. To make sure of John Carver's destruction, he must make sure that this marriage did not take place. He went steadily ahead in his brutal campaign.

"I say again," he said, "that she's very much too good for you, Swain."

The fact that he was being insulted gradually filtered to the inner intelligence of young Jerry. In an instant he was in an ugly, half-drunken rage. But the cold voice of Tom went on: "Swain, if you were simply a gambler and an idler, you might do. But not as a highway robber. That, certainly, will never do."

All the fumes of alcohol were suddenly swept from the brain of the other as a broom sweeps cobwebs clear. He peered at Tom with a working face of dread. He attempted to speak. And yet he could not continue. Even though the identity of Tom had been revealed to him by Mrs. Carver, he had hoped against hope that his own indiscretion of eight years before could not be used against him. Now he saw those hopes shaken and on the verge of disappearing.

"Highway robber?" he echoed.

But here the face of Tom smoothed suddenly as the door from the kitchen opened and Mary Carver entered. He turned the talk away. And Swain, realizing that he must not show his horror to the girl, managed to force a laugh. So she disappeared again, and Tom leaned forward once more. Jerry Swain was a thoroughly sobered man by this time. He realized that he had talked too much.

"Keene," he said, "what do you want?"

"Ah," sighed Tom, "that was what I hoped for. I simply wanted you to admit, in the first place, that you know me. In the second place, Jerry, I want you to remember that the club that I hold over John Carver . . . oh, I know well enough that they've told you . . . is the club that I hold over you!"

"Good Lord!" cried Jerry Swain. "You'll try blackmail?"

"I'll try anything."

308

"But it's eight years ago that I . . . Keene, no court in the world would believe that you'd keep silent for eight years about such a thing."

And Tom Keene knew that he was perfectly right. It was only by the power of physical fear and, more than that, sheer bluff, that he could control Jerry Swain.

"You're a fool," he said calmly. "I've waited because I had no way in which I could use you, Swain. But things have changed. I can now use you very neatly, and I intend to. You shall not marry the Carver girl, my friend. You hear me? You shall not marry her."

Jerry Swain sat gaping at him, left hand resting on the edge of the table and twitching violently. If ever there were murder in the eyes of a man, Tom was seeing it now in the eyes of Jerry Swain. But he saw a greater thing, a controlling fear, also.

"In affairs like that," Swain said, "one man can't control another. You ought to know that, Keene. You can't stop me from marrying Mary Carver. Even if I were to go to prison the next day . . ."

"You would," Tom said slowly and heavily. "You certainly would."

"Why in the name of heaven . . . ?" began Jerry.

But his host interrupted him. "Why I'm going to do it," he said, "is something you can guess when you have a chance to think. But the important thing for you to know, Swain, is that I'm a man who is determined to have his own way in the matter. You can't put me aside or alter me. My mind is made up and is as fixed as stone. I'm going to crush the Carvers, root and branch. I'm going to smash them, Swain. And here you are going to help me. Sit down."

This last was called forth by the hasty rising of Jerry from his chair as though he would seek refuge in flight—anything to avoid facing the deadly eyes and the low, muttering voice of Tom. But he slumped back at once and sat, half cowering in terror, half crouched in rage, and Tom guessed, and guessed correctly, that if his own head turned for the slightest part of a second the slender hand of Jerry Swain would fly for the revolver on his hip. For what could be easier than to avoid any ill consequences from the shooting of an ex-criminal such as he? No court would convict him.

But not for a moment did his glance waver from the evil and contorted features of the rich rancher's son.

"Look me in the eye, Swain," he ordered. "I've gone through eight years of a pretty steady torment. Do you think I'll let you stand between me and the Carvers now? No, no, man. Think again. I'll break that expensive back of yours first. You hear?"

Jerry gasped and winced back. It was impossible for him to think of gun play now. His hands were trembling far too much.

"When she comes in next, Swain," went on Tom, "I'll tell you what you're going to do. You're going to say to her . . . 'Mary, I've been talking to Mister Kenyon, and I've changed my mind. I can't marry a cook.'"

"Say that to her? I'd rather have my tongue torn out."

"That's what you think now. But you'll think otherwise in a moment. If you don't, at the least I'll turn in what I know about you to the sheriff tomorrow. That's the least, and that least means arrest and jail for you."

"It means exposure of you as a jailbird, also."

"What is exposure to me, Swain? It's nothing. I only assumed a different name so that I could get the Carvers into my power. Now the name means nothing to me. But to you, Jerry? What would your father say if that arrest should take place?"

Jerry Swain started in his chair, and his eyes became as bright as the eyes of a cornered rat.

"Keene," he said, "you devil . . . you fiend."

"But more than that," Tom said. "If you should fail to say to her what I've told you to say, you would have an immediate reckoning with me, Swain. And that might be worse than facing your father, even."

Jerry Swain stared at him with eyes so eager that they would have pierced to the meaning behind a mask, but Tom Keene, trained in the deception of prison guards, trained by living a lie for five years, a lie from which he never deviated a step, presented an unreadable face to him.

And, before Swain could speak again, Tom poured a brimming glass of whiskey and pushed it toward his guest. "Drink!" he commanded.

Automatically the other obeyed. The whiskey disappeared. And, as though at a signal—as though this were her cue to come out upon the stage—Mary entered from the kitchen. The lifting of Tom's forefinger furnished the signal, and then, as though infuriated by the predicament in which he found himself, Jerry Swain grew spotted white and red with rage. It gave a wonderful reality to his tone and to his words.

"I've been talking things over with my friend, Mister Kenyon," he said, "and I've made up my mind, Mary, that I can't marry a cook. I suppose you'll understand."

Chapter Thirty-Eight

In justice even to Jerry Swain it must be said that he had no sooner spoken than the full horror of what he had done rushed upon him. He scowled down at the table, then reached hastily for the bottle and filled himself a glass of whiskey unbidden.

Tom Keene glanced with grim satisfaction at Mary Carver. She had halted in the middle of the floor, but, as the meaning of the words of Jerry

Swain reached her, it seemed to Tom that her first reaction was one of astonishment, then joy. Only after this did she feel shame.

When she had gone out again, Jerry Swain pried himself up from the table, resting heavily upon his hands. The whiskey had all at once taken possession of him. His face was bestial.

"This isn't the end," he declared. "You and I will settle this account later on. My father . . . he'll take a hand . . . and then . . ." He could no longer speak, but, turning away, he stumbled for the door.

And Tom, following lest the other should turn around as soon as he was in concealment and attempt a shot from behind, saw his victim stagger down the steps, drag himself up the side of his horse, and slump heavily forward in his saddle. No sooner had the dark of the night closed behind his form than Tom turned back to the table and rang the bell for Mary Carver.

She came at once and stood just inside the door. Plainly she had spent the interval in thinking hard upon the probable consequences of what Jerry Swain had just done, for now she was whiter than ever, and that wretched, haunted look was in her eyes. Tom motioned her forward, and she came a little closer before she halted, always with her eyes fastened upon him in dread.

He observed this without concern. That he was being brutal in the most vicious sense of the term did not at all disturb him. What was of importance in his estimation was simply that he had succeeded in reducing her to the proper state of subjection, and that he could now use her as a tool at his will. Also, he felt he had turned the first great counterattack of the enemy with the most consummate skill. He had made Jerry Swain destroy himself.

"I'm sorry," he said to her, "but a man can't prevent his guests from making beasts of themselves. I'm sorry that Swain hurt you. You can be sure that he'll never have the opportunity to do so again."

She did not answer. She merely watched him. And that quiet watching seemed to Tom more eloquent than words. He would see that terrified and horrified glance again, he was sure; he would see it in his unhappy dreams. And yet there was an unfathomable patience about her. It was as though she had some resource of strength that was hidden away from the observation of the world, but that was nevertheless real.

"You can talk out to me," he said. "I know you want to talk. Then tell me what's going on inside your mind. Did you ever dream that there was a man in the world low enough to conceive such a thing . . . to jilt the woman he was engaged to at the table of another man? Tell me, Mary, did you dream that there were men of such caliber in the world?"

She still paused. Her glance went down to the floor, then flickered up to him. "I might as well tell you now," she said. "When you sit on this side of the table . . . where you are now . . . the other side of the room acts as a sounding board. And it throws the sound of every voice clearly in the kitchen. I heard you tell him what to say."

That was all. She spoke without raising her voice. She spoke apparently without malignant hatred. Yet, Tom felt as though he had been struck on either cheek with a light but stinging hand, so hot was his flush.

"I had a reason for it," he said gloomily, to justify himself. "I had to make him show you what a hound he is. Good Lord, Mary, you couldn't be married to a fellow like him. It would be absurd. There's more manhood in five minutes of you than in five years of Jerry Swain. And that's why I made him break with you. But what will you do when he comes cringing and crawling to you and trying to make up?"

"I don't think he will," said the girl.

"You don't?"

"I do not."

It thrilled him strangely to hear her talk. "Come," he said, "sit down here at the table and tell me what is going on in that strange mind of yours. Sometimes I feel that you're not thinking or feeling at all. But then, again, something like this happens and makes me know that you are thinking, thinking, thinking, all the time. Sit down."

She moved hastily to obey him. But she paused before she sat down. "It will be much better for me to stand here," she told him.

He did not insist. "Tell me why you think he won't come back?"

"Because," she answered, "cowards are ashamed to show that they are cowards."

"Cowards are . . . By heaven, that's deep." He leaned his heavy head upon his doubled fist. "You see he's a coward, well enough. But cowards are proud. Yes, that's true. They're proud. They dare not allow themselves to believe that the world knows what they are. So you're sure about it? He won't come back to you?"

"I think not."

"But if he did come back . . . a yellow-livered hound such as he's proven himself . . . what would you do then, Mary?"

"Go with him," she answered without the slightest hesitation. "I should follow him if he came to me."

"What? Follow him? You'd do that? Why, Mary, life with him would be torture for a proud, brave girl like you."

"There are others to think of," she said. "There are others to whom I owe a great deal."

"Your mother and father, eh? You would marry him. And then, through his father's money, they would be saved from me. Is that the way your thought runs?"

And she astonished him beyond measure by replying with the most perfect calm: "Yes."

It actually brought him up out of his chair, and he went around the table with great strides until he stood before her and towering above her.

"What the devil do you mean by that, Mary? What do you think I am here for?"

She did not answer, but neither did she wince. She faced him steadily, her eyes held firmly upon his. He could not press that question home, and he reverted to another.

"You'd go with him . . . and yet you don't love him, Mary."

"No."

"I can't make you out. It's blasphemy for you to marry a man you don't love."

She did not answer. He felt that he could only drag words from her now and then. And he felt, also, the ceaseless movement of her brain, weighing him and judging him and seeing through and through him.

"The whole truth is," he guessed suddenly, "that you are already in love. Is that it?"

"Yes." Once more she shocked him with astonishment.

"You are? In the name of . . . how long have you been?"

"For several years."

"For several years? Something carried out of your girlhood, then? Someone of whom you have never told a soul?"

"I have never spoken of him . . . only to you."

"Not even to your mother?"

"No."

"Then why is it you tell me?"

"Because it is better that I should tell you everything I can."

"That will make it easier when things come up that you can't tell me?"

"Yes."

He fell back a half pace so that he could study her with greater care, but she baffled him still further. There was a thousand times more to her silence than he had been able to guess. His imagination began to reach at the truth about her in great strides, but still he fumbled vaguely and could not be sure. Only he felt that there was something unique in her, something that no other woman in the world possessed.

"In the old days," he said at length, "you would have been a martyr, I guess. You would have been one of those who died singing . . . at the stake. That's all."

He dismissed her with a wave and went out under the stars. He could not have remained another moment in that room without pain.

Chapter Thirty-Nine

It was a sobered and trembling Jerry Swain that reached his home later that night. In the first place, he had never arrived at a point of drunkenness so complete that he did not realize what would happen if his father saw him in such a condition. Not that the stern old rancher was a teetotaler, but he despised beyond measure those who could not put a limit upon their desires for food and drink.

So he had diverted his horse from the home road and gone on a roundabout way. Before he had ridden half an hour, he dismounted beside a trough and put his head under a faucet. This refreshed him, and, when he rode on, the water, evaporating from his head and face, cooled him wonderfully.

Only one grisly danger faced him, and that was that he had to encounter his father before he went to bed. It was an old rule and an inviolable one in the Swain household that, no matter how late he came home, he must say good night to his father. He could not shrink from it. Moreover, Jerry Swain, Sr., was quite apt to be up, for, as age and disease rapidly weakened him, and as he was in constant pain, he dreaded the loneliness and the long anguish of his bed and cut his portion of sleep shorter and shorter. And still to the very last he was clinging to the regime that, in the opinion of his preceptor, was to make him die a cultured man even if he did not live to enjoy that quality. Therefore, he stole long and vitally needed hours from his sleep and gave them to his study. And here it was, in fact, that his son found him on this dreadful night. He strove to pass off the meeting casually.

He simply opened the door, depending upon the distance and the dimness of the lamplight to veil his face from his father, and upon the great effort that he made, to cover any inequalities in his voice.

"Well, sir," he said, "here I am back. Nothing important to report, though. Besides, I'm horribly fagged. I'll tell you about the trip in the morning, if you don't mind."

"Certainly, Jerry," his father said kindly. "Good night."

"Good night," breathed Jerry.

He closed the door, feeling that heaven had interceded for him. But, even as he closed it, he heard the small, sharp voice calling: "Jerry! Oh, Jerry!"

It was the breathless quality of the tone in which he said—"Good night."—that caught the watchful ear of the other. He opened the door once more, grinding his teeth. Then he mustered himself for a strong effort.

"Well, sir?" he asked cheerily.

He found that his father, suspicious, was sitting erect in the chair, but, at the sound of that cheerful, steady voice, he sank back again. But still he glared from beneath knitted brows at his son.

"Did you see Mary?" asked Jerry Swain, Sr.

"Yes. But in the morning . . ."

"Well . . . ," began the father.

And then something caught his eye. It did not make him sit up, but he settled even deeper into his easy chair and with a gesture bade the younger man approach. Jerry, Jr., with a feeling that the greatest crisis in his life was upon him, went slowly, slowly across the room. And still he acted a part as well as he could. He covered a yawn.

"Tired out from riding all day and talking," he remarked through the yawn, and he dropped his hands upon the back of a chair and rested there, directly in front of his father but, in a cunningly chosen position, deeply buried in shadow.

The long, lean-fingered hand of Jerry Swain, Sr., went out and lifted the shade from the lamp. At once the son shrank from that blasting, betraying flood of radiance. He knew, as he bowed his head, that his father had seen the stains where the water had dripped across his coat and shirt, and that the cool eye of the old man had dwelt upon the tousled, uncombed hair. He was lost, utterly lost. And he waited for the blow to fall. To his amazement, the shadow rushed again over him as the shade was replaced on the lamp. He heard his father saying, almost gently: "Sit down, Jerry."

He slumped into a chair, more unnerved by surprise and anticipation than he would have been by the actual berating that he felt to be hanging over his head.

"Look at me."

He dragged his glance up and forced it to reach to the face of his father.

"Jerry, you've been drunk."

"Drunk?"

"That's what I say. I say that you've been drunk again . . . you've made a beast of yourself again."

The alcohol half paralyzed the brain of Jerry, not by its presence, but by the aftermath. He felt a sense of weakness running to his fingertips. He knew that he was beginning to shake. Unless he got away quickly, he would be utterly lost. But what could he say? What could he do?

"You found Mary?" asked his father, suddenly leaving the subject of the drinking incomplete, and bewildering Jerry the more by the shift.

"Yes," he breathed.

"And she said?"

"Yes." The word slipped from Jerry against his will. He would have given thousands to recall it, but it was spoken.

The effect upon his father was magic. He leaped

out of his chair, rejuvenated. He ran to Jerry, caught both his hands, and wrung them.

"Heaven be praised, Jerry!" he cried. "This one good day's work outbalances all the bad ones that you've done before. No wonder you've celebrated . . . and if you've gone too far, I can forgive you this once. It's human to err. Go up to bed, then, and sleep until you're fit to walk and talk again. Then we'll go over things in detail. I want to know each scruple of everything that happened."

He fairly lifted Jerry from the chair and urged him toward the door, but, just as they reached that door and apparent salvation for Jerry, there was another change on the part of the suspicious father.

"You seem all-fired calm about it," he declared. "What's wrong with you, Jerry? What's going on inside your head?" Suddenly he stopped and halted his son. "Jerry, have you lied?"

It seemed to Jerry that he would go mad unless he escaped at once from that prying tongue.

"I haven't lied. She said she'd marry me. But then she changed her mind . . . I mean I told her . . ."

"By heaven, I think you changed yours!" He flung the taller and younger and stronger man from him. "What sort of fool are you?" he panted out.

Jerry was fast falling into a state of collapse. "It

was Keene," he said, only desperately eager to shift the blame to the shoulders of another. "It was that devil, Tom Keene."

"What? Tom Keene? The White Mask?" shouted his father. "What has that murderer to do with Mary Carver?"

"Not Keene . . . I mean Kenyon . . . I mean Keene *is* Kenyon . . ."

"Jerry, you've gone mad. Sit down yonder and straighten this tangle for me."

"No, no. I can't stay here. I've got to be alone. In the morning . . ."

"The devil fly off with the morning. I may be dead before the morning dawns. What I want to know now is what you mean by Keene and Kenyon being the same?"

"Simply because the names are somewhat the same, I mixed them . . ."

"You gave the first name, too, Tom Keene and . . . but, Jerry, you've kept something from me. Out with it, now, for I'll have it sooner or later. And if I have to fight for it, it will go all the harder for you."

The son writhed. He struggled to find some excuses, but there were no remaining loopholes for escape. He was being drawn deeper and deeper into the net.

"For heaven's sake listen to me!" he exclaimed. "I only meant that . . ."

"You've lied."

"I tell you, Keene was pardoned. I mean . . . no . . . when he thought I could save the Carvers if I married Mary, he made me tell Mary . . ."

His father raised a hand and stepped back from him. Jerry slumped into a chair and covered his face with his hands.

"I'm going crazy," he gasped out. "I . . . I don't know what I'm saying. In the . . ."

"But I do," said Jerry Swain, Sr. "I begin to get a glimpse of a very queer truth. Keene and Kenyon are the same . . . Timothy Kenyon . . . Tom Keene . . . not very dissimilar names, at that. I should have thought of it. Tom Keene is pardoned, picks up some money somewhere, and, altered by his eight years in prison . . . without that big black beard of his, for instance . . . he comes back under an assumed name to . . . to do what?"

"I . . ."

"Answer me!"

"Oh, Lord, if I tell you, they'll murder me!"

Jerry Swain stepped closer to the unnerved son. His own face was a singular study of disgust and scorn and agony as he viewed the cowardice of his son. "Who do you mean by *they?*"

"Kenyon and Carver . . . I mean . . ."

"What has Carver against you?"

"Because he knows I know him. That's what he holds against me. He's tried to murder me already. He knows that I could send him to prison in a minute and . . ." He stopped and raised a horrified and bewildered face. "Good heaven," he whispered. "What have I said?"

His father drew up a chair opposite and sat down. He struck his clenched fist sharply into the palm of his other hand. "You've said just enough to get me started. Now, Jerry, here you sit until you've made a clean breast of it. Begin talking."

Chapter Forty

It was nearly midnight when the tap came at the library door of Jerry Swain, Sr. He deliberately laid aside the book he had been reading, put the place card in it, and then called: "Come in!"

The door swung open. John Carver stepped into the room, while the servant who had ushered him in reached for the doorknob and drew the door closed. In the bright light of that room, John Carver blinked, barely making out the features of the other. Neither was he put at ease by the greeting of the rancher.

"Sit down over here, Carver. No, in that chair yonder, where I can watch you. I like to watch a man's face when I'm talking business with him. I can't have too much light on a man's face for my purpose."

John Carver took the designated chair. He sat down on the mere edge of it, his hat clasped between his hands, and his glance wandering here and there and only furtively reaching the face of his host. In quite another manner he had been used to face Swain in the old days when his own father yet lived and the fortunes of the two families were more or less equal. But now he was like a serf before a feudal lord—a guilty serf, far remiss in his dues. And indeed he felt that in the cramped, withered, dying body of Swain there was a more dangerous power than in all the brawn of his own body. And the very next speech of Swain was a bomb that shattered whatever remained of the composure of Carver.

"Carver, I've talked to Jerry, and he's told me everything." He went on, as the other flinched back in the chair: "He told me everything, or, rather, I dragged it out of him. It seems that he is a rascal. He's been keeping you poor. If this earth of ours were a place where the most perfect justice is done, I have no doubt that I should express my willingness to reimburse you for every penny you were blackmailed out of by my son. But this earth is not such a place of justice, and I believe that when a fool is trimmed, he deserves his trimming, as a rule. It makes the rest of us keep our wits about us."

Here John Carver seemed about to speak, but he could find no words. Only the cold voice of the rancher was browbeating him back toward his self-possession, and this seemed to be the result that Swain most desired. He nodded with satisfaction as the black scowl gathered on the face of his visitor.

Then he jumped to his point, leaning suddenly forward in his aggressive way and saying: "The point is, Carver, that you and I are suddenly in the same boat, and that there is one thing holding us both back. That is Tom Keene."

Carver leaped from his chair, but the raised hand of Swain literally pressed him back into it.

"Yes," he said, "I know everything. I know that you're The White Mask. I know that you sent Tom Keene to prison in your place. But be at ease. I'm not one of those who holds up his hands in horror on account of the sins of others. I have some tidy little sins of my own to ballast the ship with, you see. It is a little raw to send up the man to whom you owed the life of your daughter and who actually kept you from the bloodhounds. But I'm not the one to wail about such matters. Tom Keene played the part of a fool, and he has paid the fool's price . . . eight years in prison." He drew a long breath. "Now to come back to you, Carver. You have to get back on your feet, and you can't as long as this Keene, like a devil, keeps you under his thumb. Therefore, your enmity to him is established on a strong enough basis. For my part, I freely admit that the thing I want most is to see Jerry married to your girl. And, since I have found out the pitiful weakness of the rascal, I am keener for the marriage than ever. I have to have stronger blood to bolster up mine. My grandson must have some bone and fire of spirit, so that marriage must take place, but it can't take place on account of Tom Keene. He won't stand for it, according to Jerry, because he very rightly sees that it would mean that you and Missus Carver would be drawn under the protection of my power. This is perfectly clear."

"Are you trying to show me that Tom Keene is the man who is making my life a torment?" Carver grumbled, for the speech of his host had been long enough to permit him to recover some of his poise and self-assurance. "If I'd run into a cliff, would you think I wouldn't know what was stopping me from going ahead?"

"I wouldn't ask that. I'd simply ask if you knew how to get the cliff out of your way."

"Eh?"

"I mean this . . . since I see that you're the kind of man I can talk to . . . Tom Keene must die, John."

"Good Lord!"

"What? The White Mask, and yet you turn up your eyes at that?"

"No matter what I've done in the past, I've never done that, Swain. If that's your way, it's no wonder you've got on in the world. But I've never shot at a man except to defend myself."

"You'll start now, then," said Swain. "You're going back now to the ranch, and you're going to find Tom Keene and kill him. You understand? You're going to simply brush him out of your way and mine."

But John Carver rose slowly and stood with braced feet and doubled fists, glaring down at the rich man.

"Swain," he said, "I sure used to envy you. But I'm through with that. I see the kind of gent that you are, and it plumb sickens me. Like father, like son. That's sure true. Young Jerry ain't worth the powder it would take to blow him to kingdom come and old Jerry ain't much better. He climbed by driving other folks into the mud. Well, Swain, here's one dirty job that you'll have to do yourself if you really want it done. I'm going back, and, no matter what becomes of me, I tell you I'm a better man than you, Swain. Good bye." And he turned and stamped out of the room.

Jerry Swain sat for a time with a stunned look. At length he swept a hand before his face as though brushing a cobweb from his brain. Never in his life had he so completely misjudged a man as he had misjudged John Carver.

There remained a task that must be accomplished. He got up from the chair again and began to walk back and forth in the room, his step halting, his feet trailing in the velvet softness of the carpet. As he walked, his thoughts formed with the greatest rapidity. He had scored a great failure; he must balance it with a great success.

Ten minutes later he had made up his mind firmly, and, having made it up, he started to act at once. First he went to his room, laboring slowly up the steps. Then he changed into his riding togs and slipped a revolver into his hip pocket. Next he went to a closet full of dusty, musty, unused clothes and extracted from a box a great sombrero. When he had knotted the big sombrero at his throat and jammed the hat over his eyes, he was suddenly changed. He went back ten or fifteen years at a step and seemed to be once more that restless Jerry Swain who had been still driving on his way toward a great success with a remorseless energy.

But when he started down the stairs from his room, the pain in which he took each step warned him that he was far from his old self. Only the face remained the same, and would be the same to the last.

He went out in the darkness to the stables, but there he did not select for saddling one of those dainty-limbed, light-stepping thoroughbreds that he had brought in at a great cost to please his son. Instead, he put the saddle on a down-headed cow pony a full fifteen years old if she was a day, and then sent her shambling out into the night.

She was old, she was vicious, and she brought a series of muffled groans from her rider as she bucked to work the kinks out of her limbs. But at length she shook her head savagely, admitted the presence of the old master by pressing her ears flat along her neck, and struck into a lope that she could maintain, at will, for the rest of the night.

And the old master well-nigh demanded this feat of her, for he pressed on steadily through the night until in the dawn they were in a high tangle of mountains far from their starting point. Looking back as the rose hue of the morning grew, he glanced down to the blue distance where his home must be. There they still slept while he schemed and fought for them. What would become of the house of Swain when he was gone?

Again the chill of shame and dread pierced him when he thought of his craven son. And he gave the spurs to his mare and forced her at a gallop up a sharp slope. At the top, the ground gave back in a rough shoulder thick with trees, and behind these trees was the dim outline of a log cabin screened by the grove almost as though by night. To this house he went, dismounted, and pushed open with his foot the unlatched door.

Glancing inside, he saw no less than five men asleep on rude bunks. On opposite sides of the room four of them slept in a double tier like the berths on a ship. But along the wall facing the door was a bunk of more luxurious dimensions. The intruder, with the faint dawn light to help him, moved stealthily around and peered at every face and form.

The four were young giants of the mountains, thick-thewed, framed to give and receive the shocks of battle, with ragged beards already growing on their chins, and with their uncombed, seldom-cut hair tumbling over their eyes. They were close to the brute, indeed. Where their hands hung limply over the edge of a bunk, they were of appalling suggestiveness of power.

Jerry Swain noted all of these facts with the most consummate satisfaction before he went to the other end of the room, carefully avoiding a litter of traps and other gear of hunters. Like a shadow, he reached the fifth bunk and leaned over the sleeper, who was a man fit to be the sire of such a brood of sons. A heavy beard, black as ink—blue-black and shimmering faintly in the dull light—flowed over the great arch of his chest. His face, even in his sleep, was set in the lines of indomitable and sullen pride and ferocity.

When Swain dropped a hand on the muscular shoulder, the first impulse of the sleeper was to reach out and grapple silently with the stranger. His tremendous grip fell upon and well-nigh crushed the invalid, already suffering from the effects of the long and wearying ride. But a whisper came from the unresisting Swain.

"It's I . . . Jerry Swain."

Instantly he was released, and the trapper, fully clothed as he had lain down to sleep, started up from the bunk. Swain laid a finger across his lips as a signal for silence, then led the way out of the shack. He continued until they had passed the outskirts of the little grove. Then he faced his towering companion.

"Well, Landers," he said slowly, "you haven't changed much. Your beard is a little thicker, and I see you have four big sons instead of the four little shavers that I used to know. But otherwise your family seems to be about the same."

"It is," said the gigantic mountaineer. "But you . . . I can't say as much for you, Swain. You look plumb petered out. I'd say that you been living inside too much. If you was to try six months of this life up here, your chest would begin to stick out again. You never were much for size, but you used to have strength of your own, Jerry. Well, well, I'm glad to see you. It brings some of the old days, red-hot and boiling, back to my mind, Swain."

"Memories like that," answered Jerry Swain, "I put away where they won't get out and trip me up."

"Never fear me, partner. I keep mum."

"I'm glad you do. Otherwise, there are folks that would take a terrible lot of interest in what you could tell 'em, Landers."

The big man nodded. Then he buried his thick, dirty fingers in his beard and waited, his eyes sharp and small as the eyes of a fox in spite of the unwieldy bulk of his body. Indeed, he seemed in more ways than one to have the mind of a fox directing the leonine frame of his body.

"I'll be quiet enough," he said. "But it ain't for that that you've rode clear up here. You ain't that fond of your old friends that you'd go a-riding to see 'em, Jerry." He chuckled in great enjoyment of this small jest.

"No," said Jerry, "I've need of you. I want some work done."

"The sort of work that I last done for you?" And, at the mere thought, big Landers glanced in dismay over his shoulder at the listening trees.

"That sort of work . . . exactly," the rancher confirmed.

Landers started. "I'm through with that," he said. "You paid well. It started me off and got me fixed up with guns and traps, and I still keep a little in the bank . . . enough to keep me going fine, Swain, without no more deals of that kind. No, I don't want to talk to you about it."

"Don't be a fool," the other said scornfully. "You have more than yourself to think about. Haven't you four sons? Are you going to turn them loose with nothing but their hands to help them?"

"Have you come here trying to get them into some of your dirty work? I'll throttle you first, Jerry."

Jerry Swain shook his head impatiently. "You don't follow me," he declared.

"I follow you too well. I ain't going to listen to that smooth tongue of yours, neither. I've been honest the last fifteen years, and it ain't going to be you, Swain, that'll change me now."

Jerry Swain stepped back a trifle and looked with a smile of pity—the smile of a superior man—upon his companion. At length he said gently: "The last time that I came to talk business with you, partner, I was talking a few hundred dollars. It will be different now."

"Eh?" said the trapper,

"Why, Landers, I am now a wealthy man. How did I become wealthy? By not allowing my conscience to trouble me. But no matter for that. The important thing now is to make you see things in the new light. This would mean prosperity for you. It would mean that you and the boys could buy a small farm down on the river . . . some of that river-bottom land that you used to hanker for in the old days. . . ."

"You remember even that?"

"I never forget such things," said the other. "They are the handles by which a man may be lifted up and put down again. The little things are what rule us, Landers, eh? But no, partner, think of that farm by the river."

"I dunno what you're talking about," Landers said half mournfully, half angrily. "Couldn't touch any sort of farm down there for less'n four or five thousand dollars."

"Well?"

Landers started. "What do you mean, Swain?" he gasped out.

"I simply mean that four or five thousand dollars wouldn't scare me out. I'd still be willing to talk business."

There was a sort of groan from Landers. "Tell me what it is. If I can do it, I'll try."

"You can't. Not you alone, Landers. No, you're a good man, a mighty valuable man. But you can't do this. It will mean work for you and your four big sons."

"Then I'll let the work go. I'm going to raise 'em with clean hands."

"You're a fool. Their hands will be just as clean on the farm . . . when they get there."

Another groan came from Landers, but then he brushed the other away. "I'll not listen," he vowed.

"Yes, you will," replied the smaller man. "I'm just starting to talk."

And big Landers wheeled slowly, uncertainly, and came back and stood, vast, above the form of Jerry Swain.

Chapter Forty-One

With such violence was Tom Keene roused from his sleep that he sat bolt upright in his bed. But immediately he perceived the house to be in the grip of one of those sudden windstorms that plunge across some hundreds of miles of mountains between dark and dawn, making the tallest trees, the stoutest buildings shudder and tremble under their touch. Such a storm was now shaking the old Carver house, and Tom, having listened for a few moments, was certain that, what, in his sleep, had seemed to him like creaking on the stairs, must certainly be nothing but the effect of the violent wind. He lay back in the bed, accordingly, and no sooner was his strong body composed than, as is the gift of those who live in the open, he was instantly and soundly asleep.

His dreams, however, were by no means smooth. He passed through a confusion of dangers in that hurried sleep. Once more he wakened, and this time he opened his eyes with the certainty that, a moment before, a shaft of light had been playing upon his face. At least, the certainty was so great that he lay motionlessly upon the bed, stirring not so much as a single hand, but waiting, waiting, while his heart pounded with a foolish violence that startled and puzzled him. Then gradually, watching himself every inch of the way, he turned his head.

He knew, by the current of air that swept across his face and his bared right arm above the bedclothes, that the door to the room was open and the wind was whirling down the hall of the old house. The work of the storm might easily account for this, since he never locked that door. But a strange and profound instinct told him also that there was another human being in the room.

Slowly he began to gather himself, drawing up his legs and heaving himself by imperceptible degrees upon his left elbow. At the same time he recalled that he had not left his revolver anywhere near the bed. And at this instant there was a long, loud squeak from the floor of the room near its center.

He waited for no more. There was such a blind panic rising in him that he feared that, if he waited longer, he would be too paralyzed to move. Therefore, he flung himself out of the bed as he was, bare-handed, diving headfirst like a football tackler, and sending the bed sliding across the room with the back thrust of his long legs.

He was in mid-air from that leap when he heard fierce, quick, surprised voices—not one, but what seemed to him a dozen. The room must be full of men.

Then his shoulder and the side of his head struck a heavy man just below the hips, and the latter toppled instantly forward upon him. A revolver exploded, and by the flash Tom caught a glimpse almost too fast for the senses to register what they perceived. Four other men—men of gigantic stature—were in the room, and steel gleamed in the hand of every one of them.

But that fierce, low dive catapulted the fifth man ahead of him, and they smashed against the wall. He thought he felt the bones of the man's body crush with the impact. At least he heard the thud of his head against the wall. And then the form of the big fellow relaxed.

At the same time, with a storm of curses, the others rushed at him. He heard and felt their heavy feet coming. They would drive low, grappling to find him on the floor. Accordingly he jerked himself up and leaped out, throwing his body as high as he could.

His knees smashed against the head of a man leaning exactly as Tom had imagined he would. There was a scream of pain and rage from the other. Tom himself was sent tumbling headlong over the floor.

Luckily he rolled in the direction of the door, and, springing to his feet, he lunged for it. But at the same time three men converged in a terrific rush at that spot. They struck Tom. He felt himself wrenched and torn by mighty hands and went down under a loading, a reaching, gripping, writhing, cursing humanity. Yet they dared not, in the dark, strike with a weapon for fear of injuring one another.

Then a great voice called: "We've got him! Get a light! Show the lantern somebody!"

Under the stimulus of that threat Tom gathered himself and rose to his knees, pitching that load of three heavy men up from him. They flattened to him with shouts, and he tore his right arm loose. He struck up—there was a gasp and a groan of rage and pain. He clubbed fiercely to either side. Then he sprang to his feet, and the three pairs of arms slid from him. They were not altogether harmless, however. At least they caught his night-clothes and stripped most of them from his body.

Half naked, and drunk with the sense of his strength unloosed for the first time in his life—a strength unknown even to himself—he forgot to flee. He merely lunged out, seeking a new prey. He smashed against a man in the dark. A gun exploded, and a pain jabbed through the left thigh of the big man. He barely felt it. The flash of the gun had revealed the other for an instant. Tom reached for the image that had been printed black in the instant's light.

He found it. He found, also, a swinging fist that hurtled through the air with power enough to have felled an ox. It landed fairly on the side of Tom's face. It slashed the skin and flesh like a knife, and a warm trickle ran down his cheek. But the next instant he was in on the foeman. He lifted him up—a writhing, heaving giant—and then dashed him to the floor. There was a shout that was instantly stifled in the crash.

Then a bit of circular, cold metal was jabbed against his back—they had seen his shining body in the light of other flashes—and the gun exploded. He had whirled so that, instead of driving through his body, the bullet merely raked along his outer ribs after plowing through the fleshy part of his back. For an instant it turned him sick. Then he struck out wildly with both fists, felt his left connect solidly, and the man went down.

Here there came the grate of metal on metal, a quick sound like the scratching of a cat's paw against a window glass, and light spurted across the room. It showed the reddened body of Tom. It showed a big, bearded man in the corner, smashed against the wall and even now barely in the act of raising himself in a bewildered fashion. It showed another lying face down upon the floor with his arms outstretched and a pool of crimson around his head.

Another was doubled up and writhing in agony. A fourth was a black silhouette, leaning over the lantern. And the fifth man stood back against the wall with a revolver in either hand. He blazed away with both weapons at the shining target.

Tom felt something like the edge of a red-hot razor slash across his forehead, and another ripped his throat. Hot trickles poured out with the touches. Then he flung himself back. He seized on the man who lay writhing, and with a huge upward lift he wrenched the man to his feet in time to meet another fusillade from the gunman.

The stream of bullets that the man with the guns had started could not be instantly stopped, it seemed. He had splashed lead through the mirror, sending a tinkling and crashing shower of glass to the floor. He had scarred the planking and broken the window and cracked the bed, but now, as he got the range for the second time, the shining body was obscured by a darkness that was the form of the man who was picked up from the floor. It did not matter. The bullet drove home. There was a loud shriek and a convulsive struggle of the unfortunate fellow who served Tom as a shield. Against his chest struck a heavy blow as a slug that had torn through the body of the victim and been half flattened by the resistance of flesh and bone, now spent the very last of its force against Tom. But it made only a small cut and fell to the floor.

In the meantime, the two gunfighters, maddened at what they saw they had done, came charging in, intent on digging the muzzles of their weapons against the body of Tom before they pulled a trigger.

There was a strength of madness in Tom. He had felt the body of his victim grow limp. Now he swayed the body back and hurled it in the faces of the onrushing assailants. But even as he did so, and sprang forward to follow up the charge, he saw the big bearded man, who had fallen beneath his first blind attack, reaching for his revolver that had fallen close at hand.

Chapter Forty-Two

In the cottage behind the big house, the first of the roaring gunfire from the ranch house brought all the three inmates to their doors, quivering with the cold. Mrs. Carver carried a lamp that she shielded so that the light fell only on the wild face of her husband and the pale face of Mary at an opposite door, as she gathered her bathrobe more closely around her.

"It's Swain," groaned John Carver. "It's the hired murderers of Swain at work. Lizzie, our troubles with him are over, but the devil burn Swain. Look! There's a whole army of 'em!"

They had hurried to the side window. They could see, in the windows of the upper room where Tom Keene slept, the quivering flash of guns exploding at intervals, and a huge shouting and trampling, and the shocks of heavy bodies, until it seemed that the wall of the house must be torn out by the impacts.

"Father!" cried Mary. "Take help to him. Here . . . here's the revolver. . . ."

Her mother knocked down her hand. "Are you

mad, Mary? D'you dream that I'd let him go up there to be murdered?"

"But can we stand here and watch it? Oh!"

The last was a shriek. A light had showed in the room, and a swirl of silhouettes of many struggling men passed across the window. It seemed, in the flurry of many shadowy bodies, that the room was literally packed with men shouting and cursing, and over the uproar came the great booming voice of Tom Keene as he battled.

"Then I'll go!" Mary Carver cried suddenly. "It's murder!" She started for the door.

Her mother caught at her, but her stiff hands were utterly incapable of stopping the girl. She slipped through them and hurried on. There was a shout of dismay from her father, but, before he could get clear of the door of the cottage, she was away and had raced half of the distance to the house, clutching the great revolver.

As she whipped through the door, she saw her father halting behind her. Then she rushed for the stairs leading to the upper story, knowing that she would have to carry help alone. And she had never fired a weapon in her life, even at a mark, to say nothing of a human being. How she could be of the slightest assistance, she did not know, but she knew that in some way, when she got there, she would try to help, even if it were only with the strength of her hands.

So she flew to the head of the stairs and down

the hall. Through the open door she saw a strange picture that in a flash was printed deeply in her mind to haunt her the rest of her life. One man lay face down on the floor, his limbs twisted strangely, and she knew at a glance that he was dead, though she had never seen death before. Another man was picking himself up from a corner of the room, a mighty, bearded man whose clothes were half torn from his back, and who seemed to have been bodily flung to the place where he was now staggering to his feet.

Two others were locked in a fierce embrace with a half-naked giant whose body was a mass of open gashes. And she saw the mighty lift and knotting of his muscles as he strained at the two. He had fixed the fingers of his right hand on the throat of one, and, as the fingers dug deeper and deeper, the throttled man wrenched his head far back, his features convulsed and blackened, though he still persisted in grappling with the giant. The second of those locked with the semi-nude warrior had twined his legs with the legs of the other and was attempting to wrench him to the floor. Indeed, he had fallen to one knee, and there he hung braced. And above that sinister group of three stood a fourth man, with his wide-shouldered back turned to the door, and in his hands he was swinging up a heavy chair to batter out the brains of the defendant.

These things, which take so long in the telling,

had been perceived by the girl in one flash of the mind, and in the next she knew that the wounded fighter who was about to be crushed was the man known to her as Timothy Kenyon, cruel, implacable, strangely delighting in torturing others. But above and beyond his cruelty she saw now that prodigious strength battling for life, and with that strength a dauntless courage that filled her to the throat with wonder and with admiration.

She jerked up the heavy Colt, seizing it in both her hands, but at the thought of discharging the weapon she shrank far back into the shadow of the hall. She saw the chair heaved up to full height in the hands of the assailant, and then the eyes of the victim turned up and saw the impending ruin, not with terror, but with a shout of furious defiance.

That shout gave strength to Mary Carver. She thrust the revolver before her, and, knowing that she had no time to aim, or not even thinking of that somewhat essential feature, she pulled the trigger.

The bullet struck the ceiling exactly in the center where the old chandelier, with all its tinkling and shining fixtures of glass, was attached to the plaster above by a narrow chain. That chain was severed. The chandelier hurtled down.

But the sound of the exploding gun had made the man with the chair leap back to avoid the attack, and the blow that would have killed Tom Keene did not fall. All four of the assailants who were now capable of seeing, looked toward the door, and they saw a revolver flash and explode twice in rapid succession, very much like the firing of two guns.

The figure of the holder of the weapon was shrouded from them. What they knew was that the lantern near the door had been unhooded so as to cast a flare of light over the room while it left the hallway in darkness. In a word, they were made perfect targets, while the new assailants could shoot safely from the dark into the light. In the meantime, the chandelier had splintered upon the floor with a terrific crash. And there is nothing so appalling to excited nerves as an unexpected noise. Moreover, on the outside, John Carver, half out of his senses, was shouting to Mary to come back, and then swearing in a thunderous voice that he was coming for her.

No wonder, in that critical moment, that it seemed to the four that the hall was filled with rescuers, and that more waited in the night outside the house. They stood not upon the order of their going, but they went, and the father led the way. Straight through the high windows they plunged, then raced down over the shelving roof below, dropped to the ground, and made for their horses.

Mary Carver found herself, after all the confusion of sound, suddenly standing in a silent room with a dead man lying a step in front of her, and against the far wall the crimson form of Tom Keene sinking down and propping himself feebly upon one shaking hand. She ran to him and dropped upon her knees before him, striving to peer into his face, and feeling that in his eyes she could read whether or not he were mortally hurt.

"Mister Kenyon!" she shrilled at him. "Mister Kenyon!"

He seemed to be falling to sleep. His head dropped down with a jerk, and he was sagging toward the floor. She reached out and gripped his shoulders, shining with crimson. Under her fingers the great muscles slipped and rolled. She cared not for the stains, and, indeed, she did not even seem to see them.

"Mister Kenyon!" she cried again. "Are you . . . have they . . . the cowards . . . have they killed you?"

He did not answer. He only sank lower.

A moment later, John Carver, at the door of the room, saw his daughter, having pulled the arm of the wounded man across her shoulders and around her neck, attempting to lift him to his feet, quite regardless of the stains that dripped and were smeared upon her. He ran to her aid. Between them they half dragged and half carried the staggering bulk to the bed, and there they laid him.

"I'll . . . I'll get to Porterville," stammered Carver. "I'll bring out the sheriff. I'll prove that I ain't had any hand in this, and, heaven above, he stood off five of 'em."

"You can't go to Porterville!" cried his daughter sternly. "You've got to help me here. He isn't dying. He isn't going to die. A man like him . . . why, cowards couldn't kill him."

He was so overcome with wonder that he obeyed without a word. The blood from a scratch had been too much for her to look at. Now all this carnage seemed to mean nothing to her. She managed everything, working with a sort of frenzy until the wounds were tended, the bleeding stopped. Under her directions, her father, having helped as he could, now removed the body of the dead man with great effort and cleared the wreckage from the room.

"It's Young Si Landers!" he confided to his wife in a whisper of awe. "It must have been all of them Landers . . . the whole five of them. And the five of them giants wasn't enough to beat Tom Keene. What a man! And don't go near Mary. She's in a sort of frenzy. She won't talk. She just works. She ain't like herself."

But when the mother came to the head of the stairs and looked in, while her husband now rode for the doctor, she found Mary Carver sitting with folded hands beside the bed, her face calm, and a smile of strange happiness just on the verge of appearing on her lips.

Chapter Forty-Three

It was the middle of the next morning that Jerry Swain came again to old Carver Ranch, spurred on by the mingled admonitions and threats of his father. Though the attack on which the elder Swain had counted so much had failed, at least it had temporarily crippled Tom Keene. It would be a month, said the doctor, before he could walk again. None of the wounds had been of a vital nature. Loss of blood was the main thing that held him back, that and the shock of the long struggle maintained when he had only nerve-power to buoy him. Therefore, young Jerry Swain sneaked to the house and sought Carver.

His greeting was strangely unenthusiastic. "I'll get the wife to take care of Keene and send Mary down to you," he said. "But she's gone plumb queer about this. I never seen nobody wrapped up in a job as much as she's wrapped up in taking care of him."

"You start in and give reasons to persuade her, then," Jerry suggested angrily.

But the other shook his head. He seemed to have grown much younger and happier in the past day.

"Now that Mary has saved him . . . well, I ain't worrying so much," he said. "Mary can decide what she wants to do for herself."

"There's only one thing," Jerry said eagerly as

the rancher turned away. "Does she know that Kenyon is Tom Keene?"

"She don't. And she ain't going to learn it from you, Swain."

She did not learn it from Jerry Swain. Indeed, she learned very, very little from him. She descended to the hall and walked straight up to him with infinite contempt in her eyes.

"I know why you've come," she said, "and I've come down to tell you that I'd rather work for a man like Timothy Kenyon than be the wife of a man like you."

"He'll make a slave of you," breathed Jerry.

"I'd rather be his slave, then!" Mary cried tremulously.

When he attempted to speak again, she turned her back on him and went up the stairs. And Jerry Swain sneaked out of the house and back to his father. "They've all gone crazy," he reported. "They don't want me to marry her now."

"Crazy?" his father said bitterly. "They're just beginning to show good sense. Get out of my sight. I need to be alone."

So Jerry Swain promptly got. As for Jerry Swain, Sr., he had something new to think about, and that was what would happen if the Landers family were caught, and old Landers confessed who had hired him for the work of the previous night.

But the Landers family was never caught. The three remaining sons, separating each to a different direction, melted away among the mountains. Only the father of the family was run down, three weeks later, and cornered by a whole posse. The fight that followed was a terrible page in history, but Landers died before he would surrender. Jerry Swain was not betrayed.

It was to announce that death that Mary Carver broke the rules and entered the room of her patient in the midmorning. Since he had so far recovered that he could sit in bed, propped with pillows, he had laid down a strict law that no one should enter the room save with his meals. And now, when she tapped, he bade her enter with a sullen growl of leonine depth and power. When she stepped inside the door, she found that his scowl matched his voice. He stared silently, waiting for her to speak.

Never once had he relaxed in this attitude. Never once had he expressed to her gratitude for what she had done for him, even though he had learned from the doctor how he had been saved in the crisis, and how she had kept him, afterward, from bleeding to death.

"They did it to make sure of their places," he had told the doctor, and she had overheard.

But in spite of that insult she had continued to nurse him with perfect devotion and with a sort of curiosity, feeling that he could not keep up the barriers forever.

Now he listened without interruption to the account of the fall of Landers, closing his eyes and lowering his book while she talked. When she had finished, she slipped back toward the door, but he surprised her by calling her to him.

"I've made up my mind," he said, "that you deserve some reward for this nursing. Casting around for what it should be, I've decided to send you to Denver and let you hunt around there until you find the sort of position you're equipped for. I'll stand the expenses."

But she shook her head.

"You'd rather stay here, I suppose," he sneered, "and take care of me?"

"Yes," she said meekly.

All at once he exploded. "Don't you suppose I know what's in your mind?" he roared.

She stepped close, raising her hand with a frightened face. "You mustn't do that," she warned him. "It may throw you into a fever. I'll go out at once. I'm only sorry that I troubled you, but I thought you might wish to hear . . ."

She retreated as she spoke, but his call stopped her and brought her back to him, anxious and unwilling. As she came to the bed, he caught her wrist with his lean hand, in which there was only a ghost of his old power.

"I've been making you out a devil on the inside and a saint on the outside," he said gruffly. "It's just popped into my head that you may mean what you say. Mary, where do you get the strength to listen to me?"

"It needs no strength."

"But you've worked to save my miserable self."

"I saw you fighting like a hero," she said with a sudden warmth. "Is it strange that I have tried to help you? Oh, if you would only believe . . ." She stopped, but he urged her on.

"Talk," he said. "Get it out of your system."

"You hate everyone," she said. "You trust no one. You take your pleasure in tormenting us. But, oh, don't you see that there's a thousand times more good in you than you yourself will admit?"

"Where did you learn that?" he asked.

She stepped back again. "I'm going to show you," she said. "But if you laugh at me, then I'll hate you and despise you."

She left the room, and he heard her heels tapping swiftly as she ran down the stairs. In a minute or more she was back, a little breathless, flushed, but walking with a sort of defiant pride that he had never seen in her before. Her right hand carried something concealed in the fold of her skirt, but, when she was close to him, she drew out and placed in his hands a little battered, time-yellowed Bible.

It slid open in his hands, the thin sheets flowing like water. And his eye struck like a blow on the line so long ago familiar to him that each word was like a well-remembered human face. "I will sing of loving kindness and justice. . . ."

He crushed the book shut with such force that the binding was wrenched and torn, and that sight drew a cry of pain from the girl. She tried to seize the book from him.

"Oh," she cried, "there is no soul in you, then . . . only brute force. Give it back to me. Give it back to me!"

He pushed her away, but she struggled to get it back.

"I've thought there must be kindness and gentleness in a man as big and as strong as you," she sobbed, the tears beginning to stream down her face. "Because the man who owned that book was to me as big and as strong. . . ."

Her words suddenly were converted into a stream of musical sound with meaning in the syllables.

Through the brain of Tom Keene a thousand recollections were running. The Book that had sent him out to bring loving kindness into the world had fallen from his hands into hands of another. And what he had failed to be, she had proven. This was the mysterious source, then, of her courage, her divine patience, her exhaustless sweetness of nature.

Once more he had sat beside her and talked in another year. That spirit that had been in him, and which he had considered as empty as wind, had sown the seed in this girl, and in her it had grown. This was the source of the difference between her and her parents, the pure spirit, the self-respect, the holy dignity of young womanhood. It was something that he had given her.

There was a mighty melting of the heart in Tom. It was as though the work of the long, lazy, warm spring were done in a day, melting the winter from his nature. He had felt himself always beaten, hopelessly defeated, shamed. And now he looked back to what had been a glorious victory. Suddenly his hands were loosened, and he gave back the Book to her.

"Keep it," he said. "In the name of heaven, keep it. It was my father's before me. I give it to you freely."

It struck Mary Carver to her knees. The Bible slipped to the floor. Their faces were close. Their spirits were unguarded.

"Oh, Tom Keene," she cried, "I've been waiting all this time. Why wouldn't you tell me?"

But it seemed to poor Tom that the weight of all his sins was dropped upon his shoulder. He looked up from her.

"Lord God," he said, "I believe. Help Thou mine unbelief!"

About the Author

Max Brand is the best-known pen name of Frederick Faust, creator of Dr. Kildare, Destry, and many other fictional characters popular with readers and viewers worldwide. Faust wrote for a variety of audiences in many genres. His enormous output, totaling approximately thirty million words or the equivalent of five hundred thirty ordinary books, covered nearly every field: crime, fantasy, historical romance, espionage, Westerns, science fiction, adventure, animal stories, love, war, and fashionable society, big business and big medicine. Eighty motion pictures have been based on his work along with many radio and television programs. For good measure he also published four volumes of poetry. Perhaps no other author has reached more people in more different ways.

Born in Seattle in 1892, orphaned early, Faust grew up in the rural San Joaquin Valley of California. At Berkeley he became a student rebel and one-man literary movement, contributing prodigiously to all campus publications. Denied a degree because of unconventional conduct, he embarked on a series of adventures culminating in New York City where, after a period of near starvation, he received simultaneous recognition as a serious poet and successful author of fiction.

Later, he traveled widely, making his home in New York, then in Florence, and finally in Los Angeles.

Once the United States entered the Second World War, Faust abandoned his lucrative writing career and his work as a screenwriter to serve as a war correspondent with the infantry in Italy, despite his fifty-one years and a bad heart. He was killed during a night attack on a hilltop village held by the German army. New books based on magazine serials or unpublished manuscripts or restored versions continue to appear so that, alive or dead, he has averaged a new book every four months for seventy-five years. Beyond this, some work by him is newly reprinted every week of every year in one or another format somewhere in the world. A great deal more about this author and his work can be found in *The Max Brand Companion* (Greenwood Press, 1997) edited by Jon Tuska and Vicki Piekarski. His Website is www.MaxBrandOnline.com.

Center Point Large Print
600 Brooks Road / PO Box 1
Thorndike ME 04986-0001 USA

(207) 568-3717

US & Canada:
1 800 929-9108
www.centerpointlargeprint.com